PAST LIFE'S REVENGE

Past Life's Revenge

A DAVID HARRIS AND EMMA JACKSON MYSTERY

Angela van Breemen

Iconic Scribes Press Inc.

Copyright

First published by Iconic Scribes Press Inc. 2024
Copyright © 2024 by Angela van Breemen
First Edition - 2024

ISBN

978-1-7383130-1-3 (Hardcover)
978-1-7383130-0-6 (Paperback)
978-1-7383130-2-0 (eBook)

1. FICTION, Mystery & Detective / General
2. FICTION, Mystery & Detective / Amateur Sleuth
3. FICTION, Occult & Supernatural

Distributed to the trade by The Ingram Spark Company

Reviews

"A beautifully crafted and well-researched novel packed full of intrigue and mystique. Murder, reincarnation, suspense, and romance, it's all there."

Brenda Short, Author

"Past Life's Revenge maintains a great pace throughout, the characters are believable and had me invested, and it's brimming with different locations and rich details. I thoroughly enjoyed the story."

Mike Madill, Author

"Past Life's Revenge by Angela Van Breemen is a stunning suspenseful thriller. It's filled with unusual things like past lives and things we cannot explain. The paranormal vibe though fit well for this story. The tale was dark, twisty, and kept me on the edge. Someone knowing he was murdered, and the murderer is hanging around is the greatest catch of all. There were so many questions that popped up as I read. It made me want to keep reading until I found all my answers. Especially, who was the murderer and why. I loved reading this book. It also reminded me of one of my favorite programs, Unsolved Mysteries, a bit."

Urban Lit Magazine

"Memorable, thoughtful, and entertaining author Angela van Breemen's "Past Life's Revenge" is a must-read mystery and paranormal thriller. The shocking revelations and the equally shocking twists that take the protagonists to the edge emotionally and physically will have readers eager to delve deeper into this new series. If you haven't yet, be sure to grab your copy today!"

Anthony Avina, Book Reviewer

"With its deftly plotted narrative and hauntingly vivid imagery, "Past Life's Revenge" is sure to captivate fans of supernatural fiction and mystery alike. Van Breemen's masterful storytelling will leave readers eagerly anticipating her next literary endeavor."

Avid Reader, Critic

"Angela P. Van Breemen's "Past Life's Revenge" is a gripping exploration of the intricacies of past lives and the haunting power of unresolved trauma. From the onset, readers are drawn into the tumultuous world of David Harris, a man plagued by recurring nightmares that defy conventional explanation."

Prerna Lakhina, Book Reviewer

"Overall, Past Life's Revenge is an enthralling read that skillfully blends psychological drama with supernatural elements. Angela van Breemen's
ability to craft a suspenseful and thought-provoking narrative ensures that this book is both captivating and memorable. For those intrigued by the
mysteries of past lives and the quest for closure, this novel is a must-read."

Alan R. Warren
Best Selling Author
NBC news Talk Radio
KCAA 106.5 F.M. Los Angeles
KKNW 1150 A.M. Seattle

Dedication

This book is dedicated to my wonderful husband Peter Thomas Pontsa whose love and support have been constant.

Who do I see in the mirror?

But an ancient collage of the many lives I've led, and
an unspoken promise of the person I shall become.
ANGELA VAN BREEMEN

Acknowledgement

I am grateful to the extraordinary people who have helped make this book a reality. A special thanks goes out to the Wordsmiths writing group based out of New Tecumseth, Ontario, Canada who listened to the initial chapters of Past Life's Revenge.

Thank you so much to alpha reader and author Peter Thomas Pontsa, beta readers Brenda Short, Teri-Lyn Smethurst and Annette Bays.

The editorial suggestions made by author and editor Diane Bator were invaluable, as is her friendship and support. Thank you.

My sincere thanks and appreciation also go to award winning poet, Mike Madill for editing the final manuscript.

I'd like to make special mention that New Elgan is not an actual place, but is loosely based on the many charming towns and cities located throughout Ontario, Canada. Neither is *Amelia's Fine Dining* a real restaurant, nor is *Café Mokka*, a coffee shop. Although Lake Simcoe is mentioned, there is no South Simcoe Pier One or a Tempest Point. But that's the power of the imagination!

Finally, any errors or inconsistencies are my own, keeping in mind, this book is a work of fiction and meant to entertain.

I hope you will enjoy Past Life's Revenge!

With humble thanks,

Angela van Breemen

Contents

Copyright v

Reviews vii

Dedication ix

part xi

Acknowledgement xiii

One
The Thing 1

Two
The Café Mokka 6

Three
The Client 9

Four
The Date 15

Five
A Man In Agony 24

Six
A Visit To The Country 27

Seven
The Drive 36

Eight
Sharing The Burden 41

Nine
The Meeting   44

Ten
For The Love Of Emma   50

Eleven
The Regression   57

Twelve
George Samuel Larson   60

Thirteen
Tracking A Killer   63

Fourteen
Emma And Laura   69

Fifteen
Liam   72

Sixteen
Bianchi   78

Seventeen
The Storage Unit   82

Eighteen
Sarah Larson-Moody   87

Nineteen
The Bank   92

Twenty
Third Time's The Charm   99

Twenty-One
The Memory Card   106

Twenty-Two
The Video   111

Twenty-Three
The Lost Brother   116

Twenty-Four
What Do We Do Now?   121

Twenty-Five
Staff Inspector Bryan Grant   123

Twenty-Six
New Elgan Police Service   126

Twenty-Seven
The Wait Is Over   130

Twenty-Eight
Let's Talk Strategy   137

Twenty-Nine
Emma   142

Thirty
South Simcoe Bay Docks   146

Thirty-One
I'm Okay, Stop Fussing   151

Thirty-Two
It's All In The Genes   154

Thirty-Three
Exiled In Paradise   156

Thirty-Four
It's Good To Be Home   160

Thirty-Five
An August Evening   165

Thirty-Six
This Can't Be A Coincidence   169

Thirty-Seven
Breaking The News ... 174

Thirty-Eight
What Do We Do Now? ... 178

Thirty-Nine
Don't Go, My Love ... 181

Forty
What Now? ... 186

Forty-One
David Harris, P.I. ... 189

Forty-Two
Serenity Lake ... 194

Forty-Three
He's Gone ... 201

Forty-Four
The First Dawn Without You ... 209

Forty-Five
The Ranger's Cabin ... 214

Forty-Six
Bootcamp For One ... 218

Forty-Seven
Days Of Grief ... 221

Forty-Eight
Our Anniversary ... 225

Forty-Nine
Scared, Please Hurry ... 230

Fifty
Rebecca ... 235

Fifty-One
But Can We Turn Her?   241

Fifty-Two
Coming Home   246

Fifty-Three
We Work Better As A Team   249

Fifty-Four
Don't Think Of It As Eerie   253

Fifty-Five
The Séance   256

Fifty-Six
You Can Call Me Jazzie   260

Fifty-Seven
Jasmijn Bakker's Story   266

Fifty-Eight
What Do I Need to Do?   272

Fifty-Nine
An Offer Not To Be Refused   277

Sixty
There Are No Guarantees, Honey   283

Sixty-One
A Generous Snifter Of Camus XO   287

Sixty-Two
The Maldives   291

Sixty-Three
Where Is She?   299

Sixty-Four
Snacks, Anyone?   304

Sixty-Five
The Labyrinth							307

Sixty-Six
What's Next?							313

About the Author						317
Preview of Revenge is Not Enough				319

One

The Thing

DAVID TORE AT the tangle of sheets, entrapping his arms and legs like an overzealous wrestler pinning his opponent to the mat, until he was free. Salt tears welded his eyes shut. They burned as he rubbed at their encrusted corners. There it was again. The thing.

He flung the sweat-soaked pillows to the floor and scrabbled against the headboard until there was no more room to move.

He couldn't swallow; a thickness constricting his breathing, like a cork stopper. He grasped at his left temple attempting to calm the discordant thrumming in his head.

He tried to call out but couldn't speak. He was at the mercy of the thing, mesmerized by the dark eyes that haunted him every night.

He cleared his throat and with more bravery than he had, he cried out, "What do you want?"

Nothing.

"What unholy thing are you?"

Still no answer.

From an early age he had experienced these night terrors. His mother would murmur to him, "It was just a bad dream, honey. Go back to sleep." And secure in his mother's comforting arms, he would. As the nightmares intensified his worried parents sought help for him; the endless stream of doctors, psychiatrists and specialists reassuring him and his parents he would outgrow this, and for a long time the dreams did stop.

Now approaching thirty years of age, the debilitating dreams had returned. More intense than ever. Since December of last year, he was once more oppressed by the nightly apparition, its black bottomless eyes drawing him into its circle of evil.

As swiftly as the vision had come, it was gone. He wiped the beads of perspiration from his forehead and switched on the light on the bed stand, opened the top drawer and pulled out his journal. To keep his right hand from shaking, he grasped his wrist with his left hand and began to write.

> *Wed. July 26, 2023*
>
> *I saw the eyes again tonight. The same as always, in-fusing me with fear. The same strange shadows and mists and the mocking and cruel expression in those evil eyes. With the lights on, I can convince myself this is not real, but in the darkness of night I know better.*

Embarrassed, he scratched the last line out; his psychiatrist would never approve of him writing such a thing. Especially when he had convinced the doctor that he now believed the eyes to be a figment of his imagination, a remnant from his childhood, best attributed to the dreamworld.

He glanced at the stained sheets and soaked pillows strewn on the floor, picked them up, and threw them in the laundry hamper. Disgusted with the evidence of his weakness, he slammed the lid shut. He pulled a new set of sheets and pillows from the armoire and remade his bed. He tried to make himself comfortable under the duvet cover but knew going back to sleep would be impossible. *This has got to stop... I need a proper night's rest. Better call the doc in the morning.*

When the alarm rang at seven-thirty, he was surprised. *I must have had some sleep.* He stretched his long, muscular legs and got out of the bed. With one enormous lunge, he reached the spacious bathroom.

The bathroom's light turned on automatically as he entered. The sink, a transparent bowl flecked with gold, atop the black marble counter, shimmered under the fluorescent light.

David grimaced at his reflection in the mirror. Dark shadows like smudged eyeliner were visible below his brown eyes. He waved his hand across the sensor of the waterfall tap causing a gentle stream of water to cascade. He cupped his hands under the water and scrubbed his face vigorously, then raked his wet fingers through his wavy brown hair.

With the bright sunshine filtering through the half-closed drapes, the thought of his nighttime encounter did not frighten him as much. *Just a figment of my imagination,* he reassured himself with forced bravado, *a result of a fatigued brain.*

Exhausted as he was, he should have slept through the night. Perhaps it was time to ask for that prescription of sleeping pills his doctor kept suggesting. It would be so nice to have an uninterrupted sleep, but he was reluctant to take medication unless necessary. He had trouble admitting it was necessary.

He padded back to his bedroom and pulled on an old shirt and sweatpants before he headed to his personal gym.

The gym was laid out efficiently, with economic use of space. Against one wall was a Bowflex Home Gym weight machine, on the opposite wall stood a Concept2 RowErg rowing machine and a Nautilus Elliptical Trainer. A yoga mat lay at the center of the polished wood floor. A fifty inch large screen television occupied the far wall.

He checked the exercise chart his personal trainer had prepared for him. Rowing, weightlifting, and meditation were on the list for today. He rowed for twenty minutes, then switched to weights. For today's meditation, he decided upon a Yoga Nidra practice and thumbed through the Spotify app on his phone, and pressed play. His mind and body calmed as the soothing voice of the narrator guided him.

After the exercise, meditation, and a long hot shower, David had regained his equilibrium. Over a quick breakfast of toast and fried eggs (not the healthiest choice, he knew, but his 'go to' comfort food) he checked the newsfeeds on Bloomberg and the Canadian Broadcast Corporation. Then he answered a few emails before checking his agenda on his iPad. This morning, he was scheduled to spend a few hours at the law firm he ran with his uncle, and then meet a new client for lunch at one o'clock.

*   *   *

After his vigorous workout, he decided not to walk down the fourteen flights of stairs of his condo, but instead took the elevator. The doors slid open, and he entered the spacious lobby.

"Morning," he said, nodding to the desk clerk.

"Morning, Mr. Harris. It's a fine summer day," said the clerk. "Have a good one."

"You, too."

David blinked at the bright, sun-filled street and descended the steps to the sidewalk below. He was struck again by how preposterous his experience from the night before had been.

Did other people see strange things like he did? Surely not everyone imagined apparitions. There must be some truth to stories and sightings reported over the centuries. Phantom ships seen by hundreds of people at a time. Ghosts walking about with the ghastly evidence of their deaths; some of those sightings must be real.

Preoccupied with these musings, he didn't glance either right or left, and proceeded to cross the street. As he stepped off the curb, he was surprised by shrill and panicky honking issuing to the left of him. He looked up with astonishment and dodged the oncoming car as brakes screeched. Shaken, he stumbled over to the closest building, leaned his back against the wall, slid down on rubbery legs and sat on the ground. He gasped for breath.

A worried voice asked, "Are you all right?"

He gazed up into a pair of concerned green eyes, fringed with long lashes. They were framed by a pretty face with laughter lines at the corners of the eyes and mouth. Her smile was kind and as she leaned over to look at him closer, a tumble of unruly auburn hair fell across her face. Her long, graceful fingers pushed the wayward curls away.

"Yes, I'm okay." He gave a nervous laugh. "I wasn't paying attention. Silly of me."

"Maybe you have a lot on your mind," she said. "You do look quite shaken." She knitted her eyebrows together as if in thought then snapped her fingers. "Café Mokka isn't far from here. Let me buy you a coffee. It's the least I can do after giving you such a bad scare."

"Coffee's a great idea, but it'll be my treat. After all, I scared you, too." He gave her what he hoped was a disarming smile. "It's not every day a charming young lady like yourself nearly hits a cumbersome fool like me."

"You cumbersome? Or a fool? Hardly," she laughed. David flushed as he saw her gaze linger on his chest and arms.

"I'm Emma Jackson," she said, stretching out her hand.

He shook her hand. "Nice to meet you, Emma. My name's David Harris."

"Come on, let's go get that coffee," she said, smiling. "I think we could both use one."

Two

The Café Mokka

THE CAFÉ MOKKA was almost empty of patrons. The morning rush was over; frenetic commuters needing their caffeine fix for the day had picked up their orders and were now at work.

The twenty-something barista's name tag displayed *Megan, they/them* in bold gold letters. Their right eyebrow raised slightly as they looked at the attractive man standing by Emma's side. "Hi Em, you're in later than usual. What can I get for you and your friend?"

"Hi Megan. I'll have a green tea." Emma turned toward him and said, "And what about you, David?"

He was inwardly delighted by the soft, intimate way she'd called him by his first name. "An espresso, please."

David opened his wallet to pay, but Emma had already swiped her phone over the terminal. She placed her hand on his, and said, "Your turn next time."

A warm rush of pleasure pulsed through him at the thought there would be a next time and knew at that very moment he could easily start falling for her.

"Go have a seat, I'll bring your orders to you," said Megan.

David and Emma sat at a little table covered with a blue and white checkered tablecloth with matching seat covers, and before long they fell into easy conversation. They'd both forgotten the terrible incident that could have occurred had Emma not stepped on the brakes when she did. It was refreshing to chat with someone who shared many of the same interests, such as environmental issues, yoga, physical fitness, and global events.

* * *

Emma couldn't remember when she last had such a great time talking with someone. And yet, she noticed, he was reserved. There was a haunted look about his eyes which not even his buoyant laughter could completely hide. It was strange; he both intrigued and frightened her. How could a person be so approachable and yet at the same time, have eyes that were haggard and old beyond his years?

The more they spoke, the more curious she became. She was certain there was a heavy burden of sorrow in his life which he kept hidden, but he carried himself with courage.

Emma's thoughts were interrupted when David asked, "And what do you think of the present stand the provincial government is taking with Bill 23?"

She gasped, realizing she had lost at least half of the conversation leading up to the question. "I'm sorry," she stammered. "I was daydreaming."

To her surprise, genuine amusement sparkled in his eyes. "Don't worry, who wants to discuss the present political situation in Ontario anyway?"

She returned his generous smile with one of her own. "Sure, you're right, however, the loss of wildlife habitat and our greenbelt is of grave concern to me, as it should be to us all. We need to better manage our green spaces and building mega-highways and sprawling suburbs over our agricultural lands is unacceptable and not a solution for the housing shortage."

"It is a serious problem," David agreed. He looked at his wristwatch. "I should get going. I'm meeting a new client at one and I've got to complete some work beforehand."

Disappointed to part company, Emma stood to shake his hand. "It was great meeting you."

"I'd really like to see you again." He kept her hand in his. "I hope you feel the same."

Her face grew warm. "Sure, I'd like that."

"Great. How about this Friday?"

Trying not to sound too eager, she said, "Friday evening would be just fine." Before she could curb her enthusiasm, she blurted out, "Where?"

"How about some place nice?"

"Sure, what do you have in mind?"

"*Amelia's.* Let's say eight."

"Sounds great. I'll be there." Emma hesitated. "Do you know if they have vegetarian options on the menu?"

"Not sure." David picked up his phone, pressed on the home button, and said, "Siri, menu options for Amelia's Fine Dining." He scrolled down with his right thumb. "TripAdvisor says Amelia's has great vegetarian and vegan options."

"That's perfect."

"I see you have an iPhone too. I'll airdrop my details to you in case we need to contact each other."

Seconds later, Emma's phone chirped. "Got it. See you Friday."

Three

The Client

FOR THE FIRST time in ages, David had forgotten his troubles and enjoyed spending time with a genuine and lovely person.

His steps were light as he climbed the gray worn steps to the building where the law office was situated, his thoughts preoccupied with the beautiful Emma. He was grateful for the bizarre turn of events that had led to meeting her and was happy she had agreed to see him again.

Stepping off the elevator at the fourth floor, he opened the door to the offices he shared with Liam Foster, his mother's brother.

"Morning, Uncle Liam."

He peeked at the bespeckled man seated at his desk. His suit jacket was hanging off the back of the chair and his shirtsleeves were rolled up to the elbows. At sixty-two, his white hair was thinning at the top, but he had the energy and drive of a man years younger. Piles of folders were spread over the large wooden desk.

"Good morning, David. Unusual for you to be running late."

"Almost got hit by a car."

Liam slid his wire rimmed reading glasses to the edge of his nose and surveyed his nephew with alarm, then relaxed when he noticed he was grinning. "What happened?"

"I met a girl," said David.

"So, you were talking figuratively," Liam said.

"No, I really did almost get hit by a car." David gave a sheepish smile. "Driven by a gorgeous girl."

"Hmph. I see." Although it didn't sound like he saw at all.

"She was sorry about this whole thing, so she invited me for coffee at the Café Mokka."

"Nice girl, then."

"Very nice girl."

"Are you going to see her again?"

"Yeah, this Friday," David was unable to suppress his excitement.

"About time you met someone special," Liam smiled.

David whistled under his breath as he entered his private office, hung his coat up in the closet behind his desk and got to work.

* * *

David worked steadily until the antique grandfather clock in the foyer chimed at the three-quarter hour mark. He glanced at his watch. *Twelve forty-five. Time to leave for the meeting.* He saved his work on the laptop and placed it in his computer bag. He was ready for his luncheon date.

He was happy. The talk he had that morning with Emma had invigorated him. He felt more alive than he had for years. His senses were more perceptive than ever before, and with a light step, he bounded out the door to meet his prospective client at the New Elgan Hotel.

* * *

David was taken aback by his new client. He was a man of significant stature and breadth and had a swarthy complexion. Two faded parallel scars from the corner of his right eye meandered down to just below his right earlobe. His battered face indicated he had once been a tough fighter in his younger days, and even though well past his prime, was an impressive character and no doubt still dangerous.

The most fascinating part of the man, however, was his huge and hooded eyes. David was both magnetized and repelled by them. This was someone not to disappoint. To go against the wishes of this formidable person could be catastrophic.

Shaking off his misgivings, David extended his hand and said, "How do you do, Mr. Bianchi. I trust that you are keeping well."

"Oh, infinitely well," smiled the man through thin lips, though the eyes seemed dead and betrayed no emotion at all. "You can call me Enrico."

"And please call me David." He paused. "You mentioned over the phone that you would like to meet over lunch. Did you have a place in mind?"

The older man shook his head, and said, "It doesn't really matter. I trust your choice of restaurant."

This flattery did not go unnoticed by David. "Very well, may I suggest Manicotti's across the street? The walk is short, and their Italian food is excellent."

"Let's be on our way then," said Enrico.

* * *

Over lunch, Enrico observed the articulate and self-assured young lawyer. The only sign showing David might be ill at ease, was the nervous tic of rubbing the back of his neck when thinking or uncertain, a reflection of his type A personality. Enrico had survived and flourished in the dark world of crime by being observant and watching for the tells people unconsciously telegraphed. *How ironic that decades later I should be crossing paths with this law firm once again.*

For the moment, the young man was needed to arrange some of Enrico's more innocent business agreements. If the lawyer was required for more nefarious deals, he was sure that his enforcers would find a convincing factor like threatening a sweetheart or young wife.

The lunch began with a delicate tagliatelle with Bolognese sauce, followed by an assortment of grilled sausage, chicken liver and lamb chops. Enrico ordered a carafe of house wine, a Chianti Classico, which paired well with both courses.

The server refilled Enrico's wine glass then turned to David, who placed his hand over the glass.

"No, grazie." He was unaccustomed to drinking during the day and knew the one glass was sufficient.

The server nodded and said, "Perhaps you would prefer a sparkling water?"

"A Pellegrino if you have it."

"Yes, of course."

After the hour-long delicious meal was finally consumed, the men sipped their espressos. Enrico gave a contented burp, which David took as a signal to begin.

"So, how can I help you?" he asked.

"My company is developing an affordable residence for seniors." Enrico took a sip of the rich Italian caffé ristretto before he continued. "We need an independent lawyer to review the contracts with potential investors, so they understand what they are committing to before they sign up."

"I'll need to review all the documentation before I agree to take on this project."

"You'll want these." Enrico handed him a thick folder of documents. "Let me know your decision."

He stood, reached in his pocket for his wallet and withdrew a thick wad of cash. Peeling off a couple hundred-dollar bills, he threw them on the table and left without another word.

* * *

After lunch, David returned to his office and worked for several hours evaluating Enrico's property development proposal. As he continued to review the file, his apprehension increased.

The real estate deal appeared straightforward and he could see no problems with the plan to build the seniors' residence. Enrico was looking for investors and was offering a very lucrative yield of return, far above industry standards, which is what concerned him. There had to be a catch, but what was it?

The man's eyes had interested him. He was convinced he had seen them before. *But when?* Who did he know with eyes like that? Finally, he shrugged the vexing problem away and decided to go to the small diner downstairs for a light dinner before his appointment with his doctor.

* * *

David sat opposite his psychiatrist, Dr. Weiss, expressing his frustrations. "I'm not sure this treatment is working."

"It's important to give psychotherapy time," the doctor said. "Please be patient."

"I'm tired of all this talk. Looking for reasons behind the dreams. I had a happy childhood."

"And yet you display clear signs of trauma. This indicates an event of great significance and through the dreams your subconscious is trying to get you to work it out."

"Maybe." David frowned. "I'm not convinced."

Dr. Weiss looked at his watch, "Time is up for this session. Would you like to schedule one for next week, same time?"

"Let me think about it."

Dr. Weiss stood up and shook David's hand. "Call my receptionist when you're ready to see me again."

"I'm not sure I'll be back."

"I don't recommend stopping the psychotherapy sessions abruptly," said the doctor, concerned. "May I ask why?"

"The sessions are not helping me. I need solutions." David sighed with frustration. "Not more talk."

"You need to give this time."

"Nah, I'm done."

"If you change your mind, my door is always open."

"Thanks."

After each visit, his sense of helplessness increased. The doctor had told him to be patient, that his recurring dream would not last forever. *That's right,* he thought to himself, *maybe when I die. Or perhaps then it'll last for eternity. Who knows?*

He was tired of trying to convince Dr. Weiss that he wasn't dreaming; that what was happening to him was too real to be fabricated. His fear that he was going insane he also kept from the doctor; he had no intention of being placed in any hospital.

* * *

Hours later, he was again awakened by the eyes. This time they filled him with even more foreboding. Terrified, he switched on his night light, and recorded his experience in his journal.

Thurs. July 27, 2023

The vision was worse than ever. Should I talk to my doctor again? I don't think these sessions are helping. Strange thing though. These eyes have an uncanny resemblance to those of my new client.

The feeling of unease did not leave him that night, although he did finally sleep. When the alarm rang in the morning, he hit the snooze button and lay staring at the ceiling. Ten minutes later it rang again. He hit snooze a second time, despair washing over him in waves of apathy. Only the thought of meeting Emma for dinner at Amelia's on Friday motivated him to start his day.

Four

The Date

IT WAS EARLY Friday evening, and Emma was looking forward to seeing David again. They had had a lovely time at the Café Mokka, but what did she really know about him? *I'm being silly,* she told herself, laughing at her paranoia. *I shouldn't worry so much.* After all, meeting in a public place like Amelia's was smart for a first date.

Emma loved her mom, but one downfall of living with her was that she didn't have the privacy to come and go as she liked. Running her website design firm from home made her life even more confining, although she knew her mom tried her best to give her space.

Maybe it is time to move out, Emma thought, as she tamed her long, curly auburn hair into a chignon.

Although her mom said they should consider themselves roomies, it was still hard not to think of Laura Jackson as anyone except her mom. After Emma's father's sudden death, she and her mother had become very protective of one another.

It was going to be awkward to tell her mother that she was going on a date. I'll have to answer a thousand questions; how did the two of you meet? Do any of our family's friends know him? What does he do for a living? She knew her mom wanted her to be careful, especially after the titanic failure of her last relationship. *How was I to know the jerk was married?*

Her mom wouldn't approve of her going on a date with someone that she had met at random, so Emma decided not to say anything. She would just tell her mom she was going to meet some friends for the evening.

She opened her closet door and tried to decide what to wear. None of her clothes seemed right for the occasion. If, she reminded herself, there was an evening to come. It wouldn't be the first time she'd been stood up on a date, and she didn't want to feel foolish or vulnerable. If David didn't show up, she didn't want to be waiting in front of Amelia's Fine Dining in a long, beautiful dress, feeling silly and awkward. And she couldn't very well wear a pretty blouse and a pair of jeans to the posh and expensive restaurant either. Finally, she chose a white silk dress shirt with flowing black velvet pants, and low heel slingback shoes. She would look stylish and fashionable, but not overly dressy.

* * *

On Friday evening, David came home early from his office to get ready for his date with Emma. He was anxious, as if he was going on his first high school date. He started to laugh. He couldn't explain why he was so worried about whether he would be rejected by Emma. He made a wry grin. He decided to go to Amelia's and hope she would come. If she didn't, he could always visit some of his friends, or just go home.

* * *

Emma glanced in the mirror at the end of the hallway one more time and was pleased with her choice of attire. Yes, she really did love this ensemble, one of her mother's creations. She knocked on the door of her mother's sewing room.

"Mom, are you in there?" she asked.

"Yes, dear, I am. Come on in."

When Emma opened the door, she saw her mother sketching on her drawing board. "You're working late," said Emma. She peered over her mom's shoulder. "Wow. That looks elegant."

"Mrs. Linden asked me to design a new gown for her upcoming fundraising gala, but as usual, she's left it a little late. She didn't even come in for her first fitting till this morning."

Amanda Linden was chair of the organization called *Protecting Nature and Keeping it Green.*

"The gala is just one week away," she added.

Laura Jackson was petite and vivacious with auburn hair a shade darker than Emma's. Her olive complexion complemented her startling green eyes, the same eyes her daughter had inherited. As a seamstress, she had a sophisticated, high-end clientele. She not only designed custom clothing for her patrons, but also did alterations, often dictated by her clients' expanding and contracting waistlines.

"A tight deadline, but not impossible to meet," said Emma.

"True, but it will mean working late nights, and that's a strain on my eyes," said her mom, sighing with frustration.

"Well, I hope you are charging her a premium."

"No, just my standard fee. Mrs. Linden's one of my best clients and my best advocate." Her mom smiled and said, "You look pretty. Going out?"

"Yeah, meeting some friends downtown." Emma's phone chirped. "Mom, my Uber is here. Gotta go. I'm late. Love you."

* * *

The Uber driver drove safely, although faster than the speed limit. Emma didn't mind since she was running late. Once they reached the downtown section of New Elgan, the driver passed the second set of lights, turned right and then pulled into the roundabout driveway in front of Amelia's Fine Dining.

Rumor had it that the fine restaurant was named after Amelia Earhart who was believed to have frequented the establishment in 1918 when she became a nurse's aide in nearby Toronto. It was also rumored that Niki Davros, the owner of the restaurant then known as Niki's, was so enamored by the feisty young woman that he renamed his restaurant, Amelia's Fine Dining. Several generations later, the restaurant continued to win awards and accolades from food critics worldwide.

Emma was surprised when the Uber driver got out, walked to her side of the car and opened the door for her.

"Thanks so much," she said.

"No problem," said the driver. "Just use the app if you need a ride home."

Emma raced up the steps of the establishment, a bit breathless both from the exertion and excitement of seeing David again. Not paying attention, she tripped and fell forward on the top step, her right hand and wrist taking the brunt of the fall. She got up, wiggling her fingers and rotating her wrist to reassure herself no major damage had been done, except to her pride.

Feeling unraveled, she asked the maître d', "Could you direct me to the restroom, please?"

"Sure; are you okay?"

Emma nodded, "My pride's a bit hurt, but I'm fine. Just need to straighten up."

"It's down the hall to the right."

Emma reached the doors to the restroom, and threw herself in, nearly knocking over a matronly lady. She recognized her as one of her schoolteachers from high school, Mrs. Hunter.

"Oh my, I am so sorry," said Emma.

"Emma? Emma Jackson from my tenth-grade math class?" asked her former teacher. "I see you are as graceful as ever." Her words dripped with sarcasm.

Embarrassed, Emma hid herself in one of the restroom cubicles to compose herself and waited till she heard the last person wash her hands and exit the restroom. Approaching the sink, she looked in the mirror; her worst suspicions were confirmed. Her hair was awry, and her face was flushed; she looked like a disaster. Quickly she undid the chignon, brushed her hair, allowing her striking mass of auburn curls to hang loose around her shoulders. She sprinkled some water on her face and applied some lipstick.

She exited the restroom with as much dignity as she could muster, still chagrined at the disturbance she had caused. She walked into the reception area, satisfied at the look of surprise on the young maître d's face and knew she had reclaimed her dignity.

"Hello how can I help you? My name is Karl," he said, his tone filled with admiration.

"Hi Karl. I'm here to meet David Harris," she said. Her voice now calm, lovely and musical.

"I'm sorry, Mr. Harris has not arrived yet, but I do see he made a reservation for two at eight this evening."

Emma glanced at her Movado wristwatch and saw it was just a few minutes after eight.

"You can sit in the lounge area while you wait," Karl offered.

A brush of wind gusted by as the front door opened and closed and she heard a baritone say, "That won't be necessary. Karl, could you take us to our table?"

"Certainly, Mr. Harris. Please follow me."

David leaned close to her, and lightly kissed her cheek. He whispered, "You look lovely." He offered her his arm and said, "Shall we?"

Emma hoped David hadn't noticed the heat that flared in her cheeks the moment their arms had touched.

The restaurant had been recently renovated to maintain its high reputation for elegance and refinement. The tables were adorned with linen tablecloths, and a single rose with a whisper of baby's breath was meticulously placed in each crystal vase atop each table. The lighting was subtle and subdued, casting a romantic ambience throughout the dining area.

"It's breathtaking," said Emma.

"First time here?" he asked in surprise.

"Not since the renovations. It's gorgeous."

Once seated, the server approached their table, handed each of them a gold embossed menu, and said, "Good evening. Would either of you like something to drink?"

Emma nodded. "I'd like a sparkling water to start with, please."

"The same for me," said David.

Soon they fell into the same comfortable and companionable conversation as they had earlier in the week at Café Mokka's. They barely noticed their drinks had arrived.

The server smiled. "Have you had a chance to look at the menu yet?"

Emma glanced up and said, "May we have a few more minutes, please?"

"No problem at all. Take your time, just call me over when you are ready to order."

"We better make our dinner selection before the late dinner crowd arrives, otherwise we'll be here all night," David said.

"It's going to be hard to choose. They have some nice vegetarian options," she said.

"I'm hungry for steak tonight."

David motioned the server over, indicating they were ready.

"What have you decided?"

"I'd like the grilled portobello mushrooms topped with caramelized red onion, garlic and parmesan cheese and assorted vegetable and greens," said Emma.

The server turned to David. "And for you sir?"

"Beef tenderloin, the asparagus and roasted garlic and mini potatoes," he replied.

"How would you like it prepared?"

"Medium rare, please." David looked at Emma. "Would you like some wine with your dinner?"

She nodded. "A big bold red would be great."

"Can you bring a bottle of your 2008 Irony?

"Absolutely," acknowledged the waiter.

"Big, bold and red," said David. "I like that." He reached across the table and stroked her hand.

Emma took a sip of the sparkling water, hoping to douse the heat radiating within her, at least until after dessert.

* * *

After dinner, David told her, "They have a lovely rock garden out back. It's lit up at night and is quite pretty." David took her hand and gazed into her eyes, telegraphing he wanted to show her more than just the gardens. So much more. "Come, let me show you."

As Emma and David walked hand in hand along the pathway, she looked up at the sky with a sigh. "It's lovely out, but it's too bad you can't see the stars in the city."

"Oh? Do you live in the country?" he asked.

"Yes, I do, but many of my clients are in the city, so I drive down once or twice a week. With my web design business, it's easy to work remotely." She leaned over to take a closer look at a white trumpet-like flower that shimmered in the flood lights along the path. "Moonflower. Just exquisite. Related to morning glories, but these bloom at night."

David was surprised. "Are you a gardener?"

"Yes, my mom and I both are." She stepped closer to the trellis supporting the silky white blooms and breathed in their fragrance. "We're nature lovers. Did you know that the Moonflower attracts sphinx moths and other pollinators?"

"No, I didn't know that. Fascinating."

"I'm so happy you suggested to see this garden. Many of the flowers here are night bloomers."

"Will you be my night bloomer?" He pulled her toward him.

She playfully drew back from his embrace and gasped in excitement. "Look! That's a Queen of the Night. Only blooms once every one or two years. It's a real privilege to see this one."

This time, David caught her around the waist and held onto her tightly so she couldn't squirm away. "The only Queen of the Night I see is you."

She relaxed and snuggled into his arms and sighed with contentment. "This is nice."

"I really enjoy being with you too." His face was illuminated with a look of joy, brighter than the lamplight.

"Oh David," she said. Suddenly shy and overwhelmed by his longing and her own, she pulled away from him.

"What is it?" he asked.

"This night has been so magical. I don't want it to end."

"Neither do I," his voice was choked with emotion.

"I feel like I'm on holidays," she said, feeling the heat rise in her face again.

He drew her into his arms and whispered in her ear. "May I make this holiday one to remember?" His kisses against the small of her throat were soft and gentle.

"Please do." She pulled his face toward hers and kissed him back.

* * *

The new sweethearts were reluctant to say goodnight, and David waited with her until the Uber arrived.

He opened the passenger door for her and asked, "Will you do me a favor?"

"Sure?"

"Text me when you get home. I'd feel better knowing you're safe and sound."

"Of course." Emma's heart melted as she realized the depth of his feelings.

On the ride home, she wondered what she'd tell her mom. Her mother always noticed everything. She'd see the stars shining in her daughter's eyes. Perhaps she could sneak off to bed without seeing her. *Who am I kidding? If she's asleep, I'll wake her up! I can't wait till morning to tell her about my date.*

When the Uber driver pulled up in front of the house, she thanked him and raced up the steps.

She pulled out her iPhone and thumbed out a message: Just got in. Thanks for the great evening, E.

Good to know. Sweet dreams, D. ❤

Smiling at the heart emoji, Emma opened the door, and called out, "Mom, I'm home!"

Five

A Man In Agony

DAVID HAD FORGOTTEN about the eyes. Normally, he crawled into bed with the sinking feeling of what terrifying images he would see in the middle of the night. His happiness from having spent a delightful evening with Emma had made him forget and his sleep was without interruption. On Saturday morning, his mood was buoyant and happy, when he realized the dream or 'vision' had been absent. He pulled out his iPhone, scrolled through his contacts and called Emma.

"Emma, speaking," she said, her tone brisk and business-like.

"Hi, Emma, it's David."

"Good morning. It's great to hear from you." Warmth seeped into her voice.

"Glad you got home okay."

"It's so sweet of you to check up on me."

"I wondered… are you free tomorrow?"

"I sure am! What do you have in mind?"

"Would you like to go sailing?"

"It's been a while since I've been on the water. I'd love to!"

"Pick you up at nine in the morning?"

"That'll be great. How about I pack a picnic lunch?"

"It's a date!" said David.

Infused with energy, he spent the morning working out in his gym, and in the afternoon listened to his favorite classic car podcast while he straightened up his condo.

Thoroughly content with his day at home, he went to bed. He was shocked when his vision reappeared in a manner more terrifying and frightening than he had yet experienced. He'd gone to bed with a new book by Daniel Silva, intending to switch the nightlight off as soon as he grew drowsy. Although the lights were on, he drifted into a dreamless sleep, which became so deep, it was trance-like. It was as if a force had taken control of him and was drawing him toward oblivion.

He tossed and turned and then abruptly awoke, conscious of his damp body and drenched bedsheets.

White wisps and shadows drifted before his eyes. His throat became parched, dry, and constricted, unseen hands restricting his airways. The mist surrounded him, hemming him in, draining away his vitality. A strange pain pulsed on the side of his face, and it seemed as if there was something dripping from his left temple down to the corner of his mouth. He reached toward his face, yet it seemed like ages before his hand could reach his temple. There was nothing there. No dampness, no moisture. Nothing.

Then the eyes broke through the mist. They were cold and cruel, ready to inflict pain. He was certain the owner of these eyes could catapult him into insanity. Startled by heart-wrenching screaming, he turned toward the sound and saw a man in agony, writhing in a pool of his own blood. It was so clear, so real.

A calm realization came over David. He was the man who lay there, dying, and begging for help. The man screamed in horror and tried to crawl away, transfixed by the staring eyes.

David's attention was diverted by loud knocking. *Who could that be?* He wondered. *Strange; it's dark. I don't remember turning the light off.* His fingers groped for the light switch on the bed lamp and found it was smashed. Hesitantly, the vision still before his eyes, he inched toward the bedroom door. The light in his bedroom came back on; the bed lamp was safely on the night table and undamaged. And the knocking at the door had ceased.

He opened the door, not entirely surprised to find the corridor vacant. Puzzled and terrified, he returned to his room. Sleep was out of the question. He took the journal from the nightstand and began to write.

Sun. July 30, 2023

I dreamed I saw a man being murdered. I'd like to tell myself it was just a bad dream, but I can't shake the feeling this really happened. What's more, I think the man was me. Ridiculous, but it was just so vivid and real.

David was reluctant to remain in his bedroom and went to his den, which served as his home office. He spent the rest of the night there with the lights on to keep the shadows away.

Reflecting on this latest episode, an idea struck him. He remembered reading an article about reincarnation. At the time, he'd decided it was nonsense, just sensationalism created by charlatans to con money from frightened and foolish people.

In the middle of the night, after such a terrifying experience, he wasn't so sure. Maybe there was something to the whole idea of previous lives. He could not stop thinking that this was a memory; that this had already happened. And worse yet, that it had happened to him.

Six

A Visit To The Country

SUNDAY MORNING DAWNED clear with beautiful summer light filtering through the spaces between the blinds covering the windows. David got out of bed and raised the shades, but this time, the sun did not cheer him. His mind was in a whirl, and he was exhausted after having had little sleep the previous night. A terrible headache raged in the left side of his head. With faltering steps, he finally reached the bathroom. He looked ghastly. Dark circles ringed his eyes, and a vein at the left temple throbbed.

He leaned his arms against the base of the sink to steady himself, waiting for the wave of nausea to pass. He took a couple of tablets from the bottle of Tylenol he stored in the bathroom cabinet and swallowed them down dry, placed his hand under the faucet and drank some water from his palm to chase the pills down.

How am I going to get through the day? He had been looking forward to seeing Emma, but under these conditions, he wondered if he should cancel their date.

If he didn't feel any better after breakfast, he'd call Emma and let her know. As he sipped his chamomile tea, he prepared a bowl of oatmeal and topped it with strawberries, blueberries, and pecans.

He wished he had someone to talk to besides the psychiatrist. After years of treatment from experts like Dr. Weiss, he was fed up with the whole process. By now, one of those specialists should have found a solution for him. Meditation only staved off the dreams for a short while. He needed to get to the bottom of this and he had lost his faith in the psychiatric branch of the medical profession.

Although he hadn't known Emma long, he decided that if the chance arose, he would talk with her about his recurring nightmares. She was kind and sympathetic and he hoped she might have some insight as to what he should do.

* * *

Laura was already preparing breakfast by the time Emma came downstairs. She brushed a light kiss on her mom's cheek and began to set the dishes on the kitchen table.

Laura noticed her daughter's jovial mood and asked, "You look happy today."

"I'm looking forward to sailing with David. Oh, Mom, I'm so excited. He's so nice. I just know you'll like him!"

Laura made a soft smile. "If you like him, dear, then I know I will too."

Emma turned to her mom and gave her another little kiss on the cheek. "You're so sweet," she said. "I love you so much."

"Well, then show me and finish getting that table set. If we wait much longer with our breakfast, we'll be sitting down for lunch instead."

"Mom," Emma laughed. "It's only eight in the morning!"

"All the same, hurry up dear. I don't want you to be late for David. He'll be here in an hour."

Emma beamed at her mom. "Very good!"

"I'm getting better at it, aren't I?"

"Yes, you certainly are."

Laura was an empath. When she had been very little, she had had many experiences, but as she grew older, she lost her 'special feelings,' as she used to call them. Several years ago, she had read an interesting article on Extra Sensory Perception and was trying to resurrect these latent abilities.

To Laura's delight, Emma also displayed psychic abilities; both women would on occasion have premonitions concerning dates, times and places of events. It was an interest which the two of them loved exploring together.

They attended weekly classes held by a group of spiritualists. Students were taught to listen to their feelings and intuition and to explore connections with their spirit guides. With the guidance of sensitives more advanced than they, both were developing their intuitive skills.

* * *

After inputting Emma's address into Google Maps, David carefully reviewed the directions to her house till he had them memorized.

He grabbed his car keys for his vintage 1978 MGB two-door convertible from the table in the hallway, leaving the keys to the sailboat behind with great reluctance. Environment Canada was forecasting heavy winds on Lake Simcoe, where he kept his sailboat. He hoped Emma would not be too disappointed.

The drive would take approximately forty-five minutes to Emma's house. The roads were busy, with people headed to the country, picnic baskets and luggage piled to the brim in the back of their SUVs. As he navigated by the slower vehicles, he could see kids and parents with smiles on their faces. David, however, could not share their buoyant optimism and happiness. He was preoccupied with the events of the previous night. He tried to sort out what had happened. The more he thought about his experience, the more puzzled he became. His analytical ability was nil where this problem was concerned. He had no idea what to do.

The landscape changed gradually from skyscrapers to the rolling hills of the country. The air was fresh, except for the occasional scent of the true nature of farm work. His city nose turned up when he drove by busy little farms, relieved once he passed them, to breathe the fragrant air of a lovely summer day.

Normally a brisk ride in his MGB would lift his spirits, and although he was aware of the heady scents of mid-summer, he did not feel buoyed by them. The gloom that had choked him the night before still clung to him like an oppressive cloak. He could not shake his depression or the chill in his body, even though the sun was warm. Only the thought of Emma made him feel better. Instinctively he knew somehow, she would be able to help him, and he was looking forward to spending the day with her.

David realized his turn was coming up and soon he was traveling on a dusty dirt road. The trail of sun-filtered particles appeared hazy when he gazed through his rear-view mirror. He recoiled at the sight. The haze reminded him of his nocturnal visions.

He finally turned into the driveway, leading up to Emma's house and parked beside Emma's silver-gray 2018 Mercedes-Benz SL 450 roadster. The house was nestled in a cluster of large cedar trees. Flower gardens surrounded it, and to the right, a paved stone pathway led to a large swimming pool. The red brick of the home shined brightly in the sun, and the windows caught every particle of sunlight, reflecting their brilliance onto the stone steps that led up to a large oak door.

Impressed with the peaceful surroundings, David was calmer than when he had left the city. The door knocker was unusual in design; two exquisitely cast metal ornaments in the shape of hummingbirds, their beaks and tails touching in mid-flight formed the shape of a heart.

He was about to use the door knocker when he noticed a doorbell button on the side of the door. After pressing the button, he heard a gentle series of chimes.

His acute hearing picked up the sound of footsteps long before they had reached the door. Finally, the large oak double doors swung open, and he saw a petite woman who resembled Emma.

The woman gave him a welcoming smile. "You must be David."

"Yes, that's right."

"I'm Laura Jackson." She reached out to shake his hand. "Emma has been talking nonstop about you."

"Nice to meet you Mrs. Jackson."

"Please call me Laura. Come on in."

"Thank you. I'd love to." He paused on the threshold. "The hummingbird door knocker. It's beautiful. I've never seen anything like it before."

Laura beamed. "Thanks. My late husband designed it."

She held the door open wider and gestured for David to enter. At the end of the hallway entrance, a large mirror hung in the center of the wall and substantial two-doored closets graced each side. An intricate oriental rug lay at the front of the entrance. David removed his shoes and placed them on a shoe rack by the door. The front room was spacious, and an ornate iron chandelier hung from the high ceiling and cast its light over the entire room.

"That's a gorgeous chandelier," David said.

"Thanks. Also, one of my husband's creations." Her voice was filled with pride. "He was quite an artist."

The woman was delicate and graceful, with a vivaciousness indicating a free spirit. Her dark auburn hair was pulled back from her face and tumbled down her back. A few wisps of the hair, however, had managed to escape the hairband and framed her pretty face like lace. Her emerald eyes were as lovely as her daughter's, but it was the expressive eyebrows and smile that most reminded him of Emma. His observations were interrupted at the mention of her name.

"Emma should be down in just a few moments. Perhaps you'd like to wait in the sitting room until she's ready? She won't be long."

"Yes, certainly. If it's no trouble."

"No, of course not," she smiled. "Please follow me."

She led him through several more spacious rooms until they reached the sitting room. She motioned him to a seat, and asked, "Can I get you a coffee or tea?"

"Tea would be great. No milk or sugar."

"I'll be back soon."

* * *

Laura traced her steps to the kitchen while humming to herself. Yes, David, certainly was a very nice fellow, just perfect for her daughter. She had been impressed by his polite behavior at the door, and pleased he'd noticed her late husband's artwork. She began to softly sing, *Over the Rainbow*, under her breath as she made the tea.

A few minutes later, Emma came down dressed in a short-sleeved blouse and shorts. She had known for several minutes that David had arrived, but sudden shyness had restrained her from coming down right away.

"Do I look all right?" she asked her mother.

Laura gently tucked a wayward auburn lock of hair behind Emma's ear.

"You look very nice." Laura paused. "I hope you're bringing a sweater and a pair of slacks or jeans with you. It might get chilly on the water."

"Already thought of that," she said, as she motioned to the large duffle bag slung over her shoulder.

* * *

Emma pecked her mom on the cheek and ran out of the kitchen and through the hallway leading to the sitting room, where David was waiting. She looked in the hallway mirror, gave her hair one last pat, and then firmly grasped the door handle and entered.

"Hi David, I'm sorry I kept you waiting—" Emma's words died on her lips. She was surprised to see David sitting with his two hands covering his face, slumped over, as if weeping.

Worried, she asked, "David, are you okay?" She sat down beside him on the couch and tentatively touched his right shoulder.

David sat up with a start. Emma was shocked to see how drawn and tired he looked.

"Hi Emma." He managed a tired smile. "You're a sight for sore eyes." The dark pain behind his eyes faded a little.

"It's nice to see you too, David." She paused. "But you didn't answer my question. Are you all right?"

"Yeah. Just had a poor night, that's all. I'm a light sleeper."

Emma sensed there was more to this than a bad night's sleep but decided not to pursue it. She changed the subject. "I'm looking forward to our day together."

"About that. I listened to the weather reports this morning and they are forecasting high winds in the range of twenty-one to thirty-three knots per hour. It will be too rough on the open water. I thought we might do a little driving out here in the country instead. Would that be all right with you?"

"Sure, I understand. If it's too windy, we'd better not go."

"I hope I haven't disappointed you," said David.

"Oh, not at all. I know lots of wonderful back roads we can take. And I have a nice spot in mind where we can stop and have our picnic."

"Sounds great."

At that moment, their conversation was interrupted by the rattling of teacups on their saucers.

"She's bringing out the fine china." Emma winked. "It means she likes you." She got up and opened the door for her mom.

"Thanks," said Laura. "I brought chocolate biscuits in case you're hungry."

"Wow, this looks great," said David. "Thanks."

* * *

Emma's mom poured the amber liquid into the teacups and sat on the settee across from David and Emma.

He took a sip of tea and savored the delicate flavor. "This tea is wonderful."

"It's from our garden. One of Emma's blends," said Laura.

"Delicious. What's in it?"

"Chamomile, bergamot, anise hyssop flowers and stevia." Emma blushed. "I'm glad you like it."

"I love it. I taste a hint of licorice."

"Good taste buds. That's from the anise hyssop. I use the chamomile to smooth out the flavors."

"Very nice. I'm impressed."

Laura said, "I'm curious; what is your profession, David?"

"Mom—" Emma rolled her eyes.

"I'm a lawyer. I work for Foster and Harris. It's a firm my father and my mom's brother Liam started some forty years ago."

"Oh, do you work with your dad, then?"

"No, he passed away three years ago." A shadow crossed David's face. "Uncle Liam and I have kept the firm going, but he only works a few days a week now and plans on full retirement within the next few years."

"Do you like your work?"

"As a rule, yes. Just before I was born Uncle Liam and my dad switched from criminal law to real estate law. They used to be defense attorneys."

"That sounds like a big change."

"Yeah, it must have been. When I asked my dad about it, he said he was tired of dealing with the criminal element. Our clients are real estate firms and corporations that have been with us for years." David took a sip of tea. "It's really not very exciting work."

"All the same, it must keep you very busy."

"It does. I enjoy it for the most part, but much of the work is mundane." David looked at his watch discreetly. "Most times, I'm just glad when I've wrapped up a case, especially when it's been dragging on for several months."

Emma noticed that David had checked the time. She cleared her throat, and said, "David, maybe we should get going." Her mother had been monopolizing the conversation and she wanted to spend time with David.

"Ah yes, you two have plans to go sailing," said Laura.

"We've decided against sailing. Environment Canada's marine weather forecast is promising rough water on Lake Simcoe," said David.

"We're going for a drive in David's convertible. Thinking we'll head up to Beaver Valley, find a nice spot for a picnic along the way."

Laura saw that Emma's eyes were bright with excitement and David's eyes were just as happy.

She could take a hint; with great dexterity she placed the dishes on the tray and left the two young people together. When she was out of earshot, she began to chuckle. *Ah, to be young again.* With another small laugh, she walked to her sewing room.

Seven

=====

The Drive

EMMA ENJOYED watching David drive; he handled the vintage car with confidence. His arms were lean and strong, and the wind swept back his thick brown hair from his chiseled features. The light smile that played on his face was wonderful to see and was such a contrast to the tired and bedraggled look he had earlier in the day. She sighed and closed her eyes and relished the sensations of the sun kissing her face and the wind caressing her skin.

"Hey, Emma, why are you sighing? Aren't you enjoying yourself?"

"I sure am!" She gave a small laugh. "I sighed because I'm happy. I hope this day will never end."

"Great; I'm so glad." David blushed with pleasure. Hopefully, Emma would think it was just a sunburn. "I'm having a great time, too."

"How long have you had the MGB?"

"My dad bought it about ten years ago. We used to work on it together." He paused. "When he passed away, I kept the car. Whenever I drive it, I feel close to him."

"That's so sweet." Emma loved that he was sentimental. "I lost my dad a few years ago, too. I kept his SL 450 roadster. There's something special about driving his car."

"I'm glad you appreciate cars," David grinned.

"Your car is very nice. I like the color."

"Thanks. It's original. Inca Gold Yellow."

"I love it."

"Thanks."

They fell into companionable silence. Sunshine, convertible and being together made it a perfect summer day's outing.

An hour later, Emma asked, "Are you getting hungry?"

"I could eat," he said.

"See that turn coming up on the left? There's a scenic lookout and picnic area. We can eat there."

David navigated the turn expertly and parked.

The view overlooking Beaver Valley was stunning. "I had no idea this was so beautiful," he said.

"I knew you'd like it." Emma pointed to a nearby picnic table. "Let's set up here, we can enjoy the view while we eat."

"Perfect. I'll go get the picnic basket."

"Thanks."

David carried the picnic basket and put it on the bench of the picnic table. Emma pulled out a floral tablecloth and placed it over the worn boards of the table.

"How classy," he said.

Emma smiled and set the table with plates, cutlery, and fancy plastic wine glasses that looked like crystal. Next, she tossed a mixed green salad with olive oil and balsamic vinegar and garnished it with thin slices of Jarlsberg cheese, blueberries, raspberries and pecans, thin slivers of onion and avocado. She pulled out a miniature bread board and cut up thick slices of sour dough bread.

"When you said picnic, I was thinking sandwiches," he said. "This looks amazing."

"Thanks. I wanted to make it special."

"You sure have."

She handed the wine bottle to David. "Could you pour for us?"

"Umm, not sure about having alcohol though."

"It's okay; it's nonal sparkling wine. By Carl Jung."

"Nonal?" He looked perplexed.

"My nickname for non-alcohol." She laughed. "Drinking and driving don't mix."

"You think of everything." He poured the wine in their glasses, and said, "A toast. Thank you for this amazing day."

"My pleasure."

After their toast, he pulled out his phone. "Let's take a selfie of ourselves and this amazing spread."

"Okay! But hurry up, I'm hungry!"

* * *

Emma sensed a change in David's mood, a heavy weight descending upon her own shoulders. She tried to shake it, but the foreboding feeling intensified.

"Come on," she said and reached for his hand, hoping to bring him out of his funk. "Let's go for a walk on the trail. I've something to show you."

The day had become hot, so the shade of the maples that lined each side of the path was welcome. The tall trees blocked the sun and cast dark shadows on the rough steps which had been carved out of the hill, making it difficult to see as they descended.

After another twenty minutes of hiking, the terrain flattened out and the trees became sparser until they reached a clearing.

"There!" She pointed to a pond which shimmered in the sunshine. A canoe provided for the public rested on the shore. "Look, the wind has died down," she said, gesturing toward the water's placid surface. She tugged at his hand. "You promised me a day on the water. Now's your chance to redeem yourself. Let's go!"

"Why not?" David said laughing, as Emma pulled him toward the canoe.

Soon they were paddling on the pond. Their paddles playfully dipping in and out of the smooth water. Droplets of water dripped from their paddles like iridescent jewels in free fall, shimmering in the sunlight until they rejoined the waters of the pond.

"Feel like going ashore for awhile?" asked Emma, pointing to a small beach.

"Sure." David guided the canoe until it was parallel to the shore and then stepped out into the water and pulled it onto land.

"It's so peaceful here. Sure, beats the city," he said. He took off his shirt, placed it on the ground, unaware of Emma's appreciative gaze of his strong upper body. He sat down and motioned to Emma to come join him. "Let's sit a while."

She snuggled in beside him, her right hand resting gently on his chest. They sat there, relishing each other's company. Too shy to yet say, *I love you,* although they both already were deeply in love. Nestled together, as two pieces that belong to one another should, they became drowsy.

* * *

Lulled by the peaceful surroundings, David drifted into a light sleep. On one level of consciousness, he remained aware of his environment and sensed impending danger. The eyes were coming!

Oh my God, not now! Not with Emma here!

His last thought before his mind shut down and fear incapacitated him was to protect her. Tendrils of fog surrounded the couple. And the eyes came. He heard a gasp, wrenched his gaze away, realizing Emma was also watching the eyes through the swirling wisps of mist. *My God, she sees it, too! She shouldn't see this.* His mind screamed, *"No!"* Emma's gaze remained riveted on the eyes. *But why can she see them, too?*

"Be gone!" said Emma, her voice strong and commanding. Within moments the vision had dissipated. Emma had protected him… she had sent the eyes away.

"How did you do that?" he asked, noting with concern the dark shadows around Emma's lovely green eyes. And with clarity he understood that Emma had become him for that moment, her face now mirroring his own haunted expression.

"David?" she hesitated, her face pinched and drawn. "We need to talk about what just happened—"

"You saw them? The eyes?"

She nodded. "I knew something was troubling you when we first met, but I had no idea it was this serious."

"But how?"

"Give me a minute to collect my thoughts," she said, her voice soft. "You have been seeing a psychiatrist when all the time you should have been seeing a hypnotherapist."

"How did you know about the psychiatrist?"

"You probably won't believe me. Sometimes I just know things."

"Emma, I do believe you."

Her forehead was furrowed with worry. "My mom and I are both empaths. Our abilities are limited compared to some sensitives." She drew a heavy sigh. "Let me take you to at least one spiritual meeting. There's a past life regression therapist I'd like you to meet."

David shifted uncomfortably and scratched the nape of his neck. "I don't know, Emma."

"You have exhausted all the other resources, please try and keep an open mind."

"I suppose I could give it a shot."

"Good… you have been hurt too much already."

Emma sighed; the experience had drained her of energy. After she had regained her composure, she added, "There's a meeting on Thursday night, promise me you'll come with me. David, this may be your only chance."

Hope surged within David, the shadows of his depression receding. He drew Emma close to him, his chin resting on the top of her curly head. For several minutes they sat there, drinking in the peace of the forest, and soaking in the comfort of each other.

Eight

Sharing The Burden

LAURA SENSED SOMETHING was wrong when Emma and David returned that evening for dinner. She had prepared one of Emma's favorite meals, a green curry Buddha bowl made of fresh broccoli, cremini mushrooms, cashews, coconut cream and of course, her kick-ass green curry. During the meal, beyond the normal pleasantries, such as *please pass the salt*, little was said by either Emma or David.

David left soon after dinner.

Emma looked serious and worried. Laura decided to ask, "What is it dear, did you two have an argument?"

Emma gave a heavy sigh and quietly said, "No, Mom."

"Didn't the two of you have a good time today?"

"Oh Mom, we did until—"

"Until what? Is David in trouble?"

"Yes, he is."

"What sort of trouble? I did see a dark aura around him."

"He's been seeing visions. His whole life. I think memories of a past life are pushing their way through." Emma sighed again. "I'm really worried."

"Isn't it a little premature to be worrying about David? After all you've known him less than a week."

Emma shook her head, "Mom, I know what you're saying, but this is different. I feel a strong connection to him. From the moment we met."

"Tell me what happened," said Laura gently.

"After our picnic lunch, David became moody. I suggested we hike down to the Beaver Valley Pond and go canoeing. The distraction seemed to have worked, and everything was fine, and we were enjoying ourselves. We were in tune with each other's thoughts, though I doubt he realized this. We paddled to the other side of the pond and got out for a rest. Without any warning, I could feel him slipping; he was going into a trance. I stayed in sync with his mind and then I saw them." Emma shuddered.

"Saw what?"

"Malignant and evil eyes. Just staring." Emma drew in a heavy breath. "With all the willpower I could muster I visualized a protective ring around him."

"This could have been dangerous. You're not ready for this type of psychic energy healing work."

"I know." Emma took a deep breath. "It was hard, but I was finally able to chase them away. It left me drained and exhausted… I haven't been trained to handle this."

"Would he be open to going to a spiritual meeting?"

Emma nodded. "I've invited him to join us this Thursday. I told him he might be able to get help through our group and that he should consider seeing a hypnotherapist. He told me he doesn't sleep much at night." She wiped the tears forming at the corners of her eyes. "Mom, what else could I do?"

"You did your best. There was nothing more that you could have done."

"I'm not strong enough to keep these dreams away from David on my own. Emma's hands trembled as she drew her hair back from her face and formed it into a loose bun. "Can you work with me tonight, pray for him, and send him healing light and energy?"

"Yes, but we may need help from the entire faith healing group." Laura put a comforting arm around her daughter. "I'll call Anna in the morning and let her know you will be bringing a guest."

"You're not coming, Mom?"

"Next time. I've still got to put the finishing touches to Amanda Linden's gown."

Nine

The Meeting

DAVID'S DREAM DID not recur that night, nor the following ones. It was as if Emma was still protecting him. The thought gave him comfort. Today was Thursday and tonight he was looking forward to seeing Emma, but most of all, he hoped he might discover the underlying reason for his debilitating nightmares.

He was still grappling with the idea that Emma had seen his vision, too, and that the help he needed could be of a spiritual nature. He'd always scoffed at the idea of psychics and considered them con artists and charlatans. *But what if there was something to it?* He had spent years visiting his psychiatrist and other so-called professionals, and his visions were getting worse, not better. It was time to try something new. He'd keep an open mind toward the idea of past lives.

***

Heavy thoughts weighed on Emma's mind as she prepared herself to meet David. She was worried. Worried that David would reject the help they were offering him, worried that he might rebuff her because he might consider she was feeding him nonsense. With hardly a glance at the attractive reflection in the mirror, she brushed her long wavy hair.

She chose a simple skirt and a pull-over sweater. She made no attempt to pretty herself for the evening. Tonight was different. She was going to help David. And she needed to remain focused.

Finished getting ready, she sat on the edge of her bed and ran her fingers over the vintage rambling rose crochet bedspread. She was surprised at how serious she was getting about David. Their relationship was moving very fast. She dismissed the second thoughts she was feeling. She couldn't pull back now, not when she had promised to help. Besides, her affection for him ran deeper than any reservations she might have; more intense than she could have imagined after knowing someone for only a week.

They had arranged to meet at David's condo and head to the meeting together.

She ran down the stairs and poked her head into her mother's sewing room. "Sure, you can't come tonight?"

"No, Mrs. Linden is coming in for a final fitting. The gala is tomorrow evening."

Emma glanced at her watch. "I better get going. Love you."

Before her mother could answer, Emma was out the door, her purse dangling from her left hand, and her car keys grasped in her right.

* * *

She was always sad when she left the rolling hills of the country she loved and entered the city. Even during the summer, it was artificial, bleak, and colorless. The trees placed in strategic rows along urban streets would never make up for the loss of the fertile soil below, trapped under an oppressive mass of concrete and asphalt. Shaking these thoughts from her mind she pulled the car to the side of the road and entered David's address into the GPS unit. According to Google Map, from the main highway she had to turn left at Marple Way, and then right at River's Place.

Properly oriented in her mind, she pulled back on to the highway and continued driving. When she entered the driveway leading up to David's condo she was struck by the elegant lines of the building.

As she got out of the car, a sense of wellbeing came over her and she knew that things would turn out well for her David. She blushed at how the 'her' had slipped out so naturally.

She pushed the button on the wall to the right of the glass doors and waited for the doorman to buzz her in.

At the front desk the concierge asked, "How may I help you?"

"I am here to see David Harris."

"And your name?"

"Emma Jackson."

"One moment, please." After a pause, he said, "I have a Miss Jackson here to see you. Certainly sir." He handed the desk phone to Emma.

"Hi David, it's Emma. Are you ready to go?"

"Hi Emma, almost ready. Why don't you come up for a sec? It's condo 1403."

When she exited the elevator, a tired but smiling David was waiting for her at the corridor. "Come on in, Emma." He took her in his arms and murmured in her ear, "I missed you."

"Me, too." Emma pulled away from his embrace and searched his eyes. "Are you ready for the meeting?"

"As ready as I'll ever be. I am nervous though."

"You've got to come of your own free will, not because I told you to."

"Don't worry, Emma. I'm desperate. I'm ready to try anything."

He gestured her into the large and spacious living room and motioned her to a love-seat adorned with silken blue and gold stripes. "Will you excuse me for a few minutes? I'll be right back."

"Sure, we have a little bit of time, but we should head out soon. I'd like to get good seats. The place always fills up fast."

She sat there quietly musing. *So, this is where David lives.* As luxurious as the apartment was, she'd suffocate in a place like this, with no trees, and no garden to tend. She realized how fortunate she was to live in the country. But then of course, she countered, not everyone is happy living in a rural setting. Some people do prefer life in the city. The nightlife was a big draw, which she also liked to a point, but many of her contemporaries from college remained in the city because of more lucrative job opportunities. She was grateful her web design business gave her the ability to work remotely.

When David re-entered the room, he looked less haggard. Emma knew he was putting on a brave face and that for years his mind had been ravaged by the nightmarish visions. *And yet, he's remained strong, stronger than he realizes.*

Her thoughts were interrupted when he said, "Hey Em, I'm ready whenever you are."

She looked at him with surprise.

"You don't mind if I call you Em, do you?"

"Normally I don't like it when my name is abbreviated, but it sounds nice when you say it." She rose from the love-seat and touched his cheek.

"Em it is, then." His smile was broad and open.

⁎ ⁎ ⁎

David was beginning to regret attending the meeting. He was getting tired of all these 'mediums,' as they called themselves, stand in front of the group and guess their way through supposed clairvoyant or clairaudient proclamations.

He was working on a tactful way to leave early, when a slender looking lady in her mid-fifties came to the front of the room. Although she was attired in a simple, blue dress, and wore no jewelry at all, she was elegant. Her long brown hair was streaked with gray, piled on top of her head and secured with a long pin. There was a magnificent and regal air about her. His thoughts were thus occupied when she began to speak.

"There is a young man in attendance who has never been here before. Neither has he ever come to a meeting of this kind." The woman looked straight at him.

You fraud, he thought. *That's a safe assumption to make, anyone could have guessed that! I'm sitting here with Emma. She's bound to know I'm with her. And didn't Emma's mom call ahead to say I was coming?*

As if he had spoken the words aloud, the woman answered him, "Young man, don't be afraid to say those unkind words to my face." A spark of anger flashed in her blue eyes. "Go ahead. Say them. Don't just think them."

David decided to challenge her, "What words? Repeat them to me."

The woman remained calm, "Very well. For the past five minutes you have observed my dress, that I am simply adorned, and that I am good at guesswork. Your exact thoughts were, 'You fraud!'"

David squirmed in his chair, as if he was sitting on a nest of agitated red ants.

"Do you want to hear the rest or is this sufficient? I can always tell the good people here why you came today. I could tell them about the—"

"Stop!" David cried, "Stop." He gasped, what was happening was unbelievable. He was stunned. "I don't understand how you know this, but I apologize. Others may be fraudsters, but clearly you aren't." Embarrassed, David slumped into his chair, too dejected to say anything further.

Moments later, the woman's expression softened. "I'm sorry, too. I was harsh with you just now. After the session, come talk to me. Let's see if I can be of help to you."

Her gentle words were a great comfort to David. He turned to Emma and whispered, "She really didn't know about me?"

"No, David," she whispered back. "Mom got busy and forgot to tell Anna you were coming tonight."

* * *

Emma and David sat in their chairs quietly until the meeting was over and waited until the last person in the audience had left. She took his hand in hers and led him to the front of the room and said, "Anna, this is my friend."

He smiled shyly as he reached out to shake the woman's hand and said, "Once again, I'm sorry, Mrs—"

"The name's Miss Tungsten. I never married. You can call me Anna." Her tone was efficient, bordering on brusque. "And your name's David Harris." She slightly turned her head, "Hi Emma, how are you?"

"I'm well and yourself?"

"Just fine. How's your mom? Where is she tonight?"

"Working on a gown for Mrs. Linden's upcoming gala."

"Tell her I say hello."

"Sure thing."

Anna fixed her intense blue eyes on David.

"David, you have suffered a great deal, especially these last few months. What is bothering you is not a spirit. Your subconscious mind is trying to tell you something. It has been trying for many years."

"What can I do?"

"I suggest that you let me hypnotize you and bring you back to your childhood days, and if necessary to previous incarnations."

"Do you really believe in reincarnation?" he asked, his voice full of hesitation.

"Yes, I do," she answered disregarding David's note of reluctance. "As a past life regression therapist, I have been able to help people address issues from past lives that trouble them in their current lives."

"I have to admit I feel skeptical, but I am willing to give it a try." He couldn't believe he was considering this. "If I am going to do this, we may as well get started as soon as possible. When are you free?"

"These sessions take time. Let me check my schedule."

Anna took out her cell phone and scrolled through her calendar. "Would seven o'clock tomorrow night work for you?"

"Sure; that works."

"Here's my card, come to my home." She turned toward Emma, "You should come, too."

Ten

For The Love Of Emma

DAVID HAD TROUBLE working at the office on Friday and paying attention to his cases. He could not stop thinking about what would happen in the evening. Several times he had reached for his cell to call Anna that he had changed his mind. Each time though, he would disconnect before the call completed.

I know how disappointed Emma will be, thought David. *There's a part of me that doesn't want to find out the truth about what is troubling me.* That fear was probably why he had so little luck with the long line of treatments by doctors and psychiatrists.

I've got to find out, no matter what the consequences, David reasoned. *I can't continue this way. Before I can ever be involved with someone like Emma, I've got to have this problem solved.* David's pulse quickened just thinking of her. She was wonderful to be with. He loved her gentleness and her understanding and patience. Yes, he would go tonight, for the love of Emma.

* * *

When David returned home to his condo, he was still preoccupied with what might happen that night. Tired of arguing with himself, he resolved not to think about it further.

After the meeting the previous evening, David had been surprised at Emma's insistence she drive him to Anna Tungsten's home. When he pressed her, she had said, "You might be disoriented after the session, and it'll be better if I drive."

"Okay. You convinced me." He had smiled, changed tack, and said, "Let's have an early dinner."

"Sure. That's a great idea. What time?"

"Let's say five thirty. I'll make vegetarian wraps."

He was pleased by her enthusiastic response. "I'll bring some of that chocolate cake from Café Mokka," she teased. "That's if you like chocolate cake."

"No, I don't like chocolate cake." He enjoyed the look of surprise on her face. "I *love* chocolate cake," he teased back.

"Good. I could never date a man who didn't like chocolate!"

* * *

David and Emma sat beside each other on the couch munching on their wraps filled with chopped kalamata olives, hummus, baba ghanoush and finely chopped romaine lettuce.

"This is so delicious, David."

"I love Greek inspired food."

Emma pushed her plate away. "I don't think I can eat another bite. Let's save the chocolate cake for later."

"Sounds good. We can have it when we get back from Anna's place."

"Let's clear up the dishes."

David washed the dishes and Emma dried them. "You don't use a dishwasher?" she asked.

"Nah, not worth it for just one person."

As the last dish was placed back in the cabinet, he turned to Emma. The words rushed out. "I can't hide what I feel anymore. I'm frightened, but I just want you to know that I'm glad that you're here to help me. You're a wonderful person. I've never met anyone quite like you. I—" David's cell phone vibrated along the granite counter.

"Sorry, I have to take this." He snatched it off the counter. "This is David speaking." He listened for a while and said, "My office is closed tomorrow. We're not open on Saturdays, but I can make an exception." After another pause, he said, "Fine. We'll meet at my office then. See you tomorrow morning."

"Who was that?" asked Emma.

"Just a worried real estate agent," he said. "It's her first deal and she's nervous. She's coming by my office tomorrow at ten."

Emma's cheeks flushed bright pink with jealousy. David pretended not to notice but smiled with pleasure. *She cares for me, too.*

"Look at the time," Emma said. "We better get going to Anna's place."

"Sounds good." Whatever he was going to say before the phone rang could wait till later.

* * *

A few minutes before seven o'clock David and Emma knocked on the massive arched door of Anna Tungsten's mid-nineteenth century home. Soon they heard light footsteps move briskly to the door, and seconds later, the door opened. Anna wore a black dress with white lace at the throat. Her hair was pulled back from her head, in a tight knot, not a single strand out of place. She gave the impression of a spinster schoolteacher.

"Come in you two," Anna said, smiling. "I trust the drive was uneventful?"

"Yes, it was smooth sailing," said Emma.

"Let's head to the living room." They followed Anna through the hallway to a room furnished and decorated according to the era the home had been built. "David, please take the couch. Emma, please sit there." She pointed at a plush chair with an embroidered cushion featuring a floral pattern of roses cascading from a vase.

"Thanks so much, Anna," said Emma.

"It feels very peaceful here," said David.

"Familiarize yourselves with your surroundings." She fixed her gaze on David. "Keep your conversation light and easy. Just relax." She smiled at the two young people. "I suggest we have some herbal tea before we get started. I'll be back soon."

***

Anna returned to see that David and Emma were laughing. *Good,* she thought. *They need to be happy and relaxed, especially David. What comes next is not going to be easy for him. Emma's support will be crucial.*

As Anna poured the tea, she said, "I'd like to review a few things with you before we begin the session.

"Above all, I want you to have a clear understanding of hypno-therapy and what we plan to accomplish this evening. Treatment using hypnotherapy is done while a patient is in a trancelike state. Compared to 'talk therapy,' such as the treatment plan you've been receiving from your psychiatrist, hypnotherapy can accomplish a lot more in a shorter amount of time." She raised the dainty teacup and took a small sip of tea and continued.

"I record all my sessions. During a childhood or past life regression, my clients often do not remember everything. Listening to a recording allows them to later recall details of the session."

"Sounds like this could be a helpful tool," said David.

"Indeed. I will also be making a transcript of the recording, which I'll have ready for you in a few days."

"Thanks."

"Also, it's important you follow my instructions during induction carefully."

"Induction?" David placed his teacup and saucer carefully on the table.

"This is the process used to induce you into hypnosis."

"Okay. Like you see in the movies."

"Something like that, but not nearly as dramatic." Anna smiled, then grew serious. "Finally, here is an informed consent form for you to complete, saying you give me permission as your hypnotherapist to place you under hypnosis and to record the session. It's a standard form."

After they had finished their tea, Anna said, "Please take your time reviewing the consent form." She picked up the teapot. "I am going to refresh the tea with more hot water. I'll be back in a bit."

* * *

David read the document. "It's a standard consent form." He looked at Emma and asked, "Em, am I doing the right thing?"

"Yes, it's worth a try."

"Okay, let's do this." He picked up the pen and signed.

He turned to her and said, "I wanted to tell you later, but this just can't wait. It means so much to me that you are here. Em, I really am beginning to care for you."

She smiled. "I know David, I feel the same." She paused; a shadow crossed her face. "I want things to work out for you tonight. You won't have peace until this problem is solved."

* * *

When Anna returned, she sat across from David and looked at him with her calm sea-blue eyes. "David," she said quietly. "I want you to lay back on the couch and listen closely to every word I say. If anything becomes uncomfortable, I want you to use the safe word, 'home'. Do you understand?"

"Yes."

"Good. David, now close your eyes. Relax your body. Make yourself as comfortable as possible. I want you to feel a tingling sensation in the tip of your toes, when you feel it, tell me by saying 'yes.'"

"Yes, I feel it in my toes. No wait, it's moving upwards."

"That's very good David. But remember, just answer with 'yes.' Don't panic. Stay calm. Don't be afraid, the sensation will continue to move upwards until it encompasses your entire body. Let it flow. Do you feel it?"

"Yes. It's a bit like the Yoga Nidra guided meditations," he said, his initial misgivings and fear, dissolving.

"Very good. Just answer with 'yes.' David, you are beginning to feel very sleepy, but you are still aware of your surroundings. You are going to fall asleep by the time I have counted backward from five, but you will still be able to listen to my voice. Do you understand David?"

"Yes."

"Five, four, three, two, one. David, can you hear me?"

"Yes."

"David, you are four years old. What are you doing?"

"Playing with Mommy. I love my mommy."

"Where are you?"

"Mommy and me are at the playground. I like it here. Swing higher Mommy! Faster Mommy! Faster!" A smile of amusement briefly played across Anna's lips at the grammatical error made by the preschooler.

"Does she play with you everyday?"

"Most days. We have fun." David giggled. "I'm a bird! Weee!!!"

"What are you doing right now David?"

"I'm playing pretend. Do you like airplanes?" He tilted his head to the side. "What's your name?"

"I'm Anna."

"I like to make lots of friends. Will you be my friend?" David asked in a high-pitched eager boyish voice.

"Yes of course, David."

David yawned, "I'm sleepy. I want to go to bed." He rubbed his eyes with his knuckles and gave another yawn.

For the next few minutes David quietly slumbered, his face seemed so young and innocent. It was if he really was only four years old. Then a troubled frown appeared on his previously serene forehead. He breathed harder, sweat pouring from his face. He screamed, "No!"

Anna was concerned but decided to keep him in his hypnotic state. "David, stay calm. Do you understand?"

"Yes." David's voice was neutral and quiet, then abruptly changed to a piercing childlike voice, "Mommy?" David called out in the dimly lit room.

"She's here, honey. With me, your friend, Anna."

"I'm scared."

"You are safe, David. Did you have a nightmare?"

David moved his head up and down. "I am so scared," he wailed. "Please tell them to go 'way."

"Tell who?" Anna asked carefully.

David became impatient. "The scary eyes! I want my Mommy!" He was crying, the sobs deep and inconsolable.

Anna decided to bring him back. "David. You are twenty-nine years old. You and your friend Emma are visiting me at my home. I want you to wake up and sit up when I have finished counting down from five. Five, four, three, two, one. Wake up, David."

David sat up; his upper body swayed. "I had that dream again," he said in a subdued voice. "I feel dizzy."

Emma rose from her chair, picked up the teapot, topped up David's teacup, and handed it to him. "Here, take a sip."

David composed himself and said, "What happened?"

Anna looked at David for a moment and then said, "I took you back to the age of four. I believe what is disturbing your sleep is not something from your childhood but from before."

"You mean from a previous past life."

"Yes, that's right."

"To be honest with you I'm having a hard time accepting the idea of reincarnation." He covered his face with his hands, "I just don't know what to think anymore."

"I can appreciate how frustrated you must feel." Anna looked at him with compassion. "Would you be willing to try again tomorrow night to learn about your previous lives?"

David was about to say, *what good will it do?* but the hope in Emma's eyes stopped him. "What do you think, Em? Should I do this?"

"Your decision David, but I think it's worth a try." She gave him a gentle look. "I truly believe Anna can help you."

"Okay." He turned toward Anna. "Let's do it. Same time tomorrow night?"

"Yes, that works for me," replied Anna. "See you at seven."

Eleven

____

The Regression

AT SEVEN THE next evening, David and Emma found themselves back at Anna Tungsten's great door. She answered it with a big smile.

"Hi," she said, pulling them both into a tight embrace. "Come right in and settle yourselves in the living room. I'll be back in a few minutes with the tea."

Over tea, Anna turned toward David and said, "David, the process will be the same as before, but this time, I'm going to take you past your current childhood to your birth, and backward through the tunnel of light to your previous life. Sometimes a current life can be affected by traumatic events experienced many lifetimes ago."

"Sort of like an echo?" asked David.

"Yes; that's a good analogy. It will be a matter of work on our part to determine if it's the immediate past life, or one even before that which has been affecting you with these dreams. If at any time you are uncomfortable, say the word 'home.' And if I feel that you are under any distress, then I will bring you back out of the hypnotic state."

"Okay," he said.

"Good," Anna replied. "Let's get started."

David lay down on the couch and allowed Anna to guide him through the steps to take him to his most immediate past life.

David's face underwent an abrupt transformation. He was still a young man; however, the features were angular and the expression aggressive. Anna immediately noticed the change and said, "I'm Anna. With whom am I speaking?"

"My name is George Larson."

"Hi, George. It's nice to meet you. May I talk with you for a while?"

"Okay, if it doesn't take too long. I'm on my way to my lawyer's, then the bank."

"Can you tell me the month and year, George?"

"Don't you know?" Confusion like a trapped bird flitted behind his eyes. "It's December fifteenth, nineteen ninety-three."

"What's the weather like?"

"It's been overcast all day, and very cold."

"Where are you?"

"I'm walking on Main Street, south of Queen."

"What city?"

"New Elgan."

"What time of the day is it, George?"

"About six at night. It's dark. Strange; the streetlight should be on. I don't have time to talk. I've got to get going."

He shuddered and looked afraid, his chin trembling. He was obviously under distress. Anna decided to pursue the matter further.

"What's wrong, George? Are you ill?"

"No. I got this feeling I'm gonna die today."

"How old are you?"

"I'm thirty-two, and single." He smiled rakishly, before the expression on his face returned to one of fear.

"You're far too young to think that way," said Anna.

Anna and Emma were shocked at the expression on George's face.

"No," he screamed. "Get away from me. I told you I don't have it!"

David's body shook violently. He jumped off the couch still in his trance and stared with wild eyes at Emma and Anna. "Help me." His hand touched his left temple. "My head… Oh my God! The pain. I think I've been shot! Somebody help me!"

Emma and Anna were shocked to see tendrils of dark shadows trailing down the left side of his face, as if he was bleeding.

David's body sank to the floor, as his former self, George, screamed, "Those eyes. So terrible." George gasped. "I won't forget this… I won't forget you!" He clawed out with his hands as if in accusation, and then lay still.

"Oh my God," screamed Emma. "Do something!"

Anna had no idea that things would have gone this far. Reacting to George's death as quickly as she could, she said to Emma, "Help me get David back on the couch."

The two women struggled to get the lanky man back on the sofa. His breathing was shallow and distressed, but he was alive.

"David," said Anna gently. "Remember your safe word. Home."

Emma wept silently as she held David's limp hand. "Come back to me."

David whispered, "Home." His voice was as brittle as the late leaves of autumn.

"Five, four, three, two, one. Wake up David. Sit up." Anna breathed in the breath she hadn't realized she'd been holding. "David, you are home. You are safe. You are David Harris, it's Saturday, August fifth, two thousand and twenty-three, and you are very much alive and engaged with the business of living."

Twelve

George Samuel Larson

DAVID OPENED HIS eyes. A nagging feeling told him that something of extreme importance had occurred, but he could not quite grasp what it was. He was certain he had seen the eyes during the session.

He heard Anna say, "Wake up, David," but he was too weak and groggy to answer right away.

He saw Anna's worried eyes and said, "Something happened, didn't it?"

"Yes, we had a breakthrough, but you gave us a scare."

"What happened?"

"You relived the death of your former life. It was traumatic and I had trouble bringing you out of the trance."

"Did we learn anything worthwhile?"

"David, you were named George Larson and either worked or lived here in New Elgan in your previous life," she paused. "You died at the age of thirty-two on December fifteenth, nineteen ninety-three."

David stared ahead and said, "So you really think my dreams are not just nightmares, but actual memories from a past life."

"Yes, I do." Her expression was thoughtful. "It's unusual, though."

"What is?" asked Emma.

"Normally souls don't reincarnate so soon after death. Unless—"

"Unless?" David swallowed the lump forming in his throat.

"The trauma was so great, the soul needed to return sooner—"

David interrupted. "I was murdered, wasn't I?"

"Yes, I think so. I'll review the recording and prepare a transcript for you, but my impression is that you saw and may even have known your killer."

"This is a lot to process."

"I'd recommend you review the transcripts, and then we can schedule another session."

"I wonder…" David looked back and forth between Anna and Emma; his face pinched with concern.

"Yes?" asked Anna.

"If this is all real, and I was murdered thirty years ago, there's a good chance the killer could still be alive."

"True," said Anna. "And still be relatively young. Possibly still in his fifties. Maybe even early sixties."

"What are you thinking?" asked Emma.

"Hang on a sec." David grabbed his iPhone and typed in his query. "Just found this website called Canada Cold Cases. It's a database of unsolved murders and disappearances."

"Is there a search tool?" asked Emma, unable to hide her excitement.

"Yep. Typing in 'George Larson.' Oh my God, I've got a hit." His face turned white. He turned the display around for both Anna and Emma to read.

Canada Cold Cases: George Samuel Larson
Updated March 15, 2023

On the evening of Wednesday, December 15, 1993, between the hours of six and seven, 32-year-old Officer George Samuel Larson of the New Elgan Police Service was shot in the head.

He was off duty at the time and was killed enroute to an appointment with his lawyer, Liam Foster, of the law firm

Foster and Harris. His murder is believed to be a completely random act of violence.

In the almost thirty years since his death, there have been no suspects, and this case remains unsolved. His sister Sarah Marie Larson says, "George's untimely death, led to my mother's suicide in 1994. The killer not only took my brother's life, but also my mother's."

If you have any information relating to this case, please contact Detective Bryan Grant of the New Elgan Police Service.

"What? Isn't that the name of your law firm?" Emma said with a mixture of awe and fear.

"Exactly," David's complexion remained pasty-white. "They mention Liam Foster; he's my uncle."

"This is bizarre." Emma's face had lost its color.

"It's all so tragic; Sarah lost her mom, too," said Anna.

"Look, there's a picture of George," said Emma, pointing at the screen. "Can you enlarge it?"

David expanded the image with his right index finger and thumb. His face blanched even further. "He looks familiar."

"Not unusual for you to recognize your former self," said Anna.

"Odd, Samuel's my middle name, too." His voice was toneless.

Thirteen

Tracking A Killer

ON THE DRIVE back to the condo, David said, "Where do we go from here?"

"I don't know," Emma pursed her lips. "You want to track down your killer, don't you?"

"Yeah, I do."

"I'm not sure this would be healthy for you. I think you should let it go. But, in the end it's your decision."

"Em, I'm a lawyer," he reminded her. "Clearly, I want justice. Why else would I have chosen to be reincarnated into the very family whose law firm provided services to George?"

Emma pulled over to the side of the road and looked at him. "Isn't it enough to know what happened, so you can get on with *this* life?"

"No, I can't let this go. I won't rest easy till I find the killer." His mood was dark. "Even if the killer's dead now, I need to know what happened."

"Okay," she said.

"You mean you'll support me on this?"

"Of course. I do have misgivings, though."

"Such as?"

"Well for one, it could be dangerous. What if the killer is still alive?"

"True. So how do we approach this?"

Emma put the car into gear and pulled back into traffic. "Let's talk more when we get back to your condo." She quickly glanced over to him, "Feel like a house guest tonight?"

* * *

When Emma and David got back to the condo and settled onto the couch, Emma sent a quick text to her mom: Don't wait up. Staying at David's tonight, E.

Thanks for letting me know, Mom. xo

Goodnight, E. xo

Emma put her cell on the coffee table. "Told my mom I'll be staying the night." She frowned. "We need to come up with a plan."

"I could use a glass of wine to unwind." David's eyebrows furrowed together. "What about you?"

"Sure. We could both use the distraction."

"Red or white?"

"Red, please."

"I have a 2020 Guarda Rios from Portugal. Would you like to try it?"

"Sounds nice."

David got up and went to the kitchen. She heard the fridge door open. "I feel a bit peckish," he called out.

"Let's share a slice of that chocolate cake."

"Great idea. I'll bring a couple of forks."

David returned a few minutes later carrying a tray laden with the bottle of wine, a crystal decanter, two wine glasses and the cake. He placed the tray on the coffee table, picked up the wine bottle and poured it into the decanter, the dark claret shimmering in the evening light.

"Let's leave it to breathe for a bit," he suggested.

"Sure. But it'll be tough waiting."

He pulled her to him, and she snuggled into the crook of his arm. "This is nice," she said.

David sighed heavily. "It is, Em, I just wish—"

"I know." Emma placed her right index finger on his lips gently. "Let's relax a bit before we get to work."

David nodded and poured a glass for Emma, then for himself. He handed her the wine glass, and said, "I hope you like it. You mentioned you like robust wines."

Emma took a sip, and said, "This is wonderful. It has aromas of dark cherries, chocolate, and oak. This will go well with the chocolate cake."

Troubles pushed away for the moment, they sipped on the wine and ate the decadent chocolate cake, forks colliding as they competed for the final bit of icing on the plate.

"Mmmm. That was delish," said Emma, rubbing her tummy.

"There's more in the kitchen."

"Nah, that's okay." Her expression turned serious. "Time to track a killer."

"Okay. What have you got in mind?"

"Have you got a white board?"

"Yeah, I do. I have one set up in my study."

* * *

Emma stood in front of the white board, marker in hand.

"Let's mark down everything we've learned, starting with a list of the people involved." She drew columns on the board.

"Okay," said David. He was seated at his desk with his laptop in front of him. "I like this methodical approach. Write down George Samuel Larson. And my uncle, Liam Foster."

"Okay, who else?"

"Detective Bryan Grant of the New Elgan Police Service."

"Great. Let's check if he's still with the police force." Emma picked up her iPhone and did a quick query using Safari. "He's a staff inspector now." She added Grant's name to the list. "How about George's sister, Sarah Marie Larson?"

"Definitely."

"She may have married though and have a different surname."

"Shouldn't be hard to find her. We can start with high school alumni records. "George's family lived in New Elgan." He made a few keystrokes on his laptop and said, "There's a website called FindAnAlumni.org." He keyed in Sarah's name. "Got a hit here. Says she went to New Elgan City Collegiate. Graduated in nineteen eighty-one." A moment later, he said, "George went to the same high school. He graduated in nineteen seventy-eight."

"We can try social media, too."

David thumbed open Facebook and keyed in Sarah Larson in the search area. "No hits."

"Try George Larson," suggested Emma.

David gave her a skeptical look but keyed it in anyway. "Wow, you're right, Em. Sarah set up a memorial page for her brother. It's called Remembering George S. Larson. It's inviting people to come forward on the thirtieth anniversary of his death."

"That'll be the perfect reason to contact her."

He read further. "She goes by Sarah Moody now. Must have gotten married."

"Makes sense. How old would she be now?"

"About fifty-nine."

David frowned. "We'll have to approach this carefully. I can't just say to these folks, 'Hi my name is David and in my last life I was George Larson.'"

"You're right. We'll have to come up with a plausible reason."

David's face brightened, "The first person to approach should be Uncle Liam."

"Good. From there we can decide whether to next contact the police or Sarah."

"I could try another hypnotherapy session, too."

"I'm not sure about that. That last experience was traumatic for you." She gave David a worried frown. "Let's see what we can find out first." She stifled a yawn. "I'm getting pretty tired."

"I'll show you to the spare bedroom."

"Thanks David, but—"

"Yes?"

"I had something else in mind." She reached up and pulled his face toward hers and kissed him.

"Mmmm… I taste chocolate on your breath."

Emma took his hand, and said, "Take me to your bedroom."

* * *

On Sunday morning, David awakened very early, unwrapped his arms from around Emma, a soft smile playing on his lips as he watched her sleeping. His night had been peaceful, and even better, dreamless. He padded off to the kitchen and made a pot of Starbucks Sumatran coffee. It had been a late night, and the caffeine fix would be welcome.

He sat down on the sofa, and while sipping the aromatic coffee, went over the events of the previous night. He was conflicted and his thoughts were in turmoil. He desperately wanted to find out the identity of his murderer but realized it could be dangerous. He had a new life now, with the prospect of having a future with Emma, so why pursue this? What purpose would it serve?

Deep down he knew he would never be happy until he found out who had killed George Larson. His desire for justice overruled his misgivings. Perhaps it was growing up in a household of lawyers and his own respect for, and belief in the law, which wouldn't allow him to let go. His head was beginning to ache, and he rubbed at the back of his neck, trying to alleviate the tension. He swallowed a couple of Tylenols, crawled back into bed with Emma and breathed in the lavender scent of her hair, and waited for the pain meds to work.

* * *

When David woke up again, he had the strange feeling that he had learned something of great importance. But the more awake he became, the more the memory slipped away. Something about the client he had taken on recently. He grabbed his notebook from the nightstand and before he even had begun to write, the memory had faded away. He snapped the notebook shut in irritation, placed it back in the drawer and closed it with a rough shove.

The noise of the drawer opening and closing, and the aroma of coffee roused Emma from her sleep. "Good morning." She stretched her arms out sleepily toward David, who fell into her embrace.

"Good morning to you, too."

"What time is it?" Her voice was soft and languorous.

"Just after nine-thirty."

"Oh no!" she jumped out of the bed. "I'm late. I promised to work on mom's website and blog today."

"Can you at least stay for breakfast?"

"Oh David, I just can't. Rain check?"

"Sure. When can I see you again?"

"I'm coming back to the city on Tuesday morning to see a client."

"Would you be free for lunch that day?"

"I'd love to," she looked at her watch, "I've got to go. Can't wait to see you Tuesday." She gave him a soft kiss on his lips, got dressed and in a whirlwind of activity, hurried out the door.

Em, my love. Drive safely.

Fourteen

Emma And Laura

A SOFT BREEZE ruffled and billowed out the gauzy yellow curtains in the sunny kitchen. Emma and Laura were enjoying a late lunch, after having spent the morning working on Laura's new website. Although Emma had tried to keep the mood light, Laura noticed that her daughter was preoccupied.

"I love the new website," said Laura.

"Thanks, Mom. It needed a fresh look. We'll work on the branding for your Facebook and Instagram pages next. It's important to keep a consistent look throughout all the social media platforms and the website."

"You're making me look so modern."

"Well, you gotta keep up, Mom."

"Emma, I've been meaning to ask. How did last night go at Anna's?"

"Okay, but I am concerned about David." Worry lines creased Emma's normally smooth forehead. "Last night's hypnotherapy session was more revealing than the first one on Friday evening."

"That sounds promising." Laura searched her daughter's eyes. "But you don't seem happy about what was learned."

"Yes and no. We found out David's name from his recent past life."

"That's great news!"

"But we also found out he had been murdered. He's been reliving his previous death from as far back as the age of four, perhaps before that."

"That certainly explains the intense nightmares," said Laura. "So why are you so worried then? Doesn't David feel some relief now?"

"Well, he's got it into his head to apprehend his murderer."

"That's not a good idea."

"I know. I did my best to talk him out of it. Just knowing what happened should keep these memories at bay. He has an explanation. It should be enough."

"But it isn't?"

"No, he's determined to apprehend his killer. Doing the math, the murderer could still be alive; in his fifties, or even early sixties. David, being a lawyer, just can't let go of the idea of this man not being brought to justice."

"I might not agree, but I can appreciate his feeling that way."

"He's asked me to help him."

"Are you going to?"

"Against my better judgment, yes, I'm going to help him."

"You love him already, don't you?" Laura asked, her voice gentle.

"Yes, I do. I haven't known him long, but there's just something about him. I know I'll love him for the rest of this lifetime."

"It was that way for me and your father. When we first kissed, the soul recognition was just overwhelming." She stroked Emma's cheek. "I hope your love will be like that."

"Oh Mom, why did Dad have to die so soon? I miss him."

"He was a good man and a great father." Laura wiped tears from her eyes. "I miss him, too. Every day." She changed the subject. "What does Anna think about this?

"After I left David's this morning, I called her. She doesn't like the idea. She thinks it's better he doesn't try. He wants revenge, and she doesn't think that's a good motivation. Plus, it could be dangerous." Emma paused. "I just have a terrible feeling it's all going to go wrong."

Laura's heart was aching for the two young people. If David were hurt or killed, she was afraid that Emma would close herself off to any future happiness. Finally, she said, "Emma, David is going through a hard time, and if you love him as much as you say you do, you should support him as best you can."

Emma smiled at her mom. "Thanks."

Fifteen

Liam

ON TUESDAY MORNING Emma's phone chirped. She glanced down at the message and saw it was from David.

"Would you excuse me for a moment?" She left her client's office and walked into the corridor. Her face lit up as she read his text: Hi Em, can't wait to see you. How does Wok's Table sound for lunch? They have vegetarian options. I checked. 😊

Sounds great! It's been a busy morning. Should be there by 12:15.

Okay. See you then.

Can't wait to see you either! ♥

* * *

When Emma walked into the restaurant, David noticed admiring glances cast her way, however she seemed oblivious to the effect she had on the men in the room. When she saw him, she gave a bright smile and waved. He could feel their envious stares as she glided toward his table and took the chair opposite his.

"You look beautiful," he said.

"You don't look too bad yourself."

The server approached their table and asked them for their orders.

"I'll have a vegetable stir fry and a glass of sparkling water," said Emma.

"Perrier, okay?" asked the server.

"That'll be great."

"I'll have the Singapore noodles, extra spicy, and Perrier will be fine for me, too."

"How is your day going?" Emma asked.

"It's going great. It's been a busy morning at the office. I got a crick in my neck." He massaged the back of his neck with his hands and asked, "Say, are you free this afternoon?"

"Sure. What have you got in mind?"

"I was wondering if you'd be willing to come back to my office with me. I'm going to talk with Uncle Liam. Maybe he can shed some light on his old client. Me."

"I'll be glad to."

"It sure is crazy. I'm still wrapping my mind around this whole thing. Reincarnation. But after what I've been through, I'm convinced."

* * *

David and Emma walked into Liam's office.

"Good afternoon, David." Liam looked over at Emma, a curious expression on his face and said, "Who is your friend?"

"Uncle Liam, I'd like to introduce you to Emma Jackson."

"Nice to meet you," said Emma, as she reached out her hand.

"The pleasure is all mine," said Liam taking her hand. "You have a nice firm grip."

"As do you," said Emma.

"Please call me Liam."

Liam leaned back in his swivel chair and surveyed Emma and David with a thoughtful air. "So, what can I do you for?"

"Emma is helping me on a couple of cases," David hesitated, deciding to not yet mention the reincarnation angle with respect to George.

"Way back, you and my dad used to do criminal law and represented some nasty characters in court."

"True."

"What can you tell me about George Samuel Larson?"

Liam turned pale. "Where did you hear that name?" His voice was unsteady.

"His name came up as part of a cold case I learned about recently."

"Learned how?"

"That's not important right now."

"He was murdered." Liam shuddered. "It's a night I'll never forget. George was supposed to meet us at our office, but he never made it."

"Us?" David said.

Liam nodded. "Our firm was representing him." He got up from his desk and walked to the bar. He pulled out a bottle of Glenfiddich. "I need to steady myself. Would you like to join me?"

"Thanks," said David.

"How about you, Emma?"

"Okay, but make it a short one. I like putting water in mine."

"Ah, I see," he smiled. "You are a traditionalist."

"Yes. I find that adding just a wee bit of water brings out the subtle nuances of the whiskey. It tends to open the aromas."

Liam poured the golden liquid into three crystal tumblers. He carried a half-filled glass of the whiskey and a small pitcher of water and placed them on the desk before Emma and said, "Ladies first." He returned to the liquor cabinet for David's and his own glass.

He sank into his seat, pivoted back, and placed his feet on the desk.

"George was a police officer. On the side, he was working as an enforcer for a loan shark group run by Alfonso Bianchi. When George witnessed a brutal murder, he wanted out and obtained evidence that would have implicated the top wise guys in the organization. It would have been his 'get out of jail card.' We think Alfonso found out and sent his son, Enrico, after him." Liam took a long sip of scotch before he continued, "George was bringing the evidence to us that night but when he didn't show up, we knew something was wrong. The plan was that we would accompany George to the station and for him to turn himself in."

"What did you do?" asked David.

"What could we do?" replied Liam, with shaky fingers he wiped beads of sweat which were forming on his forehead. "We went home. The next morning the paper's headline read: 'Police Officer Shot Dead at Main and Queen.'"

"Did you contact the authorities?" David's voice trembled.

"No. We were terrified. Bianchi and his men were watching us." He closed his eyes for a moment to compose his thoughts. "We started getting threats. Your mom was already pregnant, and your dad was frightened something would happen to her and the baby. *You.*"

Emma looked at David. "The timing works."

David nodded in acknowledgment.

Liam gave them a puzzled look and continued. "We decided to move from criminal to real estate law. We finished up any outstanding criminal cases, packed the old case files in boxes, and put them in storage." He took another sip of the scotch. "It was the safest thing we could do for our families," said Liam.

David looked at his uncle, fear serpentining through his gut. "The new client I met with last week?"

"Yes?" said Liam.

"It was Enrico Bianchi." He leveled grave eyes at Liam "He's developing a seniors' residence north of Mason Street."

"My God, boy, what have you done?"

"Took on a new client without knowing this history." David paused; his brows knitted together with worry. "How could I have known?"

"It means the Bianchi family has never stopped watching our firm."

Emma interrupted. "We've got to tell him, David."

"Tell me what?" asked Liam.

David gave a big sigh, and said, "I just don't know where to begin."

Emma reached over and touched David's hand. "Go on, it's okay."

He straightened his shoulders. "Remember my dad telling you about the nightmares I had every night?"

"Yeah, I do. Your parents had hoped that you would grow out of them," replied his uncle. "I thought you had."

"For a long while I thought so, too. But over the last few months, the dreams have returned, more intense than ever. I am really having a tough time coping due to lack of sleep."

"I have noticed you often look exhausted. Especially lately."

"Emma suggested that my dreams might have something to do with either early childhood trauma or a past life. I was skeptical. She encouraged me to see a hypnotherapist."

"Well, it couldn't have been a childhood trauma, you had a happy and stable home life," said Liam.

"Except for the nightmares," David sighed. "Dad and Mom were great. They did everything they could to help."

"Your parents were very worried about your nightmares. They took you to countless doctors."

"I remember. It'd be good for a while, and then it would get bad again."

His uncle gave David a sympathetic look. "I didn't realize you were still struggling with this."

"Emma introduced me to Anna. Interesting lady. She is an empath, but also a hypnotherapist.

"She did a regression for me to the age of four and even at that age I was already having these dreams, visions, whatever you want to call them. Since we were no further ahead, she recommended a second session to regress me further to my most recent past life."

"David, I can't help but feel skeptical."

"I did too, until a few days ago. We have learned that in my former life I was George Samuel Larson."

Liam snorted in surprise. "That can't be possible."

"We had to make sure, so we did a google search to see if someone by that name ever existed," Emma said.

David thumbed open his phone and showed his uncle the Canada Cold Cases website. "Turns out he did. He died December fifteenth, nineteen ninety-three. Almost thirty years ago."

"Unbelievable," said Liam. "But that doesn't prove it was reincarnation."

"I think it's pretty compelling," said David. "How else would I know that name?"

"You could have heard the name somewhere."

"No, Uncle Liam, this feels like a memory, not something that was suggested to me."

"What do you plan to do with this? Go after Bianchi?" asked Liam, his face was ashen.

David's face hardened. "That's exactly what I'm going to do. Catch my killer."

Sixteen

Bianchi

ENRICO BIANCHI HAD been a cruel young man who, as the years went by, became even crueler. When his father Alfonso passed on two decades earlier, he took over the reins of the organization with the acumen of a businessman and the heart of a vicious killer. He might wear business suits and ties now, but the core of him still longed to inflict pain and shame on those who had disappointed him. Occasionally, he'd leave the suit at home and take pleasure in some wet work. He was an evil and sadistic man without remorse.

With great wealth at his disposal, he could have had plastic surgery to remove the parallel scars that ran from his right ear to his earlobe. Instead, he wore them as validation of his power and ruthlessness. He enjoyed the terror the scars imbued in others.

As part of a deal to merge their businesses, the head of an old Irish mob family had struck a deal with Alfonso for Enrico to marry Annabelle, the youngest daughter. She had died early on in their marriage. Some people, out of earshot of Enrico, said she died of grief because of the arranged and very unhappy union. Their gossip could not have been further from the truth.

She had been an air-head whose only use to him was that she gave him two sons. Lorenzo, the oldest, was just as useless as his mother. The younger one, Alessandro, showed promise and was expected to take over the family business when it was time. It was why he had sent his youngest to business school.

Soon after Annabelle had recovered from delivering Alessandro, she had taken to locking her bedroom door to avoid his sexual advances. "I've given you two sons," she'd said. "I've done my duty."

One night, when Alessandro was five, Enrico had smashed down the door, torn her night gown off and hurled her onto the bed. Demented by terror, anger, and years of abuse, she had repeatedly shrieked, "I hate you!" Years later, he still enjoyed the memory of how her slender neck had pulverized in his oversized hands, and the rush of satisfaction he had relished once her thrashing body finally lay still.

When it was over, he had heard a keening sound and glanced at the doorway. Lorenzo was screaming, terror contorting his face, but Alessandro remained calm, his eyes glinting with the same manic light as his own.

Enrico recognized the value of having legitimate businesses through which he could launder his ill-gotten gains from the family's loan shark operations. Together with Alessandro, he dreamed of building a real estate empire and with that wealth, hoped to gain recognition for the Bianchi family name, not just by fear but through respect.

At the age of fifty-five, his thoughts were driven by the idea of succession planning. He wanted his legacy to continue and to provide for his sons. Yes, both sons, despite the eldest being such a deadbeat.

His thoughts took him back to the meeting he had last week with David Harris of Foster and Harris. He enjoyed the irony that this was the same firm that would have destroyed him had he not stopped that stupid cop, George Larson, from squealing. He was impressed with the smarts the young lawyer had displayed. Young enough to mold and with the right grooming, and coercion, if necessary, he'd make a perfect partner for his son Alessandro.

* * *

David looked over at his uncle and said, "Do you still have the files on George Larson and the Bianchi family?"

"We kept the files, but without the crucial piece of evidence that George was going to give us, his testimony would have been inadmissible. After his death, there didn't seem much point pursuing it."

"I'd like to see the files."

"Sure, they are not here though. After we switched to real estate law, we moved all our old files to the storage unit at Kalvin Street and MacDonnell." Liam reached into his desk and handed David the key. "It's unit eleven."

"Great; thanks. I'll head over there later today."

David's phone dinged. "That's Anna. She just emailed me the transcript and the audio file of the second hypnotherapy session. I'm going to print out copies for us to review."

* * *

When David returned from the copier, he handed Emma and his uncle each a copy of the transcript and sat down with his own copy. Emma smiled as she noticed the similar mannerisms of both nephew and uncle. Both stroked their chins and leaned forward in their chairs as they read.

"This makes for some interesting reading." Liam's expression remained dubious. "I don't know, it's a lot to take in."

"I remember this from the session," said Emma. "You were screaming 'Get away from me. I told you I don't have it!'"

"Wow. I don't remember that part."

"Anna did say the recordings and transcripts will help jog your memory."

Liam said, "I do find it interesting that you said, 'I don't have it.' That reference bears an uncanny resemblance to George's missing proof."

"What's more, the transcript indicates that David, I mean George, had a good look at his killer," said Emma. "It says here, 'I won't forget this... I won't forget you!'"

"Do you remember what he looked like?" asked Liam. He was now thinking there might be some merit to David's past life theory.

"No, not really. It's just the eyes, I remember. It's always those eyes that get me," said David. "They're pure evil."

"By that point, 'George' was so agitated that Anna brought David out of the trance," said Emma.

David picked up his iPhone. "I'm calling Anna. I want another session."

"I don't know, David. Is that really such a good idea?" said Emma, her frown furrowing with worry.

"What choice have I got? Maybe we can move past the trauma of my 'death,' and I'll see my murderer's face."

"David, I'm worried—"

David held up his hand, "Hello, Anna?"

"Hi, David. Did you get the transcripts and audio files?"

"Yes, thanks for sending them. They've been very helpful." He paused. "I'd like another session."

"I would recommend waiting. There's a lot you need to process."

"I'd rather not wait, Anna." His voice broke. "I really need your help."

"Okay," she said with some reluctance. "Come tomorrow night at seven."

He breathed a sigh of relief. "Thanks, Anna."

Seventeen

The Storage Unit

DAVID TURNED TO his uncle and said, "I know it all sounds so crazy, but I have this deep conviction that we've got to find a way to have the murderer apprehended."

"Son, if Enrico Bianchi is involved, please be careful." His eyes narrowed with concern. "He is a very dangerous man and has not mellowed with age."

"Uncle Liam." David's voice softened, "Don't worry, he can hardly suspect a 'dead man' is on the hunt for him. Besides, I've no proof. Not yet, at least. I'm hoping the hypnotherapy might reveal some more details."

"Perhaps," Liam said, although his voice lacked conviction.

"I'm headed to the storage unit next. Maybe there are some clues that will lead to why George was killed." He looked at Emma, "Feel like coming with?"

Emma nodded, "For sure. I'm not letting you out of my sight." She pulled her cell out of her purse and said, "Just going to call my mom and tell her I'm staying in the city tonight."

***

David showed his identification to the security guard at the gate and drove to storage unit eleven. It was tricky inserting the key into the lock as it had not been used for some time.

"You should get some WD-40 to lubricate that lock," said Emma.

"Next time." With further coaxing, he was able to pull the lock open. He pulled the roll-up door open and sneezed. "Dusty."

"Probably from all the road construction. Summertime in the city…"

"At least my dad and uncle put their case files in sealed tote boxes." He carried an empty banker box into the unit.

"How long do lawyers usually keep their clients' files?"

"Normally, they retain the file for fifteen years after the date it was closed and then it's destroyed. A file could be held longer if the lawyer believes the file will be needed at a future date."

"And since George Larson's case was never closed—"

"It means there might be some files here pertaining to his case."

"Looks like they have a good filing system in place," she said.

"Yeah. The boxes are marked by year, and then the files are sorted alphabetically."

"Okay, so where do you want me to start?"

"George died in nineteen ninety-three, but we should go back one year at a time. I'll take that year, and you take nineteen ninety-two."

"What am I looking for?"

"Look for files labeled George Samuel Larson and check if there's anything for Bianchi."

"Okay. I'm on it."

"When we're done with those two years, you do the even years and I'll do the odd years until we don't find any more files on either party."

"Great."

* * *

Two hours later, Emma yawned. "I'm tired and I'm getting hungry."

"Me, too. We've gone back ten years and the last year there were files on George was nineteen eighty-nine and nineteen eighty-seven for Bianchi."

"This is going to make for some interesting reading tonight."

Emma and David put the files in the empty banker's box, careful to place them in chronological order.

"We should do takeout, so we can get a jump on reviewing these files," said Emma.

"Sounds good. Feel like getting Greek food?"

"Sure do."

"Let's stop at Yaya's Greek House."

"Great! I love that place! Their veggie wrap with grilled eggplant and tzatziki is calling me."

"I'll need something more substantial than that. I'll get their souvlaki on a bun."

* * *

Back at his condo, David poured them each a glass of Pino Grigio and placed their meals on the coffee table.

"Not really a date night," he said with apology, "as it's a working dinner."

"David, it's great spending time with you no matter what we do."

"Thanks for that." He grinned. "Shall we start with nineteen eighty-seven?"

"Sure."

"Okay, then. You take Bianchi's file. I'll take George's." David handed her the file for Bianchi.

"It's pretty thin," she said. She leafed through the file. "Looks like most of it is for small petty crime committed by Bianchi's people."

"Not surprising. I wouldn't expect to see anything serious there. Uncle Liam said witnesses wound up dead or missing. Enrico Bianchi was a master at leaving no tracks or evidence."

"Even the most clever criminal can make mistakes though," said Emma. "Don't you think?"

"If he did, hopefully we'll find it."

The two read the files for the next few hours, and besides the occasional bathroom break or refill of their wine glasses, little was said.

Emma broke the silence. "Too bad this stuff isn't digitized; this is such a tedious process."

"Yeah, we sure do have it easy with technology nowadays. Found anything of interest yet?"

"No, not really." Emma rubbed her eyes. "It's after midnight. It's been a long day. I'm heading back home in the morning. I'm turning in. You coming to bed?"

"Not yet, I'm going to spend a little more time on this."

"Okay." Emma leaned over and kissed David lightly on the lips. "See you in the morning."

It was nearly two in the morning, when David got to the files on George for nineteen ninety-three. As he opened the file, a small envelope fell out of the folder. On it, there was handwriting in faded blue ink.

Canadian Dominion Bank,
Regent Street Branch 66, New Elgan,
Box #712.

He drew in a sharp breath, and opened the envelope and found a key for a safety deposit box inside. Box 712 was stamped on the metal key.

David's hands shook as he entered the bank's address into the search engine on his phone. He sat back, relieved. This branch was still active. If—and this was a big if—there was a long-term lease on the safety deposit box, it might still be active.

Knowing there was nothing further he could do at this time of the night, he returned the key to the envelope and placed it in his wallet, turned off the light, and padded to the bedroom to join Emma.

* * *

Over coffee the next morning, David told Emma what he had discovered.

"Do you think this key will lead to the evidence that George planned to present to the Crown?" Emma asked.

"It's a strong possibility."

"I have some work deadlines today for a client's website." She hesitated. "I'd love to come, but…"

"It's okay. I can't go yet anyway. I have to come up with a viable reason why the bank would allow me access to the safety deposit box." He hesitated. "That's if the box is still open. If the box was rented on a long-term lease, then it could still be in existence."

"What if the bank knew George Larson was deceased?" she asked.

"Still may be held by the bank for years, even decades, if a family member hasn't claimed the box."

"What about his sister, Sarah? Would she be allowed access?"

David nodded. "Yes, if there is a will in her possession naming her as George's heir. It would be quite simple."

"And if there is no will?"

"If there are no other next of kin besides Sarah, then I could prepare a legal document on her behalf showing she is his rightful heir."

"You've got your work cut out for you today."

"Yeah, I do. I'll need to contact Sarah to get her permission to access the box."

"You could reach out to her via Facebook Messenger," Emma suggested.

She picked up her cell and looked at the time. "I'm running late. See you at six? We can have a quick bite to eat and then head over to Anna's."

"Thanks, Em."

"See you tonight, sweetheart." She picked up her purse and tablet and playfully blew him a kiss.

She called me sweetheart. David had never imagined his heart could ever be this full.

Eighteen

Sarah Larson-Moody

FROM THE WINDOW, David watched Emma climb into her Mercedes. He was amused at how she always angle-parked the car, declaring any spot with a curb on one side as primo parking. "No one else can park on at least one side. Trying to keep the car from getting dings," she'd explained.

When he saw her put the car into gear, he was satisfied she was safely on her way back to her mom's place.

Since spending time with Emma, he'd neglected his workouts; it was high time to get back to his exercise routine. With the goal of making good use of his time, he first opened the Facebook Messenger app on his iPhone and formulated a message to Sarah Larson.

Dear Mrs. Moody,

This is David Harris of the law firm Foster and Harris. I found your contact details on the Facebook memorial page you set up for your brother George Samuel Larson. Our firm represented George prior to his death. Going through our archives we recently discovered a key for a safety deposit box which George rented at the Canadian Dominion

Bank. If you are amenable, I would like to schedule an appointment for us to meet at our offices. Message me back if you are interested.

Sincerely,

David Harris

Foster & Harris Law Barristers & Solicitors

Pleased with the message he'd formulated, he headed to his workout room to row.

An hour later, David had shaved and showered, and dressed in a short-sleeved shirt and dress pants. Even this early in the day and with the air conditioning on full blast in the condo, the temperature was muggy and oppressive, his clothes already sticking to his skin.

While locking the condo door his phone pinged, and a Messenger notification flashed across the screen. Sarah had replied.

Hello Mr. Harris,

Thanks for reaching out. I am open to meeting with you. What day and time do you propose?

Best,

Sarah Moody

David couldn't be bothered to go back inside, so he leaned against his door and typed back his reply: Thanks for the quick response. I have time to meet this afternoon. Does 2:00 p.m. work for you?

That works for me, Sarah.

Great. See you then. Sending you the address, David H.

David texted her the address, put his cell in the rear right pocket of his pants, and headed toward the elevator.

* * *

Sarah Larson-Moody was fifty-nine years old and had retired several years ago from teaching high school music and math. A widow of five years, she found channeling herself into the rigors of exercise kept her physically and emotionally fit. She was lean with sinewy muscles. She had participated in various marathons and duathlons and was currently training for next year's Long Distance Triathlon BC Championship. Triathlons combined the three disciplines of swimming, biking, and running; she was looking forward to the personal challenge.

For this reason, she climbed the stairs as opposed to taking the elevator and several minutes later had reached the fourth floor which was home to the law offices of Foster and Harris.

The office was not ostentatious in nature and was equipped with functional and practical furniture and cabinets, dating from the late 1980s. A grandfather clock rested against one wall, as if in homage to an earlier era. A young man in his late twenties rose up from the front desk where he had been sitting and said, "I'm David Harris. You must be Mrs. Moody."

"Yes; please call me Sarah."

David reached out to shake her hand, and said, "Let's go to my office."

David guided Sarah to a glass partitioned office and motioned her to sit. Once she was comfortably seated, he said. "Can I get you anything? I just brewed some coffee a few minutes ago."

"I'd like a glass of water if you have it."

"Sure thing. I'll be back momentarily."

When David returned, he handed her the water. "Here you go. Can I get you anything else?"

"No, this will be fine." She looked at him with sad, gray eyes. "Have you been with Foster and Harris long?"

"For about eight years. I joined right after I graduated," said David. "My uncle and father started this law firm nearly forty years ago. Initially, they practiced criminal law and represented unsavory characters in our society."

"Everyone deserves the right to a lawyer."

"True. Were you aware that George was a client of Foster and Harris?"

"No, George didn't confide in me much. My mom and I knew he was in some sort of trouble." Sarah sighed. "But he wouldn't talk about it. Mom and I figured he got mixed up in organized crime."

"Might be why he became a client."

"George was a good kid and a good cop at first. But we needed money. Our dad had cancer and needed treatments the Ontario Health Insurance Plan wouldn't cover."

"That's tough."

"Suddenly, there was money. Lots of it. My mom didn't want to ask any questions, but my dad refused to take any of it." She pressed her lips into a thin line. "He said my brother was a dirty cop and he'd rather die than take any that money. By May of nineteen ninety-three, our dad was gone."

"It broke my mom's heart when our dad died. But after my brother was murdered in December of the same year, it was too much for her. She killed herself a few months later, in March of nineteen ninety-four."

"I am so sorry," David said.

"Thanks. In under a year, I lost my dad, my brother, and my mom." She wiped tears from her cheeks. "I know my brother was not a saint, but his motivation was pure. All these years later, I still want justice."

"Your brother's untimely death unnerved my dad and uncle so much that they made a sudden change to real estate and corporate law."

She leaned forward in her chair and asked, "But what does this have to do with me?

"I can't get into the specifics, but some information has come to light that led me to dig into our archives." David was reluctant to reveal the details of the past life regression to a stranger even if she was his sister, no, *George's* sister.

"Go on."

"We found a key to a safety deposit box. We think the contents might help us find out what George was up to." He paused. "Maybe even why he was killed."

"If that's the case, shouldn't you just go to the police?"

"We could. But since we don't know what's in the box, we thought as George's last known relative, you might want to be the one to open it."

"Thanks. I appreciate that."

"Since so much time has passed, the bank will want legal documentation proving you are George's sister and that you have a right to access the safety deposit box." He leveled his gaze at Sarah. "I have taken the liberty of preparing an affidavit on your behalf." David slid the papers across the desk, turning them around so Sarah could read them from her position.

"Okay. Give me a minute to read these over."

A few minutes later, Sarah's voice was hopeful. "All these years, the police never came up with anything." She picked up the pen resting on David's desk and signed. "When can we go?"

"Now if you like."

"Good. Sitting on this for even one more minute is something I just don't want to do."

David glanced at his wristwatch. "The bank closes at five today. It's only three-thirty." He rose from his chair "Shall we?"

Sarah smiled and said, "Absolutely."

"We'll take my car."

Nineteen

The Bank

THE SKIES WERE overcast, and the air heavy with humidity, promising rain for the afternoon. Just as David and Sarah pulled into the parking lot, the downpour began. David hurried out of the MGB and quickly pulled the canvas convertible top over the seats.

"Sarah, can you give me a hand?"

"Sure, thing."

Expecting to show Sarah how to secure the canvas top, his eyebrows raised in surprise when she hooked the cover's eyelets onto the supporting studs at the back.

Next, he got in the front seat and pulled the two clamps of the convertible frame securely onto the windshield frame and got out of the car. "Thanks. You know your way around an MGB."

"It's been a lot of years since I've been in one of these old British cars. Fun on a sunny day, but not so much when it rains." She paused. "My brother used to own one just like this. Same color too. Nineteen seventy-eight?"

"Yeah, it's a seventy-eight." David was nonplussed at this information and hid his face from view.

"Funny, it's even got a small dent right in the fender. Just like my brother's old car."

"My dad bought it about ten years ago. When he passed on, I took it over. It's had a few owners over the years." He made a mental note to check the Ministry of Transportation of Ontario report he had kept that listed all the car's previous owners. *Could this have been George's car?*

"It's raining even harder. I'll see you in the bank," she said.

"Hang on a sec, Sarah, I should have an umbrella in the boot." He opened the trunk and was relieved to see it was still there.

Before he could hand the umbrella over to her, it was caught by a rogue gust of wind and was turned inside out. "Sorry," David said.

"No worries, let's just go!" Sarah replied.

David ran ahead of Sarah to the bank's entrance, and opened the door for her.

The bank had been built at the turn of the last century. Their shoes tapped an irregular tattoo on the polished marble floors, unlike modern banks, it had a weighty feel of solemnity and propriety.

When they stopped at the reception desk, the attendant glanced up, casting them a look of disapproval at their wet hair and damp clothes. "Good afternoon, how may I be of assistance?"

"Hello, my name is David Harris, from the law firm, Foster and Harris. And this is my client Mrs. Sarah Larson-Moody." David handed her the paperwork. "Mrs. Larson-Moody would like access to the late Mr. George Samuel Larson's safety deposit box. Number seven-one-two. The deceased was her brother."

The desk clerk nodded, turned to her computer, did a quick search and frowned. "This safety deposit box has been inactive for almost thirty years." She reached for the phone. "I'll need to call the manager." She gestured toward some leather chairs. "Please have a seat."

Half an hour passed. The phone on the clerk's desk rang. "Certainly. I'll let them know." She replaced the phone in its cradle. "The manager will be right down to see you."

A few minutes later a heavyset man with a thin moustache came down the stairs. His hand was outstretched before he had even reached them. "I'm Albert Cartwright. You must be David Harris."

"Pleased to meet you," said David.

"Likewise. And you must be Mrs. Larson-Moody."

"Yes. That's right."

"Would you follow me, please?"

Once they were settled in Albert's office, he said, "May I please see your paperwork?"

"Certainly." David handed him the affidavit.

"Great, thanks. And Mrs. Moody, may I see your driver's license?"

There was a slight tremor in Sarah's hand as she dug through her purse and produced her ID.

After a few minutes, the bank manager looked up. "Everything seems to be in order. It's rather irregular, because so much time has passed, but this isn't unheard of. Sometimes family members have no idea that their loved ones have left behind safety deposit boxes." He stood up. "Would you follow me please?"

He led them into the safety deposit box room, and produced the key and slid it into the slot for number 712. Then David took the key from his wallet and did the same. The manager removed the box and placed it on the table.

"When you're done, just ring the buzzer, and I'll come get you."

* * *

After the bank manager left, Sarah drew a deep breath and said, "I feel nervous."

David put his hand on her arm to reassure her. "It'll be all right."

"Okay, let's take a look. Maybe I'll finally find out what my brother was really up to." She lifted the lid.

The sole content was an envelope, with the same handwriting in faded blue ink as the one that had contained the safety deposit key. It read: *Attention: Sarah Larson.*

Sarah sucked in her breath. "It's addressed to me. After all this time, I'm afraid to open it." Her voice was uneven.

"It might provide the answers you've been looking for." He gave her a sympathetic smile. *And answer my questions, too,* he thought.

"Okay." Her hands trembled as she tore the flap off the envelope. As she removed the note, a digital memory card fell on the floor.

"Wow. That's an SD memory card." David gently picked it up on the edges so as not to damage the circuitry, then placed it on the table. "It's so large compared to what we have nowadays."

"State of the art at the time," said Sarah.

"What does the note say?" asked David.

Sarah read the note and gasped, then handed it to him. "Here. You should read this." She was visibly upset, and her thin shoulders were shaking.

> *Dear Sarah,*
>
> *In the event of my death, bring this memory card to the law firm Foster & Harris. Bring the video camera, too. They'll know what to do. Tell Mom I'm sorry.*
>
> *I love you Sis,*
>
> *George.*

David placed the memory card back in the envelope. "Do you still have the camera?"

She nodded. "I never could get rid of George's things." Her eyes took on a faraway look. "I remember he bought the camera a few months before his death."

"My mom and dad had a video camera when I was growing up. They used to plug the camera into the television with RCA composite cables so we could watch family videos. Sometimes my mom would transfer them to VHS tapes. Pretty old tech."

"Not at the time. The Ampex DCT was the first digital data compression video camera of its kind. It could tape for hours."

"What do you think is on the memory card?"

"Not sure."

David glanced at his watch. "I've got another meeting in an hour." He paused. "Where can I drop you off?"

"I parked down the street from your office. Can you bring me to my car?"

"Of course."

"Would you be willing to meet again at my office tomorrow morning?" he asked. "Would ten o'clock work for you?"

"Sure."

"For security, I'll put the memory card in the office safe over night." He put the envelope in his pocket.

"Good idea."

"Can you bring George's camera with you?"

"Absolutely."

"Do you know how to work it?"

"Yeah, I think I remember. George was so proud of it and he showed me how it worked. It's been years since I looked at it though." She paused. "It'll need charging. I'll do that tonight."

"Thanks Sarah."

"No problem."

"Okay. Let's get going then." He pushed the buzzer for the bank manager.

* * *

Albert removed the ornate phone from its cradle on the oak desk and called his brother-in-law.

"Enrico. It's Albert."

"Haven't heard from you for a while," Enrico said.

"True. How's the family?"

"Family's doing great. Alessandro's helping me with the biz."

"And Lorenzo? Doing any better?"

"Nah., I don't buy into this bipolar shit. Big disappointment, that one."

"Yeah, I hear you. Kids."

"So, what can I do for you?"

"You're not gonna believe this." He paused for dramatic effect. "You were right. Remember when you asked me to keep an eye on George Larson's account?"

"Will you just spill it?" Enrico's voice was becoming impatient.

"George's sister and her lawyer are here." He eyed the card that David had given him. "Some David Harris from the law firm Foster & Harris."

Albert could hear Enrico inhale sharply. "Can you delay their departure?"

"Sure can. Right now, they are still in the vault."

"Keep them there as long as you can. I'll send one of my men to follow them."

"Sure thing."

"Thanks. I owe you one. You and Jessica should come over for a barbecue this weekend."

"Love to."

* * *

David looked at his wristwatch, trying with little success to keep his annoyance in check. "Where is the manager?"

"It is a long wait," agreed Sarah. "Do you think he forgot about us?"

"Not sure." David eyed the emergency release lever on the inside of the vault door. "I have to get back to the office, secure the SD card and then get to my next meeting."

Just as David reached for the lever, the doors to the safety deposit vault swung open.

"I do apologize to have kept you waiting," said Albert with an ingratiating smile. "I was called away unexpectedly."

* * *

From his black sedan, the man watched David and Sarah hurry out of the bank into the rain, jump in the yellow British car and take off.

He eased into traffic, keeping several car lengths of distance behind the sportscar, the wiper blades on his car beating in cadence to the pelting rain. *This is an easy tail,* he thought. *Who could miss that color?* A short distance later, the MGB pulled in behind a late model Honda and the woman got out of the car. He pushed the phone icon on his steering wheel to make a remote call.

"They're parting company. Who do want me to follow? The man or the woman?"

"Get the license plates for both vehicles but follow the man."

Twenty

Third Time's The Charm

EMMA WAS TERRIFIED by David's decision to undergo a third hypnotherapy session with Anna. She could appreciate that he needed to know more about the circumstances of his death, but worried he was exposing himself to significant mental trauma and duress.

On the drive into the city, she tried to comfort herself with the knowledge that Anna would not have agreed to another sitting if she had thought the risk was too great.

Emma pulled into the parking lot of the local grocery store. She purchased fresh romaine lettuce, a block of parmesan cheese, a head of garlic and a bottle of good quality extra virgin olive oil. Her next stop was *Eggplant Paradise* where she picked up an order for two of eggplant parmigiana. She eyed the desserts at the front counter and decided against it.

Just before six, she arrived at David's condo, got out of the car, and holding the cloth grocery bag in one hand, and balancing the takeout meal in the other, she walked toward the building. A woman with sandy colored hair dressed in jogging clothes arrived at the condo entrance at the same time, waived her keycard over the electronic eye and held the door open for Emma.

Emma was surprised the concierge was not at his desk, but thought, *Probably on a quick restroom break.*

At the elevator, the woman pushed the button and the door slid open. They both entered and she said, "Looks like you got your hands full. What floor?"

"The fourteenth please. Thanks so much."

The woman smiled pleasantly and pressed seven and then fourteen.

At the seventh floor, the woman got out and said, "Have a good day."

"Thanks. You, too."

At the fourteenth floor, Emma exited and walked over to 1403. She placed the grocery bag on the floor and just as she had her hand raised to knock, the door to the elevator dinged, and she heard, "Em, you're here already. I was running late. I hope you haven't been waiting for me long."

"No, not long. Actually, I just got here. I was about to knock on your door."

"How did you get in the building without a key?"

"The concierge wasn't at his desk, but a nice woman let me in. Lives on the seventh floor. She's in great shape. A blond. Do you know her?"

"No, I don't." David took his keycard, opened the door and said, "After you."

"Thanks. Do you mind grabbing that for me?" She motioned toward the grocery bag sitting on the floor.

As Emma and David walked to the kitchen, she said, "Can you put the oven on warm and put this in?"

David eyed the takeout container that was covered with aluminum foil. "Smells wonderful. What did you bring?"

"Eggplant parmigiana from Eggplant Paradise."

"One of my favorite restaurants!"

"Mine, too. One more thing we have in common." She rummaged through the kitchen drawers. "Where do you keep your chopping board?"

"Here you go."

"Thanks."

"What are you making?" he asked.

"Caesar salad with my own dressing. Hand me the garlic?"

It had been a long time since David had been in his kitchen, preparing a meal together with another person. He relished how easy-going and comfortable it was to be with Emma.

Dinner conversation remained light. Neither Emma nor David wanted to broach the subject of the third hypnotherapy session David had requested.

Emma pushed her plate away. "That was so delicious. I'm glad I didn't bring dessert, too."

"You mean no chocolate cake today?" He teased.

She became serious. "It's almost a quarter to seven. We better head over to Anna's place."

* * *

Once David had settled himself comfortably on the couch, Anna said, "We must be very careful how we approach this. I want you to observe rather than experience George's death. To avoid any emotional trauma, it's important that we have you remain objective and dispassionate."

"I understand."

"Remember, your safe word remains 'home.'"

"Okay."

"Ready to get started?"

"As ready as I'll ever be." He reached over to take Emma's hand. "I'll be fine. Don't worry."

Anna took David through the steps of induction, before she said, "You are now in a different life, one you have lived before. You are now reliving the life you lived when you were George Samuel Larson. It is five forty-five on the evening of Wednesday, December fifteenth, nineteen ninety-three." She waited a moment and said, "Hi George. It's Anna."

"You, again. What do you want?"

"Can you tell me where you are?"

"I'm on my way to the lawyers," he said as a tone of irritation crept in his voice. "Told you that before."

"Now, George, I want you to listen to me very carefully. Something very bad is about to happen, but I want you to remain calm. If you feel frightened listen to my voice. It is your anchor; it is your safe place."

"What the heck, lady. What are you talking about? I'm busy."

"George," she continued, "I want you to tell me everything that happens, but in a calm and relaxed voice. Remember you are watching, not experiencing."

"Sure. Whatever."

Within seconds, his face contorted and he screamed, "No! Get away from me. I told you I don't have it!"

"George, I know this is frightening, but stay calm. Tell me what is happening."

"He's got a gun." George's voice had become flat and remote.

"Who does?" Anna asked.

"Alfonso's punk son. Enrico Bianchi."

Emma and Anna exchanged shocked glances.

"What's he doing now?"

"He's gonna shoot me. Told him I don't have it."

"What don't you have George?"

"I don't have the video."

"What's on the video George?"

"Evidence. I got the murdering prick on video."

"Who was murdered George?"

"Chris Beacon."

"Oh, my God, I've been shot. Please, somebody help me!" George lifted his hand to his left temple, pulled his hand away and looked at his fingertips with disbelief and said, "Blood."

"George, you are observing only, you are not feeling any pain."

"Okay. No pain."

"What's he doing now?"

"He's leaning over me. He's searching my pockets." George's eyes looked vacantly into space. "I told you I don't have it you asshole."

David's hands clawed vicious strokes in the air.

"What's happening George?"

"I scratched the sonofabitch's face." His voice was faint. "It's getting dark here. So dark—"

Anna said, "Five, four, three, two, one. Wake up David."

Emma moved to sit beside him and helped him to sit up.

David took a few beats to remember where he was. "My killer was Enrico Bianchi. Funny, I just met him a few days ago. Wanted me to draft up paperwork on some real estate deal for him and his son. Even tried to get me to invest in it."

He shook his head. "I kept having this nagging feeling I knew him from somewhere. And he's got two double scars on the right side of his face. Where I—" He shook his head, still struggling with this knowledge. "I mean, where George gouged his face."

"What do we do now?" Emma asked.

"We should go to the police," said Anna. "I know someone who might be sympathetic. I consult for the police every now and again."

"You're kidding! The police use psychics?" David's voice was incredulous.

"Well, the way it works is I give them impressions of where a body might be buried. But it's up to them to use forensic science to see if there are any clues on the body or at the crime scene to help discover the killer."

"While I agree we should go to the police, I don't want to go just yet," said David.

Anna and Emma looked at him with surprise. "Why not?" They both said together.

He looked at Emma. "Remember that safety deposit key I found in George's file?"

"And?"

"I met with George's sister Sarah today. We went to the bank together. I presented the paperwork proving Sarah was next of kin and they gave us access to the safety deposit box."

"Okay? You're killing me with suspense."

"Well, we found an SD card."

"The video that George referred to in the session?"

David shrugged his shoulders, "It's entirely possible."

"Anyway, Sarah is meeting me at my office at ten tomorrow morning. She's bringing George's camera. Apparently, she kept it all these years. We'll know for sure then."

He turned to Emma. "I'd be grateful if you could come tomorrow. He paused. "Anna, you're invited, too."

"Great. I'll be there."

Emma pulled Anna into a hug and said, "Thanks so much, Anna."

"My pleasure. Glad to be of help." The older woman embraced Emma a second time. "This hug's for your mom. Tell her to stop working so hard."

"Will do. See you in the morning."

As Emma and David walked back to the car, they didn't notice the shadowy figure lurking in the dense shrubbery at the edge of Anna's driveway.

***

Back at David's condo, Emma suggested, "I think we should update the whiteboard."

"Good idea."

She picked up the marker and wrote Chris Beacon. "We need to find out more about him." She underlined the name for emphasis. "What else?"

"Once we know for sure what's actually on the video, I'd feel more comfortable going to Staff Inspector Grant."

"Since you, I mean, *George* scratched his killer, is there any chance there could be DNA evidence they collected from under the fingernails?"

"It's certainly something to ask Staff Inspector Grant."

Emma pulled out her phone. "What was that cold cases website you used to search for George Larson?"

"Canada Cold Cases."

"Right. Thanks."

She pulled up the website and typed in Chris Beacon.

David peered over her shoulder and caught a whiff of lavender. "You smell nice."

"Seriously, David." She playfully nudged her elbow into his ribs.

"Ouch."

"You're faking. That did not hurt." Her face became serious. "Look—I've got a hit."

"Says here Chris Beacon was a real estate developer who disappeared in early nineteen ninety-three. He was last seen leaving his office at six on the evening of March tenth. He was to attend a business dinner after work at the New Elgan Golf and Country Club but never made it there. Left behind a wife and three kids. Two girls and a boy."

"That's so sad."

"Staff Inspector Grant was in charge of this case, too."

"After we see that video tomorrow, he's definitely going to be the next person on our list to visit."

Emma stifled a yawn. "It's been another exciting night, David. But I am just bushed."

"Me, too. Let's turn in." He pulled her into an embrace. "You think it was fate?"

"What was?"

"You almost running me over?"

"Yeah, I do."

"I got something for you."

"Oh?"

He reached into his pocket and pressed a keycard into her hand. "This is a key to the condo. Can't have my girl standing in the hallway outside my door."

Her cheeks flushed pink. "Thank you, David. This means a lot to me."

"Em, you mean a lot to me. More than you'll ever know."

The two lovers held hands and made their way to the bedroom.

Twenty-One

The Memory Card

DAVID AND EMMA arrived at the offices of Foster and Harris just before nine. It had rained itself out over night, and the early morning sun cast a golden hue on the surrounding buildings. Steam rose off the pavement, promising another hot and humid day.

"That was a good twenty-minute walk," said Emma.

"No kidding. With this humidity, I'll need to change my shirt already." He nodded at her bare shoulders. "You look comfortable in your sundress."

"I see your office is air-conditioned."

"Yeah, it sure is."

"Well, thank goodness for small mercies." She motioned to the bag slung over her shoulder. "I'm glad I brought a sweater in case it becomes too cold for me."

"Nah, don't worry; it won't be an icebox. It will be pleasant in here."

"David, I've been wondering. What if that video camera doesn't work anymore?"

"I was thinking about that, too. Couldn't sleep last night, so I got up in the middle of the night."

"Oh no, I didn't notice." She gave him a concerned look. "Was it the dream again?"

"No, it wasn't that. I was just pumped up about what we're going to find out today. I went online and found out that with an SD to USB adapter, we could view it on my laptop as well."

"We could save it to a thumb drive. Then you'd have an extra copy. For added precaution, you should save it to the Cloud, too, that would be even more secure."

"Good thinking. There's an Office Depot just down the road."

"Shall I run out and purchase the video adapter and a thumb drive?" Emma offered, reading his mind before he'd asked her.

"If you wouldn't mind."

"I don't mind at all."

"Thanks, Em."

She picked up her cell and glanced at the time. "I should be back in plenty of time for the meeting at ten." She gave him a quick peck on the cheek and in a fireball of motion, was out the door.

* * *

While Emma was out, David decided to change his shirt. He went to his closet behind his desk where he kept spare clothing and selected a matching spare shirt and tie. The Bonobos business casual shirt was light blue in color and one of his favorites. Remembering the high humidity forecast for the day, he replaced the navy-blue tie back on its hanger.

He heard the office door open, and a moment later his uncle said, "Good morning, David."

"Good morning, Uncle Liam." He smiled at his uncle with affection. "I know this was one of your days off, thanks for coming in."

"No problem. It's still early. I can hit the golf course later." He settled into the leather chair in front of David's desk.

David raised his eyebrows in surprise. "You're going out in this humidity?"

"Yeah, shouldn't be a problem. I'll dress lightly and keep myself hydrated."

"With water I hope," David teased.

"Oh, sure. Lots of water." His uncle laughed. "Your message was intriguing. You told me that you found evidence. Relating to George Larson's death."

"Possibly. But it's thirty-year-old technology. George had opened a safety deposit box unbeknownst to his sister, Sarah Larson-Moody. I found the safety deposit box key from the files in our storage unit. Then I contacted Sarah. I drafted up paperwork yesterday, to present to the bank showing that Sarah was next of kin, and we were able to access the safety deposit box."

"What did you find?"

"An old SD card. But of course, no way to view it last night."

"Sarah is coming this morning with George's video camera." David leaned back in his chair. "Emma and I had another idea. What if the camera won't work anymore? She left a few minutes ago to pick up an adapter so that we can watch the video on the laptop."

"Hopefully, we will get answers as to why George was murdered."

"I hope so, too." David hesitated. "I did go to the third hypnotherapy session last night."

"How did that go?"

"Well, I haven't seen the transcript yet, but because Anna regressed me in a way that I wasn't emotionally invested, I remembered most of the session."

"Go on."

"It looks like George was on his way to you and my dad to get the safety deposit box key and then retrieve the SD card from the bank." David leveled his gaze at his uncle, his expression perplexed. "Any idea why the key was in the Foster and Harris files for George?"

Liam's voice was guarded. "He gave the key to us for safe keeping." His Adams apple bobbed up and down. "After George's death, we boxed up everything to do with George."

"But why not give the key to the police as evidence?" asked David. "It could have led to the arrest of George's killer."

"In retrospect, not our best decision," Liam acknowledged. "After what happened to George — we were terrified."

"I get it." David pursed his lips in frustration. "There's more."

"More?" A worried expression shadowed his uncle's face.

"During the last regression I saw the killer's face."

"And?"

"It was Bianchi. Enrico Bianchi."

"Oh my God." His uncle wiped perspiration from his face. "This was always our worst fear."

"Without concrete evidence, a past life regression is no proof," David cautioned.

"I agree. Right now, all we have are suspicions."

"Depending on what's on that SD card, we might be able to get the police involved."

"I've never run across a case that got solved from beyond the grave. This will be one for the record," said Liam.

"Well, let's not get ahead of ourselves. We just don't know—"

Emma tapped on David's office door and said, "Hello, gentlemen, I'm back. I got the adapter for the SD card and a couple of USB drives."

"Hi, Emma," said Liam. "It's nice to see you again."

"It's really nice to see you too, Liam," she said with warmth in her voice. She walked over to him and gave him a hug. "David and I have only been dating a short while. You don't mind the hug, do you?"

"More than okay." Liam beamed at the gesture of affection.

She turned to David and handed him the SD to USB adapter "We still have a few minutes before Sarah gets here. Time to get things set up."

"Good plan. Let's make sure everything is working. We'll set up in the board room."

Emma and Liam followed David while he carried his laptop and the adapter to the boardroom. He pulled the adapter out of its packaging and plugged it into his laptop. After the device had gone through the installation process and driver updates, David said, "I'll screen cast from the laptop to the Samsung TV."

Liam nodded his approval. "Should be able to see more detail on the big screen."

When Emma's phone pinged, she picked it up, read the message and frowned. "Just got a text from Anna. She says she can't make it today."

"It's not the end of the world" replied David. "Although it would have been nice if she had been able to attend."

"It's strange though. It's not like her to cancel at the last minute like this." She keyed in the number for Anna. "It's gone to voicemail. I'll try her later."

"It's almost ten. Sarah should be here any moment now," said David. "I put some fresh coffee on earlier. It should be ready by now. Would one of you mind bringing coffee, sugar, and creamer to the boardroom?"

"Sure, no problem," said Emma.

"I'll give you a hand," said Liam to Emma.

"Thanks."

"Great. I am just about finished setting up here. We should be ready to go once Sarah arrives," said David.

Twenty-Two

The Video

AT PRECISELY TEN o'clock Sarah arrived with a camera bag slung over her shoulder. As she entered, she was greeted by Emma who carried the coffee pot, while Liam held a tray laden with coffee cups, sugar and creamer.

"Hello there, you must be Sarah." Liam beamed at the fit and attractive woman. "I'm Liam Foster. I'd shake your hand but as you can see, my hands are a bit full right now."

"Nice to meet you." Sarah returned an equally engaging smile.

"And I'm Emma. We've been expecting you. David is waiting for us in the board room."

Once the four were settled into comfortable chairs surrounding the board room table, with their coffees, David said, "It's time to get started."

"About that," said Sarah. "I charged the video camera over night, but I just couldn't get it to work." She sighed with frustration. "I brought it with me in case we could figure out what was wrong with it. I've kept George's things stored in the basement all these years, and I wonder if the humidity damaged the circuit board. I'm so sorry."

"We considered that this might be a possibility. Emma went to the local office store, and she picked up an SD to USB adapter. We've waited for you to arrive before trying it out, but we think we should be able to view the SD card through my laptop. I have mirrored my computer to the big screen so we can watch it there."

Sarah sighed with relief. "I have been agonizing over this all morning. Hopefully your solution works."

David turned on his laptop, then inserted the SD card into the adapter. A few moments later a jerky and uneven image appeared on the screen. David hit the pause button. "I suggest the first time we watch this video; we refrain from making comments. Everybody, watch as closely and carefully as you can, for every detail possible."

The video showed a dark, wooded area, then focused in on a man on his knees begging for mercy. "I told you I'd get you the money. I just need a few more days." He was crying uncontrollably.

The video pulled away from the frightened man and zoomed in on a sinister man in his mid to late twenties. "It's too late now."

He raised a crowbar and hit the man across the face, knocking him to the ground. The screaming was unbearable and went on for several minutes as he was repeatedly bludgeoned until he lay still and was silent. Even so, the killer continued to hit the man again and again. The camera panned back to the killer's blood splattered face which showed manic eyes and a cruel mouth. Beyond Liam's sharp intake of breath, no one said a word.

The silence was oppressive. Everyone was too shocked to speak.

Liam was the first to break the silence. "That was Enrico Bianchi."

Sarah placed her left hand against her mouth, removed it and spoke next, "Oh my God! Who was that poor man?"

David's face was solemn. "We think it's missing real estate developer Christopher Beacon."

"I remember reading about that in the papers thirty odd years ago," said Sarah. "His body was never found."

"Yeah, it was big news at the time," Liam agreed.

"So, this is why my brother was killed. He videotaped a murder being committed by this Bianchi character?"

"And somehow Enrico found out about the video and killed George," said Emma.

The group sat in uneasy silence.

"I don't know about the rest of you, but, after this, coffee is not going to cut it." Liam got up from his chair and left the boardroom. A few minutes later he returned with four crystal tumblers and a bottle of Macallan single malt.

He poured generous amounts of the golden ambrosia into each glass and handed them to David, Sarah, and Emma. "Oh, sorry I forgot the water, Emma."

"Don't worry about it. I need it straight up today."

David wiped away the beads of perspiration that clung like dew drops to his forehead. He shuddered and nervously scratched the back of his neck, then took another sip of the scotch. "Okay, everyone, I suggest we watch it one more time." "Maybe we can figure out where this video was taken."

David slid the cursor to the beginning and selected play. When they got to the screen where the victim's face was shown, Liam said, "Can you pause it, please, and go back?"

David stopped the video.

His uncle leaned in to take a closer look, then glanced at David and asked, "Can you make a screenshot of this?"

"Maybe." He looked at the screen wondering where to accomplish this when Emma got up, went to the computer, and pushed print screen, then saved the image as 'possibly Chris Beacon.'

"Thanks," he gave a sheepish grin. "Shall we continue?"

The group nodded.

Sarah spoke softly, "I think that's Miller's Pond in the background. When we were kids, my mother and father used to take us there on picnics." She pointed at the screen. "Look, you can see the old tree fort right there."

"It was probably deserted at night," said Emma. "I've never heard of Miller's Pond. Where is it?"

"It got developed going on thirty years ago. It's called Miller's Haven Estates now."

"That I have heard of. Pretty swanky gated community. Some of my mom's clients live there."

"Oh, what does your mom do?" asked Sarah.

"She's a high-end clothing designer."

David cleared his throat, his voice laced with impatience. "Shall we get back to the video?"

"Of course. Sorry about that," said Emma, her cheeks flushing red at the admonishment.

Following the steps Emma had shown him, David took a screenshot of the trees and pond. The third screenshot taken was a close-up of Enrico Bianchi's face, the fourth of him raising the crowbar, about to strike the victim and the final shot was of the victim lying in a dark pool of blood.

Watching the video, a second time had not been any less painful for them, however the initial shock had dissipated somewhat. No doubt due to the scotch, which had given them some liquid courage.

"For security reasons, I've saved this video on a USB drive as well as on the cloud," David announced as he removed the SD card from the slot in the adapter and replaced it in the envelope. He turned his laptop off, walked to the wall safe, keyed in the code, and placed the USB drive in the safe.

He was sure he'd aged a decade. Everyone in the room wore somber expressions, the mood oppressive and sad.

"So, what do we do next?" Sarah finally asked.

"We go to the police. This is concrete evidence of a crime," said Liam."

"I agree," said David. "It's what we were looking for."

Emma cleared her throat. "Before we do go to the police, David did you want to talk to Sarah about your recent experiences?"

Sarah looked over at David. "What experiences?"

"Where do I begin?"

"Well, they always say at the beginning." Sarah chuckled. "I know it's a bit of a cliché but it's true."

"Sarah, I don't know how to explain this to you—" He stopped in mid-sentence.

"Yes?"

"What are your thoughts on reincarnation?"

"Well, it's nice to think that something like that is real, but how do we really know? When someone passes on, how are you ever really going to know, there's even an afterlife?" She took a deep breath and continued. "I lost my father, my brother, and my mother when I was in my late twenties, so I've had a lot of time to think about this sort of thing. I wish something like that existed, but who knows?"

"I think it exists," David told her in a very quiet voice.

She looked at him, eyes wide with curiosity. "What did you want to tell me, David?"

Twenty-Three

The Lost Brother

UNABLE TO CONTAIN himself, he blurted out, "I believe I'm your brother."

Sarah looked at him in disbelief. "What are you saying?"

"Sarah, I'm George."

"I'm out of here." She pushed her chair away angrily, got up and ran out of the room.

Emma went after her, and said, "Please stop." When she'd caught up to her, she placed a gentle hand on Sarah's arm. "You should hear him out, it's important."

Sarah turned around and said, "Do you know how ridiculous this all sounds?"

"I understand. It's a lot to take in. Would you please come back? David is very sincere about this."

Sarah looked into Emma's compassionate eyes. "All right. This is just crazy. But all right."

Emma put her arms around the older woman's shoulders and guided her back to the boardroom. She took the empty crystal glass and filled it with more of the Scotch and handed it to Sarah.

Sarah squared her shoulders, as if ready to go into battle, and said, "Okay, David, I'll hear you out."

"Thank you so much." He took a deep breath. "All my life, I've been plagued with nightmares. Since at least four years of age and probably earlier than that. My parents were at their wits' end not knowing how to help me. I've seen countless doctors and psychiatrists over the years.

"When I met Emma, I told her about my recurring nightmares. She suggested I see Anna Tungsten, a respected hypnotherapist. During the first session of hypnotherapy, it was confirmed that I had had these nightmares from an early age.

"Anna recommended a second session to regress me to my most recent past life. I was skeptical, just as skeptical as you are now. During the second regression, I experienced my murder. It was discovered during this session my name was George Larson. I was still not convinced, so we did a search online and found George's name listed on a cold case website. I was shocked."

Sarah's attention was riveted by every one of his words. "Go on."

"On the cold case website, they mentioned your name and that the staff inspector in charge was Officer Bryan Grant of the New Elgan Police Service." David took a sip of the single malt. "We didn't have anything to take to the police. Why would they believe some nut who had nightmares and had a past life regression done? I had to find solid evidence. I couldn't shake this burning desire to get justice for myself, I mean George."

"What did you do next?"

"Emma and I went to my uncle. I told him about the past life regressions and my suspicions. I showed him the transcripts of the hypnotherapy sessions. When I mentioned the name George Samuel Larson my uncle explained that he had been a client. On the night he died, George was to bring him and my dad evidence that he was going to take to the Crown to use as leverage to gain lenience in some shady dealings he had with an organized crime group led by Enrico's father, Alfonso Bianchi."

Sarah fixed her gaze on Liam. "What evidence?"

"My partner—David's dad, and I never knew. We thought whatever it was had died with George," Liam said.

"I see." She returned her attention to David.

"This office practices real estate law now, but at the time my dad and my uncle were criminal defense lawyers."

Liam interjected. "It's true. After George's death, we were so unnerved that we switched to something less risky."

David continued. "My uncle and dad boxed up everything and put the files into storage. Two days ago, Emma and I went to the storage locker and retrieved all the files relating to George as well as anything on the Bianchi organization. Going through the files for nineteen ninety-three, we found the safety deposit box key—"

Sarah interrupted. "So that's why you contacted me. Because of the key you found?"

"Yes. We hoped the key might lead to us to evidence concerning George's death." David massaged the back of his neck as he continued. "And now it turns out there were two murders. The one George witnessed and videoed and his own death."

Sarah looked at him thoughtfully. "My brother always was such a risk-taker." She shook her head in disbelief. "Still, it's a far stretch to say that you're my brother reincarnated."

"Of course," David said with sadness in his voice. "I anticipated you might have reservations."

"But whether or not you are George, your efforts have made more progress than the police have done in the last thirty years."

He pulled a file from his briefcase. "The MGB. It bothered me when you mentioned the small dent in the fender."

"Yes?"

"Well, here is the record from the license bureau. Look at the third page. Guess who the owner was in nineteen ninety-three?"

"No? Really?" She grabbed the records from him. "George Samuel Larson."

"Look, I know this all can't be coincidence." He ticked off the points on the fingers of his hand: "I was born into the family who ran this very law firm that represented George. I have had recurring dreams of my own murder since early childhood. And now I own the very same nineteen seventy-eight Inca Gold MGB."

Sarah's eyes widened with surprise. "You sure handled the car the way my brother used to."

Emma interrupted. "David, you didn't talk about the third regression."

"That's true. During the final hypnotherapy session, it was discovered that George knew his killer was Enrico Bianchi and that during the murder he scratched him. We're hoping the medical examiner collected DNA evidence—"

"I read just recently police in Toronto arrested a sixty-one-year-old man with first-degree murder in the grisly killings of two women in Toronto. They used familial DNA technology to find their killer. Arrested nearly forty years later," said Liam.

"Maybe we'll get lucky," added Emma.

"What's more eerie is that about ten days ago Enrico contacted me to work on a real estate deal for himself and his son." David shook his head in disbelief. "The man has scars on his face in the same spot, where I... I mean where George scratched him. At this stage, I don't believe in coincidences anymore."

"This is all very compelling," said Sarah. "We should contact Bryan."

Emma noted Sarah's use of the staff inspector's first name. "Bryan? As in Staff Inspector Grant?"

"Yes, that's right. After George died, Bryan stayed in touch. Over the years, my husband John and I became good friends with him." She put her hand on David's. "I am beginning to believe you. But it might be wise to not mention the hypnotherapy sessions to the police."

Liam said, "She's right. Now that we have the video, it shouldn't be necessary to reveal what led to it being discovered."

Emma said, "I think so, too."

"Let's just say, we were going through our archives, found the key, and contacted Sarah here as George's next of kin. We helped her to access the safety deposit where we found the SD card, and we were shocked to see what was on it," suggested Liam. "Everyone in agreement?"

Sarah, Emma, and David all nodded.

"Okay let's do it." Just as David reached for his phone to key in the number for the New Elgan Police Service, it pinged. He read the message, and then read it again.

"What is it?" said Emma.

"It's a text message from Enrico." The expression on his face was serious, worry lines edging the corners of his eyes and mouth.

"Why would he be contacting you?" said Liam.

"Because he got to Anna," said David. "He knows I've got the video."

"What?" Emma's hand flew to her mouth.

David swallowed at the phlegm clogging his throat, his voice wavering slightly as he read aloud, "Anna was quite talkative before she died. Not buying that reincarnation shit. Bring me George's video or Emma's next. Tonight at ten o'clock at the South Simcoe Bay Docks. Pier One. Come alone. E.B."

"Anna's dead? No, that can't be!" Fingers trembling, Emma reached for her phone. "I'll try her again." Her voice was unsteady, her face streaked with tears. "Still no answer."

Twenty-Four

What Do We Do Now?

DAVID, EMMA, SARAH, and Liam sat in stunned silence for a few minutes. David said, "We can't just ignore Enrico's text."

"No, but you can't possibly go there on your own." Emma's voice cracked. "He'll kill you."

"I agree," said Liam. "It's too dangerous."

"But what do we do?" said Sarah. "I don't want to lose my brother a second time." She smiled gently at David.

"The threat to Emma's life is a real possibility," said Liam.

"And Enrico might get to Emma through her mom," said David.

"Agreed. He's ruthless," said Sarah.

Liam took charge. "Emma, call your mom. Tell her Anna's missing—"

Emma interrupted, "But Anna may be dead—"

"We don't know that for sure. I'd advise you not to say anything to your mom just yet. I'm going to put you both up in a hotel here in New Elgan."

"Thanks," said Emma. "But we can't let David go to the meeting place alone."

"Don't worry, we'll come up with a plan," Liam reassured her. "Together."

Emma picked up her cell and called her mom. "Hi, Mom." There was a pause as Emma listened. "Don't go to Anna's. It could be dangerous.

Come to David's law office instead." She waited another moment. "I'm texting you the address. I love you, too. See you soon."

Emma disconnected the call and said, "My mother and Anna talk every morning. She got worried when Anna wasn't home. She was getting ready to go to her place, but I told her to come here instead."

"Good," Liam said. "Now, let's get to work on that plan."

"Clearly, I've got to go to that meeting," David told them.

"And even though Enrico's warned us about not involving the police, we can't ignore that they could be our best option," added Sarah.

Liam laid his hands on the table. "Okay. This is what I think we should do. Emma and her mom will go in hiding at the hotel." He took a deep breath. "Sarah and I will go to the police."

"I'll stay here at the office." David rubbed the corners of his itchy eyes with the tips of his index fingers, making them feel even more irritated.

"We'll bring the original SD card with us." Liam steepled his fingers together.

David handed the envelope containing the SD card to his uncle.

"Thanks. David, can you forward the text message from Enrico to me?"

"Certainly."

Liam then turned to Emma. "When your mom arrives, take a taxi, not an Uber, pay cash and check into the New Elgan Hotel and Conference Center. The reservation will be under my name, Liam Foster."

"Will do," said Emma, grateful a plan was now in place.

"Time to call Staff Inspector Grant," said Sarah, reaching for her cell.

Twenty-Five

Staff Inspector Bryan Grant

STAFF INSPECTOR BRYAN Grant gazed at the crime scene photos in disbelief. *Anna Tungsten. Gone.* She had on occasion worked as a consultant with the department and was well-respected by himself and his colleagues. Now she was gone. *Gone.* He had trouble accepting that this vivacious woman was dead. Worse yet. Murdered.

Bryan was of medium height with gray eyes that were as solemn as those of a funeral director. He had just celebrated his sixty-third birthday and although his arms and legs were still strong, over three decades of late and sleepless nights devoted to crime solving had taken their exacting price. He wore a gray conservative suit that matched his eyes and bulged slightly at a waist which was now past middle-age and on its way to its senior and less robust years.

His fellow officers had been skeptical about her empathic skills, but when her psychic impressions had helped them find direct evidence that led to solving the disappearance of victims, whether they had succumbed to misadventure or murder, their attitude quickly changed. Anna soon became the sweetheart of the department and he suspected that many of his fellow officers were half in love with her quick wit and quirky ways.

Bryan had first met Anna when she had contacted the New Elgan Police Service several years ago, insisting she speak to the staff inspector in charge of a missing teen case. Melissa Kurtz, sixteen years of age, had disappeared on her way home from school ten years ago. Anna said she had information as to where Melissa's body could be found.

Bryan had told the dispatcher, "Take her number. I'll deal with this crank call later."

Distracted by more urgent and current cases, Bryan ignored the pink message slip on his desk until it was buried under a massive pile of more pressing messages. Several weeks later, while straightening up his desk, he found the note. *What the heck?* he thought. *May as well call.*

When he spoke with Anna, he was struck by the sincerity of her words, and although he was very skeptical, he agreed to meet her. Expecting some new age mystic, he was pleasantly surprised by her straightforward nature.

He asked, "So why should I give this any credence?"

"What have you got to lose?"

"Time and resources the department doesn't have."

"If it's money and resources that's the problem," she paused. "I'll pay for it."

He smiled at the memory of her dogged determination and had said, "That won't be necessary."

Anna had smiled with relief and said, "Good. Melissa was the victim of an accidental hit and run. The driver panicked and buried her at Tempest Point just north of South Simcoe Bay."

He had received a lot of ribbing from his fellow officers when he had decided to follow up on the flimsy lead based on a psychic's impression, but they soon came around when a skeleton of a young female was found. DNA and dentistry records established it was Melissa's body and the coroner's results confirmed that bone fractures showed signs that the teen was likely hit by a car.

Anna's skills had not led to an arrest, but Melissa's family took some solace that her body had been found and that she could be given a proper burial. It was some closure, but the hit and run killer was still out there.

Anna had been apologetic that no more 'impressions' were forthcoming in the Melissa Kurtz case, but she had helped with other cases where arrests and convictions had resulted.

She was going to be missed.

Bryan's reverie was interrupted by the receptionist. "Sir, there's a Sarah Moody on the line for you. It sounds urgent."

Twenty-Six

New Elgan Police Service

WHEN LIAM AND Sarah arrived at the New Elgan Police Service, Staff Inspector Bryan Grant was waiting for them in the foyer.

The impressive building was built in 1912, and at the time was the finest edifice in New Elgan and the envy of surrounding towns and cities. Two massive columns and two pilasters were situated on each side of the main entrance. The station comprised three stories and a spacious basement: enough space for a court room, a law clerk office and magistrate offices.

In the era it was constructed, separate cell blocks for men, women and juveniles were considered a major advancement. Over one-hundred years later, the building was showing its age. The security of the holding cells was a matter of heated debate during many recent council meetings.

Historians were clamoring to declare the antiquated structure a historical site building. The police force was anxious to move into their new headquarters, but budgetary constraints had prevented them from breaking ground.

Bryan approached Sarah, and pulled her into a hug, "Good to see you, Sarah. We're getting close to the thirty-year anniversary of George's death."

She nodded; her expression was sad. "Yes, we are."

He turned to Liam next, gripping his hand. "Haven't seen you in years, Liam."

"Bryan. It's been a long time," agreed Liam.

"Your message was intriguing. I understand you have information concerning George's death?"

"We do," said Sarah.

"Let's head to my office."

Liam and Sarah followed Staff Inspector Grant down the sparse hallway; he pointed to the third door on the right. "Please, make yourselves comfortable."

"Before we begin, can I get you folks anything to drink? Coffee, tea, a soft drink?"

Sarah said, "Water, if you have it."

"Coffee, black, for me," said Liam.

When Staff Inspector Grant had returned with the beverages, and coffee for himself, he directed his gaze at Liam. "Now what's this all about?"

"We follow the limitations act of 2002 and keep our client files for fifteen years after a case is closed." Liam took a sip of the scalding coffee and winced. "On a routine basis we go through our archives to destroy any client files that are no longer active. Sometimes, files are kept longer if the case is still ongoing or unresolved.

"My nephew David, who works with me, came to me concerning information he'd received claiming we had evidence relating to George Samuel Larson's murder." Liam took a sip of the tepid coffee. "Since David's dad and I had represented George at one time, I suggested David and his girlfriend Emma Jackson, who has been helping him, go through the archives of files locked away in our offsite storage unit to see if they could find anything to substantiate this claim."

Bryan leaned back in his chair. "Go on."

"They found an envelope containing a safety deposit key from the Canadian Dominion Bank in George's file."

Bryan sat up straight, then leaned forward slightly. "I'm intrigued."

"David searched online for next of kin and found that Sarah Larson-Moody had set up a *Remembering George S. Larson Facebook* page. He verified that Sarah was George's sister, then contacted her concerning the key."

"After that, David and I went to the bank to access the safety deposit box and found another envelope," Sarah added.

"Inside was a personal note addressed to Sarah, and an SD card."

Liam slid the envelope containing the note and SD card across the table to Bryan.

Bryan opened the side drawer of his desk, pulled out a pair of Nitrile gloves, gently opened the envelope and removed the note and card.

"Have either of you handled these?"

"Yeah, David and Sarah handled the card and note." He swallowed nervously. "I did touch the envelope."

Bryan's frustrated sigh was explosive, more upsetting than if he had shouted. "You of all people should have known better." His gray eyes were reproachful as he glared at Liam.

"I know. Lapse in judgment."

"Did you watch it?" Bryan asked.

"All four of us did. Emma, David, Sarah, and myself. We had no idea what was on it," said Liam. "We were shocked."

"And what we saw, we'll never be able to unsee." Sarah shuddered.

"Enlighten me." His look was stern. "Why didn't David and his girl-friend accompany you to the station?"

"As head of our firm, I told David I'd approach you first."

"I see." Bryan's face was grim and impassive. He returned the SD card and note in the envelope, placed the contents in an evidence bag, rose from his chair, and said, "Wait here."

He slammed the door on his way out, leaving his coffee cup behind.

"Cranky guy," said Liam.

"Not usually. Do you think he plans to view it right now?"

"I am sure of it," said Liam. "He will certainly ask you and David for your fingerprints." He pressed his lips together. "They'll already have George's on file from his time on the force. Elimination prints."

"What do we do now?"

"Not much we can do but wait," said Liam.

"He didn't give us a chance to tell him about the threat David received," Sarah said.

* * *

It was approaching early afternoon, and the staff inspector still had not returned.

"I'm getting hungry," Sarah said.

"I'm feeling a bit peckish myself," replied Liam.

"I noticed some vending machines in the hall." Sarah got up from her chair. "I'll see what's in the vending machines. Any preferences? No guarantees of course. Depends on what's there."

"I could use a sandwich. Turkey or beef, but I'm not picky."

"Okay then. See you in a bit."

Twenty-Seven

The Wait Is Over

WHEN STAFF INSPECTOR BRYAN Grant returned to the interview room, he looked grim.

Bryan sat down heavily and said, "Can you explain how your nephew came to obtain this information concerning George?"

"You'll find it hard to believe."

"Try me."

"David has suffered from debilitating nightmares his entire life, which we now believe were fragmented memories of a murder having been committed in a past life."

"Huh?"

"His girlfriend, Emma Jackson, suggested he see Anna Tungsten, an empath and hypnotherapist." He took a sip of the soda Sarah had brought him, the roast beef vending machine sandwich roiling uncomfortably in his stomach. "We think the killer is Enrico Bianchi."

Bryan exhaled deeply, pulled a photograph out of his folder, and placed it face down on the table. "A situation has developed. Did either of you know Anna Tungsten?" His voice was neutral, and his eyes appraised both of them with cold detachment.

The pulse at Sarah's throat was visible. "You're speaking in the past tense?"

She searched Bryan's eyes for a reaction, but the staff inspector remained silent and impassive.

"No, I didn't know her," said Liam. "Only what David and Emma have told me about her."

Sarah shook her head. "We've never met."

"David's girlfriend, Emma, said Anna is a close friend of her mother's," said Liam.

"Has something happened?" asked Sarah.

Staff Inspector Grant gave a heavy sigh and said, "Yes, I'm afraid so." He slid the photo to the center of the table, flipped it over and placed it so that Sarah and Liam could both see. Liam reached over and put a comforting arm around Sarah's shoulders and winced. The photo showed a close shot of a woman's pale and lifeless face, slack and expressionless in death.

"Oh my God. The poor woman." Sarah's hands flew to her mouth and her face paled. "So, it's true then."

"Sarah, what aren't you telling me?" said Bryan, puzzled.

Liam replied instead, "I've told Emma and her mom, Laura Jackson, to go into hiding. They're in danger. We believe Enrico Bianchi is after them."

"Why do you think that?" Bryan asked. "And why, for that matter, do you suspect Enrico Bianchi?"

Liam tapped on his phone to access the text message from Enrico that David had forwarded to him earlier, slid his cellphone over to Bryan and said, "Because of this."

The shock and anger on the staff inspector's face was palpable as he read the threatening message Enrico had sent to David concerning Emma.

"Where are Emma and Laura Jackson now?"

"At the New Elgan Hotel and Conference Center. For their safety, under my name, Liam Foster."

"And David?"

"At our law offices. He's following his regular workday pattern in case Enrico's men are watching him."

Bryan cleared his throat and said, "Okay. It's imperative that I interview David and Emma right away."

He stroked his chin in thought, "I'll get the tech department to set up encryption video software so I can interview David online, and I'll personally visit Emma and Laura at the hotel."

He looked at Liam. "Despite the mishandling of the video card, I admire your forward thinking. For everyone's safety, let's keep everyone separate from each other.

"Sarah and Liam, please stay at the station. We'll have you participate in the video conference call from here." He glanced at his wristwatch. "We have four hours left to formulate a plan."

Bryan reached for his phone to request a video technician to set up the links necessary for the encrypted call which would be recorded using state of the art MaestroVision software. The interview recording system had been adopted by the New Elgan Police Service recently and had already proven to be user friendly for officers, who no longer had difficulty setting up, operating, or managing the recordings in the interview room or offsite. It had proven trustworthy, flexible, multifunctional and very secure. And within five minutes, a recording could be produced and be trial-ready.

* * *

Emma sat on the edge of the hotel suite's sofa, trailing her fingers along the satin cushions. Although the room was plush, she and her mother were not enjoying the luxurious accommodations.

She looked at Staff Inspector Bryan Grant, who sat opposite from her and said, "We left Anna's place about nine last night." Her face filled with anguish. "I can't believe this."

"We, as in exactly who?" asked Bryan.

"David and myself. She wiped tears from her eyes and tried to regain her composure. "We agreed to meet at David's office this morning. At the end of last night's session, Anna said she was coming, but this morning she sent a text saying she couldn't make it. I texted back to see if she was okay, but she didn't answer any of my texts."

"We believe Anna was killed last night. It's likely the killer used her phone to send you that text."

"Oh, poor Anna," Laura buried her face in her hands, quiet sobs racking her body. Emma put her arms around her mom in a protective embrace. "Anna was my best friend."

"You mentioned a session?" asked Bryan, his voice quiet.

Emma looked up at the crisp and clean video feed of the panelists on the monitor. David was shown on one panel, sitting at his office desk, while Liam and Sarah were shown together in the feed from the police station. She exchanged a nervous glance with David, her eyes telegraphing permission to speak.

David nodded. "Go ahead. It's okay."

"Umm, Anna is an empath and a hypnotherapist. David was seeing her to try and resolve a recurring nightmare." She gave a worried look at the staff inspector and continued. "The hypnotherapy involved past life regression."

"I am aware of Anna's skills."

Emma looked up in surprise. "Really?"

"Over the last several years, she has helped with quite a few investigations." He paused. "It's led to arrests and closure for family members."

Bryan continued, "This is the area where she was found." He screen-shared the image so everyone on the panel could see.

The picture showed Anna had been dumped by a small lake with magnificent homes on large estate lots encircling its circumference.

Emma frowned. "That's Miller's Haven Estates. Sarah told us about the place. The site of the murder on the video."

"This can't be a coincidence," said David. "It's some kind of a sick message from Enrico."

Emma cleared her throat. "That's the same clothing she wore last night."

"It's the kimono I designed for her. My own floral pattern. It was her Christmas gift last year." Laura moaned.

Emma interrupted, "What's that rectangular white shape on her chest?"

"Looks like a piece of paper," said Laura.

Bryan silently cast the next photo to the screen. "They left a note. Stabbed it with her hair pin to her chest. Right through her clothing."

When she saw the note, the color bled away from Emma's face until it was as white as the note. *The video or Emma Jackson's next.*

Bryan met her gaze with solemn eyes. "I doubt you and David randomly found the SD card. Time to start explaining in more detail." His tone was kind, but firm.

David shook his head in disbelief. "I never imagined pursuing this would lead to Anna's murder. She was a gentle soul."

Over the next half hour, David described his debilitating nightmares, how Emma had suggested he see Anna for hypnotherapy, and how the sessions had revealed what were latent memories of his past life. He explained the sessions had revealed his previous name and the third and final regression had revealed his killer's face. Knowing that this was not evidence, David and Emma went to David's uncle for advice. David was shocked to learn that his uncle and Dad had been the representatives for George Samuel Larson in a criminal case. They searched the archives which led to the ultimate discovery of the SD card.

When David had finished, he said, "My uncle and I believe we now have solid evidence which could lead to the apprehension of Enrico Bianchi."

Liam agreed. "George's death had hit us hard. He was bringing us evidence the night he was killed. He said it was something that would put Enrico away for good and get him out of a jam with the Crown."

"You never said anything to us." Bryan's tone was reprimanding. "We always suspected that bastard of a dozen grisly murders, but we could never find the proof. He was his father's enforcer, Alfonso Bianchi."

"We feared for our lives. So, David's dad and I packed away the files and switched to real estate and corporate law."

"I always thought that was a strange switch," said Bryan. "Figured you both grew consciences and got tired of representing the low-lifes."

"My sister, David's mom, was pregnant with David, and we wanted to protect our family."

"Based on the note left with Anna's body, anyone who has seen this video is in grave danger. Emma, specifically, as she's been threatened directly." He hesitated, "Word has it that his youngest, Alessandro, has the same proclivity for killing."

Sarah, who had remained silent for much of the video conference, looked directly at Bryan. "So, where do we go from here?"

"I recommend you and Liam do not go back home. Emma and Laura, please stay at the hotel. Under no circumstances are you to leave. When you get hungry, order from the hotel restaurant." He paused a moment to collect his thoughts. "David, please remain at work, I'll be in touch soon, while we work out the best strategy for you to approach Enrico tonight."

"But why does David even have to meet Enrico? Isn't the video enough evidence to arrest him? Or at least question him?" said Sarah.

"The face in the video is indistinct. Although we suspect this is Enrico, and we think it looks like him, we need to run it through a face recognition analysis program first, to see if there are enough facial markers that match current photos. Maybe then. But this will take time."

"This is so disappointing. We risked a lot getting that video," David said.

"And it still may be worthwhile. We need confirmation first," said Bryan. "Sarah and Liam, thanks for attending the meeting, I think we are done here for now. As I said before, for your safety, I suggest you each book yourselves into hotels."

Liam nodded with reluctance.

"I'd rather go home," Sarah said. "Snuggles, my ginger cat, is on meds and needs to be fed. He's a real fusspot when his litter isn't cleaned on time."

"Don't you have someone who can check on the cat?" said Bryan.

"Yeah, I guess I could call my friend from Katzy Meow. Macey's got a key."

"Great. That's settled then." Bryan nodded to the technician to disconnect the video feed for Sarah and Liam. Only David's image remained. "David, I'll be in touch later with further details."

"Okay," replied David.

Bryan next turned to Laura and Emma, and said, "I'm heading back to the station. Again, I cannot stress enough, do not leave your hotel room for any reason."

"I have some ideas on how to help—," said Emma.

Bryan shook his head. "The less you know about tonight's plans the safer you'll be."

"But—" Emma tried again.

David interrupted her. "Please, Emma. Promise me you'll stay at the hotel. I can't bear to lose you."

"But what if I lose *you*—?" Her words died on her lips. The look of fierce determination on David's face gave her pause. "Okay then."

She bowed her head, unable to hide her disappointment.

"Look Emma, it's for the best. If you or your mom need anything, call me." Bryan handed her his business card.

Twenty-Eight

Let's Talk Strategy

BRYAN LEANED BACK in his chair with a thoughtful look on his face. He was not comfortable with the involvement of civilians in an undercover operation; however, he recognized the delicate balance between yielding to Enrico's demands and ignoring them. Even so, he was confident that the danger was limited to David and Bryan's own team of seasoned officers. He was relieved Emma had promised to stay at the hotel with her mother, and that Sarah and Liam had agreed to book rooms of their own.

Bryan was waiting for the lab results to come back on the fingerprints found on the SD card and note. If the prints had not been damaged, it would reinforce the fact that it had been handled previously by George and then later by Sarah and David.

It was important to find all crucial evidence so that the past life regression would not play a factor in the apprehension of the suspect. A successful conviction of Enrico Bianchi would depend on using concrete evidence, and not something based on a psychic's impressions. The defense would have a field day with something like this. No, it had to be done exactly by the book.

He had put in a requisition for a search of DNA on the clothing that George had worn the night of his murder. Based on David's past life memory regression, he was also hoping that there might be DNA evidence underneath George's fingernails. He was pleased when the forensic pathologist confirmed that fingernail scrapings had been made during George's autopsy and that there should be enough DNA to analyze. The next challenge would be to compare this to any other known databases, such as Canada's convicted offenders' index.

Also at his disposal, although very expensive, would be to access the DNA repository of people doing genealogy searches. It was a long shot, but worth a try.

He recalled the case of a sixty-one-year-old man who now faced two counts of first-degree murder for the grisly killings of two young women in Toronto nearly four decades ago. Advances in DNA technology helped identify the man by using a technique called investigative genetic genealogy to identify the suspect's family tree. By cross referencing DNA found at crime scenes with DNA samples voluntarily submitted by popular DNA ancestry organizations and uploaded to open-source databases, the exhaustive research had led to the eventual arrest of the man.

He was sure the superintendent would approve the expenditure since Enrico Bianchi had been on the department's radar for many years. In this case, they already had the suspect's name.

He picked up the phone and called the police clerk. "Derek. Bryan here. Would you go through all known public databases and get me a list of Enrico Bianchi's relatives?"

"Sure. No problem." Derek hesitated. "How soon do you need it?"

"As soon as possible."

"Okay, I'll get right on it."

"Thanks."

Bryan picked up his mug and took a sip and nearly choked on the cream that had coagulated in the cold coffee. *It would be good if they could finally apprehend that slippery crime master.*

* * *

Ever since he had spoken with Staff Inspector Grant, David had looked at his watch countless times over the course of the day and found it difficult to concentrate on his work for more than a few minutes at a time.

His thoughts vacillated between the upcoming meeting with Enrico and that Emma was upset with him. He was remorseful for shutting her out of the plans, but his need to protect her had won out. Emma was a modern woman, and he knew she had been hurt and offended by having been excluded, but he agreed with the staff inspector that she was in danger and should remain in hiding.

He glanced at his watch again. It was approaching eight in the evening. *One hour to go,* he thought as he recalled the conversation with Bryan.

Upon Bryan's return to the station, he had reestablished the secure video link with David. He shared a screen showing an aerial view of Pier One of the South Simcoe Bay Docks and moved his cursor to indicate points of interest.

"I will have men stationed here at the north entrance, behind this copse of trees to the west and in behind Pier One to the east."

David viewed the screen with rapt attention. "What about the lake?"

Bryan nodded. "Just off the pier, we will have men posing as fisherman in two boats."

"Nighttime fishing?" David looked doubtful.

"Not implausible," said Bryan. "Some of the best fishing for walleye is done at night. During the summer months, when it's hot, the walleyes prefer deeper cooler waters, but at night, while they are hunting, they'll come close to the surface amidst the weeds. So, the best catching is right after dusk and into the night."

"I did not know that. I never really got into fishing, but I've been sailing my whole life. Ever since I was a kid." He smiled at the memory of his dad's hair swept back from his face, his look proud, as he taught him how to navigate the fifteen-foot dinghy. He shook himself from the reverie, and thought, *the only time I ever felt peaceful was on the water. With my dad.*

"I'm going to same-day courier you a bulletproof vest. It's lightweight and you can wear it under your clothing. Text me when you get it."

"Okay."

"Next, we need to monitor the meetup. I don't want you to wear a wire that Enrico might discover." He took another sip of his cold coffee. *Darn. I gotta empty this out.* He swiveled in his chair and placed the offending mug on the credenza behind him.

"What do we do instead then?"

"There is new encrypted spy software which will turn your cell phone into a bugging device. It's sophisticated spyware which will monitor your activity. As soon as our spotters see Enrico approach you, we will call your cell."

"Won't Enrico hear that?"

"No, your phone won't be ringing whatsoever. But we will be able to listen into your conversation remotely. Even though it's turned off, it will be still acting as a bugging device."

"What if he takes my phone?"

"Won't matter. It'll still be listening."

"And if he pulls out the SIM card?"

"The app will still do its job."

"Okay." David was wary. "But I'm very nervous."

"That's normal. But to reassure you, we have used this technology in dozens of successful operations."

A few seconds later David heard his cell chirp. "Just got your text."

"Great. First, accept that by installing this software you agree to authorize the New Elgan Police Service to monitor your phone."

"Got it. Done."

"Next, click on the prompts and follow the instructions to install it."

"Right. Installing it now."

"Great. Let's do a test, so we're sure it's working."

Several minutes passed. David eyed his phone with suspicion, but it appeared to remain inert. He busied himself with some paperwork, every now and again, glancing at it and muttering about the invasiveness of today's technology.

When his phone rang and he answered it, he heard Bryan say, "Do you always mumble to yourself?"

David's face darkened with embarrassment. "Oh, you could hear that?"

"Yep, loud and clear."

Twenty-Nine

Emma

EMMA WAS AGITATED. She could not sit still.

"Honey, why don't you settle down?" said her mom. Laura looked at her daughter with worried eyes.

"Mom, I just can't. David is going to that meeting alone."

"He won't be alone. The police will be there."

"What if something happens to him?" Emma was inconsolable. "I should be there."

"How so? You've received two threats to your life." Laura wiped tears of grief from her tired eyes. "I can't stop thinking about poor Anna. She didn't deserve this. I couldn't go on if something like that happened to you."

"That's exactly why I can't just sit by. I can't bear losing David." She took a heavy gulp of breath. "It's all my fault. Anna would be alive if I hadn't meddled and suggested he go see her."

"You couldn't have known this would be the outcome. You were trying to help." She enfolded her daughter into her arms. Her back stiffened. "But how did Enrico find out about Anna? This is what I don't understand."

"I don't either," said Emma. She grabbed the hotel card key from the hall table and walked to the door. "I can't stay here another minute!"

"Emma. Please, stop!"

"Mom, I need some fresh air. I feel like I'm suffocating."

"Wait. I'll come with you." Laura was determined to not let her impulsive daughter out of her sight.

* * *

The late afternoon sun refused to release its oppressive hold and the humidity in the air made breathing uncomfortable. The pavement shimmered like mirages on the Sahara Desert, its heat permeating into their feet through the soles of their sandals.

"Wait up." Laura was out of breath by the time she caught up with Emma. She grabbed her daughter's arm to steady herself. "I'm not as young as I used to be."

"Oh, Mom, I'm so sorry." Emma blinked fresh tears away from her eyes. "Maybe we better head back."

"Well, now that we're out. Why don't we go for some ice cream? There's a Dairy Queen up ahead."

"I don't think that's a good idea." She placed her arm around her mom's shoulder to guide her back to the hotel. "Come on, let's go."

"It might cheer us up."

"Mom, ice cream won't fix our problems!"

"No, but it sure can comfort." She linked her right arm through her daughter's left arm and said, "Besides, I'm hungry."

A kid on a skateboard slipped by and pushed against Laura. During the commotion she didn't feel the small sting on her bare arm.

Emma yelled, "Hey, watch where you're going!"

The ice cream shop was filled with the unbridled laughter of children exhilarated and emboldened by weeks of summer fun and freedom, the yoke of school a vague and distant reality.

"You look tired, Mom," said Emma.

"Suddenly, I am. Nothing a little sugar kick won't fix." She smiled.

"Shall I get the usual?"

"You know what I want."

"Two Peanut Buster Parfaits it is."

"Thanks, honey." Laura settled into her seat by the window. "I'll wait here."

The lineup was long, and it was almost ten minutes later when Emma returned with the sundaes, only to find an empty seat. Emma looked around but didn't see her mom anywhere. Trying to control the gorge of panic rising in her throat, she placed the sundaes on the table and gazed at the chattering crowd of kids and adults, trying to catch a glimpse of her mother.

Maybe she went to the restroom. She broke into a run and pushed open the door to the women's washroom. Doors to both metal cubicles hung open indicating the absence of occupants. *Oh my God. She's not here.*

She ran back out and scanned the room one more time. *She's gone.* Emma's hands trembled as she searched frantically for Bryan Grant's business card, found it, and keyed the number into her phone.

Her anxiety rose by the second as she was finally connected to the staff inspector's office.

"Staff Inspector Grant, speaking."

"Bryan. It's Emma. My mom's missing."

"From your hotel?"

"No, not exactly." She bit her lower lip.

"You left the hotel?" His voice was incredulous. "After I explicitly asked you not to?"

"It's all my fault. I was going stir crazy. I rushed out of the hotel and mom followed me." Her words gushed out as she sobbed. "Then we thought let's go for ice cream at the Dairy Queen just up the street. Lots of people around. What harm would that do?"

"Slow down. Take a deep breath."

"She was sitting there at the table while I was getting our ice creams. I was only gone ten minutes. When I got back to our table, she wasn't there."

Bryan was speechless.

"Bryan? Are you there?"

"Go to the manager. Ask if you can wait in the office. I'm sending a uniformed officer to escort you to the station."

"What about my mom?"

"There's a strong possibility that Enrico's men have grabbed her."

"Oh my God what have I done?" She bordered on hysteria.

"Your actions may have compromised our operation tonight. And put your mom into unnecessary danger," he said, his voice was stern. "I'll see you at the station. Promise me you'll wait for the officer and not take off."

"I promise."

Bryan disconnected the call, then keyed in the number for David. This was not a conversation he would enjoy.

Thirty

South Simcoe Bay Docks

DAVID'S PHONE VIBRATED. A video call from Bryan Grant.

Seconds later, Bryan's officers in their adjoining work cubicles looked up in surprise at the explosive outburst emitting from the video monitor mounted in his office.

"You have got to be kidding!" David shouted. "Laura is missing!" The throb in his left temple intensified. "I should've known better."

He rubbed the back of his neck vigorously, his fingers clawing harsh marks into the skin.

"Had I realized she was this stubborn, I would've stationed one of my men at the hotel room door." Bryan sighed with chagrin. "She's an adult, so, short of tying her down or locking her up there really wasn't much we could've done to stop her from leaving the hotel."

"What steps are you taking to find her mother?" David's tone was demanding, his fury barely contained.

"Emma had the *find my phone* option activated on her mom's iPhone. Apparently, she was forever misplacing it."

"And have you been able to locate it?"

"We traced the location of the phone, but Laura wasn't with it. She'd left it behind in the hotel."

"Bloody hell. I can't believe this."

"It's a mess," agreed Bryan.

"What else are you doing to locate her?" David struggled keeping his emotions in check.

"I have my officers out in full force looking for her." He cleared his throat. "They are canvassing area businesses, including the Dairy Queen, where she was last seen, for any video footage and eyewitnesses. New Elgan does have some city street cameras, so my video technicians are reviewing those for clues."

"It's only another hour before my rendezvous with Enrico." A shadow of fear passed over David's features. "Will this affect our plans for tonight?"

"Yes, I believe it might. If Enrico has Laura, he may use her as leverage against you."

"What do you suggest?" David asked.

"You'll still have to make the meet."

Bryan glanced at his watch. "You'd better get going. And don't forget to put on the bulletproof vest."

"Right," David said finally. "At least I'm doing something now. Sitting around today, trying to concentrate on my work was just useless. I'm glad the waiting is over."

"Now remember; just act normal. Don't look for us, but rest assured we'll be there."

"Thanks." Although David was anything but reassured.

* * *

The brutal heat of the day had dissipated, leaving the evening air moist and warm. A gentle breeze tousled David's brown hair as he drove the MGB to South Simcoe Bay. It could have been just another pleasant summer evening drive, except for the dread that weighed David down.

He maneuvered the compact car into the parking lot, got out and shut the door, taking care not to make any noise. He followed the signs for Pier One and walked to the edge of the pier. He fingered the SD card in his pocket. In the package Bryan had couriered him was a duplicate of the SD card; one that had been manufactured the same year. The original was squirreled safely away in the evidence room at the police department. It was essential that the copy look legitimate in every way.

He tried to stay calm, but his nerves were rubbed raw by anxiety.

"So, we meet again," someone spoke from the shadows.

David recognized the disturbing voice that had taunted him in his nightmares for almost three decades. He swallowed hard before he said, "Again?"

"Cut the bullshit. I don't really get how you know about George's little video project. I'm not buying this stupid story of past lives." His laugh was sinister and cruel. "I enjoyed extracting that info out of Anna. Too bad she succumbed so soon. Not much tolerance for pain. The fun we could have had would have been epic."

"You bastard," David snarled.

"Watch your language. That's no way to talk in front of a lady." Enrico, moved into the lamplight and shoved Laura forward. Her hands were bound behind her, and a filthy rag had been forced in her mouth to gag her. Her large emerald eyes were desperate with fear and terror.

"Don't you hurt her."

"You are in no position to make demands."

David pulled the SD card from his pocket and held it out in his open palm. "I brought it with me. Like you asked. Please, don't hurt Laura." David took a few steps forward.

"Easy now." Enrico motioned with his hand for David to stop. A younger man, of the same build and stature as Enrico, melted out of the darkness. The light from the lamppost cast sinister shadows across his face.

This must be Enrico' son, Alessandro, thought David; his undigested meal rose to the back of his throat. *This can't be good. They're not even trying to hide their faces.*

"Search him," ordered Enrico. "But get the SD card first." The gangster snatched the SD card from David's hand and brought it to Enrico, then continued his search of David's person.

A few minutes later, the man said, "He's wearing a vest."

"Really, David. Don't you trust me?"

David remained silent, unwilling to provoke the psychopath. Next, the man pulled his cell phone from his vest and looked toward Enrico for direction.

Enrico said, "Throw it in the lake."

The phone broke the surface of the water, creating a radial pattern of rippling waves that soon dissipated, the water absorbing the object as if it had never existed.

Enrico held the SD card up to the lamplight. "No other copies?"

"No." David tried not to stammer.

"Excellent. Great doing business with you." He turned to Alessandro and said, "Bring her with us. I could use a bit of recreation."

His son smiled and said, "I love fun and games."

Enrico gave a sinister laugh. "Stupid kid got the wrong Jackson woman, this one's a bit past her prime, but we can always come back and get the younger one later."

Although Laura's terrified scream of protest was muffled by the gag, to David it was deafening.

"No!" David shouted.

"Shut up, you stupid shit." Enrico raised his gun and fired.

David fell backward into the water, its black embrace, deep and encompassing.

* * *

Bryan was shocked at how quickly the situation had deteriorated and watched in disbelief as David was launched backward into the water by the force of the gun shot.

He remained calm, knowing the men posing as fishermen in the two boats positioned off the pier would rescue David.

He switched the floodlights on, pulled out his bullhorn and announced, "Attention. This is the police. You are surrounded. Surrender yourselves now."

The light illuminated the startled faces of the two men. The younger one began dragging Laura along with him.

"Forget her," Enrico picked her up as if she weighed nothing and threw her off the dock into the water. "Let's go," he shouted as his son fired at the floodlights. The lamp exploded, like fireworks, the only illumination coming from the pier mounted lights.

Disgusted and frustrated, Bryan barked into his comm. "Status report on David and Laura?"

"Teams from the water are retrieving them now. Nine-one-one has been called," said the team leader.

"Ten-four," said Bryan, using the universal code for okay. He stood up from his hiding spot, firmly planted his feet and fired at the fleeing men, who were already making their way off the pier. Satisfaction flowed through him as one of the men stumbled and got up awkwardly. The subsequent Special Investigations Unit paperwork and investigation for having discharged his firearm was a secondary consideration. He holstered his weapon and took chase, trying to urge his sixty-three-year-old body to run faster.

The subdued light from the streetlights lining the path leading away from the pier silhouetted one man supporting the other. Then the lamp shattered into darkness, glass fragments cascading like a waterfall to the pavement.

Enrico shouted, "Hold on to me, son."

An outboard engine rumbled to life. Moments later, Bryan could see the faint outline of a speedboat racing across the bay without its running lights.

Thirty-One

I'm Okay, Stop Fussing

LAURA WOKE UP in unfamiliar surroundings, disoriented and confused. Emma's green eyes widened with relief when her mother regained consciousness.

"Mom, you gave us quite a scare."

"I'm in the hospital?" Laura became agitated at the sight of the IV lines running into her left arm. "But, why?"

Staff Inspector Bryan Grant stepped closer to her bedside His voice was gentle and kind. "Hi, Laura. What do you remember?"

"Emma was going stir crazy. We went to the Dairy Queen. Lots of people, we figured it would be safe." She frowned in concentration. "I was tired and sat at our table. Emma was getting our favorite: Peanut Buster Parfait."

"Anything else?"

"Yeah, actually, I got very woozy." Her eyebrows knitted together. "I remember thinking I should go to the restroom, wash my face—" She sat up in alarm. "I don't recall a thing after that."

Emma tried to hold back her tears. "Mom, you were abducted."

"Really, are you sure?" Laura looked at Bryan for confirmation.

He nodded. "In fact, a blood analysis shows traces of a slow acting barbiturate in your system," he said.

"There was kid on a skateboard who bumped into my mom," said Emma. She drew her breath in and gasped at the realization that her mother had been drugged in public.

Laura nodded. "Oh my God, soon after that I got dizzy."

Bryan took Laura's hand in his and explained how she had been kidnapped by Enrico's men and used as collateral to coerce David into handing over the video; how he had positioned his men at South Simcoe Bay to apprehend Enrico and his son. He sighed. "We didn't count on the diversionary tactic he used." He paused. "He shot David in the chest and deliberately threw you, bound and gagged, into the water."

"David was shot!" Laura tried to get up, and then sat back as a wave of vertigo overwhelmed her. She reached for her daughter, her face filled with worry and concern. "Oh Emma, is David—"

"He's okay, Mom. Thanks to the insistence of Staff Inspector Grant here, David wore a bulletproof vest."

"Did you apprehend them?" Laura's asked, her voice hopeful.

"No, they got away." Bryan's sigh was pregnant with frustration. "It was saving you and David, or go after them."

"Where is David now?"

"This ward, one room over."

Laura turned to her daughter and said, "Let's go check on him."

"Mom, you should rest."

"I'm okay, stop fussing." Laura pulled the intravenous pole toward her, careful not to tangle the IV lines and slowly stood up, and said to her daughter, "Help me up."

Emma gently took her mother by the elbow and guided her toward the door.

* * *

David's face brightened at the sight of Emma and Laura entering his hospital room. He held out his hands and took Laura's hand in one and Emma's in the other.

"Laura. It's good to see you up and about," he said.

"You, too. Although until a few minutes ago, I had no idea what had happened." She released David's hand and groaned as another surge of dizziness passed over her. She leaned forward and coughed.

"Mom, please sit down." Emma pulled the lone utilitarian chair toward David's bed, helped her mom settle in it, then sat on the side of the bed.

"The doctor said you may have occasional dizzy spells until the drug is out of your system." She hesitated. "You did breathe in some of the lake water. They want to keep you under observation. With your history of bronchitis, they want to be sure you won't develop a lung infection."

"I just hate not remembering anything from these last few hours," said Laura, frustration lacing her voice. Once she had regained her composure, she asked, "David, how are you feeling?"

"Except for a cracked rib, I'm fine. The vest saved my life." He, too, sounded frustrated. "Still waiting on some final tests before they release me. Can't wait to get out of here."

Thirty-Two

It's All In The Genes

BRYAN SIGHED AGAIN. What a mess this case was turning out to be. His informants had been combing the streets to get information on the location of Enrico and his son, Alessandro, but fear of retaliation prevented his men from learning anything useful from their contacts.

Bryan had instructed his people to bring in Enrico Bianchi's oldest son, Lorenzo, for questioning. With any luck, he would know where Enrico and Alessandro might have fled. It was common knowledge Lorenzo was intensely jealous of his younger sibling and Bryan planned to appeal to the older brother's vanity, greed, and poor self-esteem to spy on the organization.

Another option would be to try and get DNA from Lorenzo, such as from a coffee cup, to establish a familial DNA match to what was found under George's fingernails.

His phone alerted him to a new message. It was from the forensic pathologist. He opened the message hoping for some positive news or clue which would help move the case forward. His excitement mounted as he read the message: *DNA collected from under the fingernails of George Samuel Larson during his autopsy dated 12-16-1993 has been analyzed. We are comparing results to all known databases. As requested, we have reached out to DNA Genealogy data bases and will keep you updated as we learn more.*

While he was tapping out his thanks to the pathologist, his cell chimed again. It was from Inspector Angie Turani: *Lorenzo Bianchi has been brought in for questioning. Would you like to observe? Angie.*

Bryan thumbed out his reply and hit send: I'll be down in five. Offer him coffee.

Thirty-Three

Exiled In Paradise

THE GIRL SCREAMED in agony as Enrico tightened the tourniquet fashioned from the belt of his silk robe around her neck. He seethed with an anger that smoldered deep inside. Not even the infliction of extreme pain on the helpless teenage sex worker was assuaging his fury. Violence was the only salve that would soothe his wicked soul. If only for a while. But not this time. His thoughts kept returning to how he and his youngest son had been forced to flee Canada.

Several years ago, he had asked Alessandro to find him a vacation home away from the miserable Canadian winters. He had scoffed when his son told him, "Dad, there's no extradition treaty between the Maldives and Canada."

"That shouldn't be necessary," he had said. "We've kept up appearances that our activities are clean. Our lawyers have seen to that."

"Even so. You never know. I suggest we invest in property down there."

During their first foray to the Maldives, several years ago, they had flown under assumed names and purchased a private atoll with a luxurious villa built like the Parthenon in Athens, from the Greek billionaire, Angelo Adrianakis. They had taken their time exploring the Maldives and had spent nearly a month away bonding.

His oldest son, Lorenzo, held the title of vice president and was officially in charge while Enrico and Alessandro were away, but his title was more symbolic. He was kept insulated from the real work done behind the corporation. Control of Enrico's real estate empire remained firmly in his hands as CEO, and Alessandro as CFO. Decisions were handled remotely by them both, with key trusted personnel who took care of their direct orders.

Enrico was displeased when Lorenzo tried to take over the company in their month-long absence and upon their return, had removed him from his position as vice president and reduced his pay significantly. This did nothing to improve the surly and entitled attitude of his oldest son. Lorenzo was not smart but could be vindictive, which is why his father and brother told him as little as possible. He did not even know their false identities, where they had traveled, or their purchase of the tropical estate in the Maldives.

Enrico was exhausted. They had flown via Emirates with one stopover. The overnight flight from Toronto Pearson International had left at two-thirty in the afternoon and took nearly thirteen hours. It was eleven-thirty in the morning local time when the flight landed at Dubai International Airport. Their layover was a long one. They didn't leave until just after two in the morning, finally arriving at Malé International Airport, also known as Ibrahim Nasir International Airport, at almost eight in the morning.

Enrico and Alessandro had flown using the same false passports they used on their first trip, as they now had identities established with local authorities. Even so, they had booked round trip tickets, to avoid alerting immigration they had no immediate plans of returning. It also would make their trail cloudier should Canadian authorities try to trace their escape route.

Enrico was proud of Alessandro. After he had graduated business school, he had transformed a significant portion of the family's dirty money by investing in legitimate real estate in Canada. Another portion had been siphoned off into cryptocurrency.

"Your retirement fund," Alessandro had grinned.

The only good thing about this entire situation, he mused, was the fact that in a few more hours they'd be sipping drinks at their villa. *It'll beat the crappy winters,* he thought, but he was furious at the prospect of exile in paradise.

His thoughts returned to the present and he looked at the girl writhing beneath him. He had lost interest and was no longer hard, the prospect of snuffing out the young thing's life no longer exciting. He released his hold on the belt, pulled himself off her and threw her off the bed. There was a sickening smack as her head hit the side of the bed stand. *Oh well,* he thought, as she rolled senseless to the marble floor, a dark pool of blood forming a halo around her head. A sick thrill permeated his lower extremities.

He picked up the phone and dialed housekeeping. "I'm done. Come clean up the garbage."

Wrapping the silk robe around his husky body, he tied the belt around his waist and walked out to enjoy the view.

There were worse places to be in exile, he thought, as he looked at the tropical scenery before him. In the lagoon there were lazy ships bobbing in the water. His eyes rested on the one-hundred-foot yacht anchored from shore ready to take him to his island.

He picked up the phone again and called Alessandro. "How are you feeling?" His voice was tender. Because of the gunshot wound to his son's upper thigh, the arduous thirty-hour trip had been hellish, despite the luxurious first-class accommodations.

"I got a few good hours in," replied Alessandro.

"We should get going."

"Agreed," his son said. "I'll send word to the captain to get ready to sail in an hour." Enrico could hear him breathing heavily.

"We'll both rest easier once we're at the villa." He disconnected the call and shook his head in admiration at his son's strength. During the journey his son had refused all painkillers, saying, "Dad, I need to stay alert."

* * *

Once Enrico and Alessandro had arrived at the villa, Enrico pulled out his tablet and searched for news back in Canada.

Just as he had predicted, Lorenzo, his useless piece of shit of a son, was being held for questioning by the police.

Enrico knew his oldest was too stupid to ever have understood the machinations of his business, and the police would come up empty, trying to interrogate him.

He walked onto the balcony which was supported by the massive columns and looked at the enticing ocean, the sun refracting on its surface, blinding him with its brilliance. He adjusted his Burberry sunglasses and looked at the expanse of blue. He decided being exiled in paradise wouldn't be that hard to take.

But before he could relax, he was going to have to do something about David Harris, the man responsible for his involuntary expatriation.

Thirty-Four

It's Good To Be Home

THROUGH THE HIGHPOWER oculars of the M107 Semi-Automatic long-range sniper rifle (LRSR), the blonde woman in the tracksuit watched David and Emma settle on the couch in his condo. She adjusted the amplification on her military grade bionic ear buds and leaned forward to listen.

* * *

"It's so good to be home," said David. "I really appreciate that you sprung me out of the hospital early."

Emma said, "No problem."

"And thanks for picking up the B for me."

"The bee?" she asked.

"The MGB."

"Oh right. That was a fun drive home. Although bit stiff with the manual steering and suspension."

"That's what I love about it."

Emma frowned. "Wish I could have taken my mom home, too."

He squeezed her hand. "I understand; it's for the best though. They need to make sure that your mom doesn't develop pneumonia or bronchitis."

"She's going to hate being stuck there."

"I wouldn't worry about her." David chuckled. "She'll probably re-design the hospital gowns by tomorrow morning."

"Wouldn't be surprised. I was always the best dressed kid in grade school." Emma laughed at the memory. "I feel like a glass of wine. How about you?"

"Sure, I have a bottle of your favorite on the wine rack in the kitchen." She flushed with pleasure at the thought that he had gone to the trouble to stock her favorite red wine.

"You stay put. I'll go get the wine."

She rose from the couch and went to the kitchen, and a few minutes later came back with two crystal wine glasses held in one hand and a bottle of 2021 Martin Ray Pinot Noir Sonoma, in the other.

She struggled to unscrew the metal cap from the top of the bottle. "Just not the same since they started using metal screw caps instead of cork."

"True, but there is less chance of the wine going bad."

"Here, can you try?" She handed the bottle to David and with a quick twist he had removed the cap.

"Thanks." She took the bottle from him and poured liberal amounts in each glass. "We really should let the wine breathe."

"I can think of an activity to do while it does that." He placed his arm around her shoulders.

"Oh, wait a minute! I nearly forgot!" She jumped up and went back to the kitchen and returned with a bar of chocolate.

"Chocolate. Again?" David grinned, unable to contain his amusement. "Are you a chocoholic?"

"My only vice."

He pulled her toward him and kissed her with passion, then drew back to regain his breath. "Well, I hope you have one or two more," he murmured softly.

She kissed him back, then pulled away giving him one of her engaging smiles that was like sunshine peeking from behind the clouds. "Don't you know chocolate goes great with full-bodied red wine? I'll have you know this is not ordinary chocolate. It's ninety-percent cocoa, imported from Costa Rica."

She opened the package and broke off a few squares.

David took a nibble of the chocolate, and then took a sip of wine. His eyes widened in surprise. "You weren't kidding; this is delicious." He took another sip and savored the richness of the cocoa combined with the dark cherry overtones of the wine. "Exquisite."

"KokoArt Chocolate. I discovered it on my trip to Costa Rica last year. You can even buy it through Amazon."

"Thanks for this treat. Got anymore?"

She nodded and broke another substantial piece of the sumptuous, dark chocolate and handed it to him.

"What's it like?"

"What is what like?"

"Costa Rica?"

"Like nowhere else on earth. Pristine beaches, lush rainforest, and Pura Vida."

"Pura—?"

"Pura Vida. Pure Living. It's what the locals say. An expression most visitors soon adopt."

"I like that." David gave a contemplative look. "When this is all over, let's go. You can be my tour guide."

"I'd love to, let's do it!"

Her face grew serious. "How did you sleep last night?"

"Great. Since we identified my killer from my previous life, I've been sleeping better than I have my entire life. Even after what happened last night, I still slept well." He looked directly at Emma, "It's thanks to you."

"I'm glad you feel that way David, but it could've turned out so much worse. I could have lost you. And my mom too." Her voice was tinged with remorse. "I put everyone in danger by leaving the hotel."

"It's over now."

"I guess." She didn't look convinced. "And I feel so guilty about what happened to Anna." She wiped the tears from the corners of her eyes. "Do you think they'll ever apprehend Enrico and his son?"

"With the wealth he's amassed it's hard to say. By now, he could be anywhere in the world."

"Do you think we're still in danger?"

"I don't know." He twirled the stem of the wineglass between his thumb and index finger. "Maybe. He's a vindictive man."

* * *

The assassin, listening from the apartment across the street, reached for her iPhone, which had been installed with KryptAll® firmware. She punched in a series of keys from memory and waited for the call to be routed through its secure global network, with servers that were encrypted with three different algorithms. This level of security made it impossible for outsiders to intercept her call. And should anyone ever get their hands on the Voice Over Internet Protocol (VoIP)-enabled iPhone and try to open it, an auto destruction process would be initiated. Corrosive acids would destroy the phone's hard disk rendering it useless. It was the ultimate guarantee in privacy.

Moments later she heard her boss's commanding voice. He wasted no time. "What have you learned?"

"David survived the attack. His girlfriend Emma took him home today."

"And the girl's mother?"

"Still in hospital."

"And my son?"

"They released him earlier this morning."

"Any news from our contact inside the police department?"

"Lorenzo kept his mouth shut."

"Easy enough; he doesn't know anything."

"There's more."

"Go on."

"They are testing the DNA sample scraped from under George Larson's fingernails." She took in a sharp breath, concerned about the old gangster's reaction, then continued. "Lorenzo. They offered him coffee, which he drank. He left his cup behind. That means—"

"They have his DNA. That stupid idiot!" Enrico exploded. "Then they'll have a familial DNA match. Linking him to me."

"Yes, and then to the crime."

She held the phone away from her ear until the volley of curses had subsided. "What do you want me to do, boss?"

"Kill them."

"Who exactly?"

"David's entire family. Kill. Them. All."

"In any order? Or method?"

"Be creative. And make it painful." He swore again. "Target Liam Foster first. That's his uncle. Then his girlfriend's mom, Laura Jackson. Emma after that. Then Staff Inspector Grant." His sinister laugh made even the hardened sniper cringe. "Cut him off from everyone he knows and loves. And trusts. Then kill him. Slowly and painfully with lots of knife work."

"It'll be expensive. Putting a team together."

"Whatever you need. Whatever the cost. Name it."

A surge of pleasure rushed through her at the prospect of her fattening bank account.

Thirty-Five

An August Evening

THE AUGUST BREEZE held a tinge of coolness in the air. Although it was warm outside, the wind promised colder weather in the autumn nights to come.

The dinner had been simple. Corn, fresh from the farmer's field, had been cooked in a kettle over the fire, and an assortment of vegetables, harvested the same day from Emma and Laura's garden, had been grilled. For the meat lovers, chicken had been roasted to perfection over charcoal.

After several weeks of calm, Liam and Sarah, Bryan and Laura, and David and Emma had fallen into a comfortable rhythm with each other, and the six had become friends. When Laura found out David's thirtieth birthday was on August twenty-eighth, she had suggested a barbecue at her country home.

Their growing bond and common enemy had forged their friendship. This connection had helped them deal with the aftermath of Anna's death, the traumatic kidnapping of Laura and the assault on David during her rescue. A birthday celebration was the perfect antidote to the sad times through which they had gone.

Sarah and Liam held hands as they gazed into the fire, the flames dancing with merriment in the sturdy metal fire pit that Laura's husband had constructed years ago. From time to time, they would look up from the flames and smile at each other; content in just being together.

David glanced over at his uncle. He had never seen him so happy. It was incredible to think how much life had changed for them all during the last five weeks. David looked at Emma; the woman with whom he hoped to grow old. Things would have been so different if they had never met. He had imagined a life haunted by persistent nightmares, his life in a downward spiral, poised to succumb to insanity. His heart was brimming with gratitude. He knew the threat Enrico Bianchi presented might not be over, but no matter what, he would do everything in his power to keep her and her family safe.

A soft smile played on Emma's lips as she watched her mom's face, bright and happy, the light from the August moon softening her features. She whispered to David, "I haven't seen her this happy in years."

Laura stood off to the side, with Bryan behind her, his arms cradled around her, her own hands held his, over her heart, in a gesture of deep affection. It was an evening of tenderness and love, of new beginnings for the six of them.

"It feels as if we have all known each other from previous lives," said Emma, her tone soft and shy.

"I would never have thought this until recently," said Sarah. She looked at David. "I can't believe I found my big brother, George. It gives me a lot of comfort to know that this life is not all there is. Just one of many."

"I agree," said David.

"I'm convinced we're all part of the same soul group," added Laura.

"How wonderful to be together in this lifetime. Right now," said Emma.

"And reassuring that we will find each other again in a future life," said Liam. He pushed with his arms to get up from the Muskoka chair. "It's been a great night. The food was fantastic and the company even better." His eyes focused on Sarah. "Ready to head back to the city?"

Sarah tried to stifle a yawn, nodded and said, "I am getting sleepy." She reached out her hand. "Help me up?"

Liam gently pulled Sarah from the chair.

"Thanks. I love Muskoka chairs, but once settled in, they are a chore to get out of," said Sarah.

"That's the idea," replied Laura, laughing. "They're meant to keep you seated, so you'll relax."

"Well, that we did," said Liam with a broad smile.

"You know, we have plenty of spare bedrooms. You can head back in the morning," said Laura.

David noticed Liam and Sarah exchange a private glance. "Thanks for the offer, but we should get back," said Liam.

Sarah went to Laura and gave her a hug, "You've become like a sister to me."

"I feel the same."

"Come on, Sarah," said Liam. "Time to head out. Laura, we had a great time." He turned to Bryan and grasped his hand. "See you later."

Emma got up. "David and I will walk you to your car." She pulled a compact flashlight out of her pocket and switched it on.

At the car, Sarah kissed Emma on the cheek, and gave David a huge hug. "I'm glad we found each other, brother."

"Me, too." David could barely contain the feeling of joy. He turned to his uncle. "See you at the office Monday morning, Uncle Liam."

"See you then." Liam gave his nephew a bear hug. "I love you."

"I love you, too." David was touched by the rare display of emotion shown by his uncle.

* * *

Bryan looked at his watch. "It's getting late. Almost midnight." He sighed. "I should get going, too." He began to release his arms from around Laura.

She grabbed his hands tighter and said, "Stay tonight."

"You're sure?" A jolt of joy coursed through him.

"Yes, I am. It's been a long time since I've been happy." She looked down, awkward. "Not since—"

Bryan brushed his lips against her neck. "It's okay, my love." He turned her toward him and kissed her gently. "You deserve to be happy."

"Come on," she said. "Let's go in. The fire is almost out. Time to start a different one."

"What about Emma and David?"

"They're adults. They'll understand."

* * *

Emma and David waved, called out their goodbyes to Liam and Sarah one final time, and watched the taillights of the car fade in the distance.

"I really like those two," said Emma. "I feel like they've been part of the family from the very beginning."

"I'm glad you like Uncle Liam."

"And Sarah, what a sweetheart. It's so nice they've found each other."

"Emma—"

"Yes?"

"I don't want this evening to end." He pulled her toward him and kissed her. The feeling was so intense, unlike any either had experienced before. Maybe it was the moonlight and the stars or the soft wind that played on their faces like gentle caresses, but David was sure he was floating. After a moment, he pulled away, and saw the same astonished look mirrored in her eyes.

"Did you feel that?" Her voice was filled with awe.

He nodded. "As if we were levitating."

"It was more than that... as if our souls recognized each other."

"Emma, I—"

She reached up and cradled his face with her hands. "I know. I love you, too."

Thirty-Six

This Can't Be A Coincidence

BRYAN'S CELL VIBRATED on the bedstand. It took a few minutes for him to realize where he was until he saw the sleeping form beside him. Laura. He pulled his phone toward him to check the time. Almost three in the morning. It was unusual for him to be rousted out of bed; early morning calls were rare and something he'd left behind many years ago after having been promoted to staff inspector.

The call was from Inspector Angie Turani. Without bothering to listen to his voice mail, he pushed the redial option.

"Angie, what's going on?"

"Sir, there's been a serious car accident."

He kept the tinge of annoyance from his voice, wondering why she would be calling about a traffic accident. "And you're calling because?"

"I wanted you to be the first to know." He could hear the hesitation in her voice. "The victims; they're friends of yours."

He could feel beads of sweat trickle down the back of his neck, even though the night air blowing through the open window in Laura's bedroom was cool.

"Go on."

"Identification in the victims' wallets indicate a Sarah Larson-Moody and a Liam Foster. Neither survived the crash."

"Do you have positive IDs?"

Angie's gulp was audible over the phone. "It was bad, sir. They'll need to check dental and DNA records."

"Where did it happen?"

"The intersection of Maven and Green Avenue."

"On my way." He disconnected the call and got out of bed, trying not to wake Laura. He reached for his clothing, which was draped over the leather wing chair in the corner of the bedroom.

"Wow, you're up early." Laura smiled and reached for him. When he didn't come to her for the embrace, she turned on the Tiffany lamp on the bed stand and asked, "What's wrong?"

"Laura." He sat heavily on the bed and held her hand. His slate gray eyes were dark, and his expression was grim. "It's Liam and Sarah. There's been an accident."

"What?"

"They're gone."

Laura placed a hand over her mouth. "Oh, no! How?"

"Car accident. On their way home from here last night."

"Are they sure it's them?"

"Inspector Turani thinks so, but we'll get confirmation when the autopsies are done."

"Oh my God. Why didn't they stay the night?" Laura began to sob softly. "Poor David."

"I gotta go," he exhaled in short breaths.

"Do you want me to come with you?"

He shook his head. "This may be an accident—"

She interrupted him. "You don't think so, do you?"

It was if she could see right through him.

"No, I don't. This can't be a coincidence."

"Oh my God. *Enrico?*"

He nodded slowly. "I think so. Don't say anything until I get back."

"Of course." He looked in her emerald eyes and became calm. "Will you help me break the news to David when I return?"

Laura nodded, the light in her eyes grave. "I'll help any way I can."

Bryan was grateful for the support. He had come to respect Laura's empathy for other people. From his years of experience on the police force, he knew a death notification not given with kindness and compassion could affect the psychological health of surviving family members for years to come.

He had never gotten used to delivering sad news, and considered this a strength, not a weakness. He took pride that he had not been hardened by the job. Normally, notifications were done by two officers: the investigating officer and or a superior officer such as himself. Sometimes, the police officer might take a civilian with him in certain circumstances. In this case, Bryan thought it would be best if Laura would help him break the news to David as gently as possible.

She pushed the covers away and got out of bed, putting her arms around him, and said, "How long will you be?"

"Not sure." He kissed her gently on the lips. "I'll text when I am heading back to you."

* * *

Laura was preparing a pancake breakfast in the kitchen, grateful that Emma and David had slept in. It gave her time to compose and prepare herself before Bryan came back to give David the sad news about Liam and Sarah. She was upset for David. He had finally resolved the issue of his recurring nightmares… and now this. She knew David loved his uncle and that Liam had been a strong and positive force in the young man's life. She mused, *How will this news affect David?*

Her thoughts were interrupted by her daughter's buoyant voice. "Morning, Mom." Emma removed the plate cover keeping the breakfast warm, breathed in the delicious aromas and said, "Yummy, you made my favorite: pancakes." She replaced the cover, padded over to the coffee maker, poured a cup, and asked her mom, "Refill for you?"

"I'd love one."

A few minutes later David came into view and headed straight toward Laura and gave her a tender kiss on the forehead. "Morning, Mom." Laura reached out and touched where he had kissed her, feeling nonplussed at how he had addressed her. "Say again?"

"You betcha, *Mom.* I asked Emma to marry me last night."

Laura looked over at her beautiful and happy young daughter and tried to stifle the fear stirring deep inside her. She pushed away the unsettling feeling and opened her arms and drew both Emma and David into her embrace.

"How wonderful," she said, smiling, although her heart was aching for them. *Their timing couldn't be more unfortunate.*

Emma broke free first and looked around. "Where's Bryan? Didn't he stay the night?" Her daughter's face was the picture of innocence.

"Umm… he had to go into work." Laura's fair complexion turned a shade rosier. "He said he'd stop by later this morning."

"Great. We can tell him when he gets back," said Emma, squeezing David's hand.

"I've got to tell Uncle Liam the news. And Sarah, too." David had grown very fond of her in the few weeks he'd gotten to know his sister from his previous incarnation. He pulled out his cell and pushed the contact icon for his uncle. "They may still be together this morning. We can tell them both at the same time."

Together in more ways than you can imagine, thought Laura. She wiped the moisture from her eyes.

Her daughter noticed and misread the tears. "Mom. You know, you're not losing a daughter, but gaining a son."

"Honey, I know. These are tears of joy." She hated lying to her daughter and had never done so until today, even though this was a forgivable white lie. *How was she ever going to help Bryan break the news to these two?*

"Uncle Liam's not picking up. Must be busy." He grinned. "Love is in the air."

I hope Bryan comes back soon. Laura was smiling on the outside but screaming inside. "Emma and David, would you set the table, please?"

"Sure."

"Good. I'm starving and have been up for hours waiting for you two lovebirds to get up."

"You don't need to ask me twice," said David. "Since I met you two, I've never eaten better."

* * *

Emma pushed back her chair. "Mom, that was so delicious."

Laura smiled back at her daughter and said, "I cooked, you two should clean up."

"Sure thing." Emma looked over at David. "I'll wash; you dry."

"Let me try Uncle Liam first." After several rings, David frowned and hung up. "Still no answer."

"Have you tried calling Sarah?" asked Emma.

"Yeah, and she's not picking up either."

Laura noted the mounting concern in his voice, but refrained from saying anything, keeping her promise to Bryan to wait. Instead, she refilled her coffee and said, "I'll be in the garden out back."

She left via the kitchen door, walked down the stone paved pathway, and sat in her favorite wicker seat overlooking the gardens. Even the explosion of late summer yellow, gold, and red flowers could not provide the usual salve to her soul. *Bryan, where are you?*

Thirty-Seven

Breaking The News

LAURA'S THOUGHTS WERE interrupted when Emma called out, "Bryan just turned into our driveway."

"Great. Coming."

Laura cut around the house in time to see Bryan get out. His posture was of a man much older than his years, the weight of Liam and Sarah's deaths having drained him of energy.

Bryan's eyes said it all when they looked into hers.

Her hands flew to her mouth. "It's true then?"

He nodded. Unable to speak at first, he swallowed at the thick and viscous lump which was blocking his vocal cords. He cleared his throat and said, "It's them."

"Was it an accident?"

"No, I don't think so. Our auto accident forensic investigators are reconstructing the scene; it looks like they were forced off the road." He shook his head. "I can't believe it. So alive and vibrant one moment, then the next—" He was so overcome, he couldn't finish the thought.

She gestured toward the house. "They're busy in the kitchen cleaning up after our late breakfast. I've not said anything, but David is getting anxious that his uncle is not answering his phone."

"Let's head in then. In my experience, it's best to give the facts up front. Plain words. No sugar coating. I'll need you to provide support as they take in the news." He paused for a moment. "Oh, and please make a pot of tea."

"Tea?"

"Doing normal things like drinking tea or coffee or water gives the victim's family a sense of normalcy. It helps distract from the full impact of the grief."

"I see; that makes sense." She waited a moment. "There's some news you should know first."

"Go ahead."

"David asked Emma to marry him. She said yes." Tears sprung in Laura's eyes. "He's been trying to reach his uncle all morning to give him the happy news."

"Life's equalizer. A happy moment wiped out by tragedy." Bryan's voice was bitter. "Those poor kids."

"Why don't you go into the sitting room? I'll prepare the tea and ask them to join you there."

* * *

When Emma and David entered the sitting room, Bryan stood in front of the large bay window, his arms clasped behind his back. So as not to startle him, Emma cleared her throat. "Ahem."

Bryan turned around and gazed at her with sad gray eyes. "Hi Emma, David."

They exchanged concerned looks. He was not the cheerful and carefree man from the previous evening.

"Mom will be just a minute. She's bringing in the tea, and some scones she baked yesterday."

"Good, have a seat you two."

Emma thought it odd for him to tell them to take a seat, in her own home, thinking his behavior unusual. Something was off and she began to feel uneasy. *But what?*

The three looked toward the doorway at the sound of rattling teacups and saucers on the serving tray. Her mother's hands were not steady, as if she was nervous. She rose to help her mom, took the tray from her, and arranged the dishes on the coffee table.

"I'll pour," said Laura. Once the tea had been served, Emma and David looked at Bryan expectantly.

"There's no easy way to say this." Bryan sighed. "David, I am sorry to tell you that your Uncle Liam and Sarah died in a car crash last night."

"No!" David's face was pale, his voice filled with anguish. Emma put her arms around him, but he shrugged them away. He got up and began pacing. "Where?"

"At Maven and Green Avenue. On their way home from here."

"I can't believe this," said Emma. She looked at Bryan and then her mom. "Ah, you already knew. How could you keep this from—"

Bryan interrupted. "I asked your mom to keep it to herself until we were sure."

"I want to see my uncle's body." His expression was desolate. "Sarah's, too." He folded his arms in a defensive position.

"I don't advise it. Their faces were badly damaged in the collision."

"Then how do you know it's them for sure?"

"It is highly likely, based on the car being registered in your uncle's name, and the identification in his wallet, and in Sarah's purse." He took a sip of tea. "Autopsies and dental records will confirm what we believe."

Laura got up and took David by the hand and guided him back to his seat. "Come sit down." When he sat down heavily, she handed him the tea. "Here, drink this."

David took the cup from her and put it down without taking a sip. "Got something stronger?" His voice was hoarse, as if his vocal cords had been stripped raw with sandpaper.

"Sure. Camus, okay?"

"Yes, thanks."

Laura walked to a black lacquered cabinet adorned with flying cranes carved in mother of pearl. She pulled out a carafe of amber liquid and poured the cognac into a crystal tumbler and brought it to David.

"It's strong. Drink it slowly." He nodded and took a sip.

"Anyone else want one?" Laura asked.

"I'm on duty, so no," said Bryan.

"Emma?"

"Yes, please."

She returned to the cabinet and poured two more drinks, one for herself and the other for Emma.

David took several more sips, the color in his face returning. "Was it really an accident?"

"We have our suspicions." Bryan cleared his throat. "The accident scene is being analyzed, but it appears Liam was forced off the road. They hit the concrete barrier and were killed instantly."

"My uncle was a cautious driver. Never took a drink whenever he knew he'd need to drive." He shook his head in disbelief. "Last night was no different."

"You don't think it was—" Emma stared at Bryan.

"Yeah, I do. And I think David, you and your mom are in danger. Enrico Bianchi is a ruthless man and won't stop until he's destroyed you all."

Thirty-Eight

What Do We Do Now?

"WE'RE NOT RUNNING!" David's hands were clasping Emma's tightly. He stared intently at Bryan. "Federal Witness Protection? Really?"

"Look, I know it's not ideal, but you have your whole lives ahead of you. You're getting married. Why take the risk?" said Bryan.

He had expected David to be against the idea of going into hiding. The Federal Witness Program was administered by the non-investigative branch of the Royal Canadian Mounted Police (RCMP) with a dedicated staff which was separate from the investigative arm of the RCMP to maintain impartiality. Participation was voluntary, and could be for life, if required. The program was available to all law enforcement agencies across Canada.

"I have never run from anything in my life, and I am not starting now," said David.

Emma squeezed his hand in reassurance and said, "I agree. I wasn't raised to be a coward." She hesitated, "I might be convinced otherwise if mom would join us."

"Emma, this is not the same thing. Your lives are in danger," said Laura.

"Mom, don't be a hypocrite. You are in just as much danger. Enrico nearly killed you. If you are rejecting Federal Witness Protection, then so am I." Emma was frustrated, and her face was red from crying. "I'm with David. I am not giving up my life because of that bast—"

Bryan tried another tack. "It would be just until the perpetrators are caught, and you've testified."

"If they're caught," said David.

"Yes, there's that." Bryan acknowledged with reluctance.

"I still think you and David should go," Laura told her daughter. "My life has been full. I am settled and comfortable. I don't want to go through the upheaval."

"Mom, I am not going without you." Her eyes filled with tears. "I love you too much to leave you."

"I know honey." Laura's eyes softened. "I love you, too."

"And I am not leaving without Emma," said David. "We're going to have to face this together."

Bryan was conflicted, feeling both relief and guilt. He was deeply in love with Laura, and the thought of losing her outweighed the common sense of her and her family going into hiding. He was worried sick about the three of them and vowed he'd keep a close eye on all three as much as he could.

* * *

The assassin dialed the encrypted number and heard the curt response.

"Report."

"Liam Foster and Sarah Larson-Moody were eliminated last night."

Enrico enjoyed the delicious sense of power flooding through his body. "How?" His voice sounded greedy and anxious for the details.

"Single car accident."

"Tell me more."

"At the corner of Maven and Green Avenue. One of my men forced them off the road and they hit the concrete median."

"Dead on impact?" Enrico could not keep the glee from his voice.

"The woman, yes. The man, no. Which was good. My operative injected cocaine into his forearm. He lived long enough for the substance to be pumped throughout his body."

"Excellent."

"Thanks. You should know Staff Inspector Bryan Grant has his suspicions. He's got a team of accident forensic specialists examining the scene."

"But when the autopsies are done—"

"The medical examiner will see evidence of substance abuse and rule out foul play."

"Outstanding." Enrico chuckled with delight. "I'll wire the funds to you immediately."

"Still want Laura Jackson to be next?"

"Yes. Continue as planned."

"Okay." The assassin disconnected.

Thirty-Nine

Don't Go, My Love

A MONTH HAD passed since the tragic deaths of Liam and Sarah, and once cocaine had been discovered in Liam's bloodstream, the coroner, although reluctant to do so, ruled their deaths as accidental.

On the drive over to Laura's house, Staff Inspector Bryan Grant recalled the conversation he'd had with the coroner.

"I think it's too convenient an explanation," Bryan had said in frustration. "Liam and Sarah were with us that evening, and there was no way Liam was abusing cocaine that night, or any other night. He was a well-respected lawyer and citizen in our community."

The coroner had smiled at him with sympathy. "I hear you, but unless you can find out when and how the cocaine was injected into his system, I am going to stay firm with my position that this was a tragic accident as a result of substance abuse." He placed his hand on Bryan's arm. "Look, we've known each other a long time, your instincts are probably right. If you find any evidence to the contrary, I will be happy to reconsider."

Bryan was annoyed. Although the forensic pathologist had confirmed the DNA collected from under George Samuel Larson's fingernails was likely that of Enrico Bianchi, due to the familial match of his son's Lorenzo's DNA, finding Enrico was proving difficult.

The video evidence for which George had forfeited his life thirty years ago indicated that Enrico was the killer of Chris Beacon, the businessman. Tying him to the recent deaths of Anna Tungsten and his friends Liam and Sarah, however, was a challenge.

As to where he had run to, there were no leads at all. No doubt Enrico Bianchi would be living under an assumed name and could be anywhere in the world.

As he pulled his car into Laura's driveway, Bryan shook himself out of the reverie. He was looking forward to seeing her tonight and didn't want their time together tainted by his concerns.

He knew there was a strong chance that Enrico might make further attempts on the lives of Laura, Emma, and David and feared this was not a hypothetical if, but a definite when.

As he rounded the last turn in the laneway, it was approaching seven in the evening and the intense blues of the crisp September day were yielding toward deep shades of indigo. He noted with a measure of unease that the lights at the front door were not on, nor were there any lights on in the house.

Worried, he turned the key Laura had given him in the lock and entered. The usual aroma of delicious food being cooked or baked in the kitchen and the hum of her sewing machine as she created yet another avantgarde design were missing. The house was silent.

"Laura?" There was no cheerful response to his call. His police training told him to remain calm, but worry was causing him to panic. He called out again, anxiety mounting in his chest and his throat was closing in. "Laura! Where are you?"

Bryan ran throughout the house continuing to shout her name. *Where was she? She should be home.* They'd spoken that afternoon confirming their get together for this evening.

His search of the house was complete, and Laura was not inside. He switched on his flashlight and went outside to search the property.

The flashlight's beam showed Laura slumped over in her favorite wrought iron chair, her wavy hair obscuring her face. The fingers of her right hand were draped over the side of the chair, reaching toward her blue rescue inhaler which was lying inches away.

"Oh my God, no! Laura!" He rushed over to her and checked one of her carotid arteries and was relieved to find a pulse. He reached for his cell and dialed 911.

* * *

Bryan rode in the ambulance with Laura, watching her chest rise and fall with each breath. *Don't go my love. I need you.*

The emergency medical technicians transferred Laura to the hospital bed and took her to triage. Once he had answered the triage nurse's questions, he made way to follow her to the emergency room cubicle.

The nurse gently pushed against Bryan's chest, stopped him, and asked, "Is she your wife?"

"No, my girlfriend."

"In that case, please have a seat in the waiting room. We need to examine her now," she said.

"I want to be with her." He flashed his badge.

The nurse shook her head. "Staff Inspector Grant, we'll call you as soon as we can. Does she have family you could call?"

"Yes, her daughter, Emma."

"Good. Why don't you call Emma while you wait? I am sure Laura will be happy to see you both when she wakes up."

Bryan sat heavily on the hard and uncomfortable waiting room chair and punched in the number and waited for Emma to answer.

"Bryan! What a nice surprise." Emma's voice had the same lovely timber as Laura's. "Are you with my mother? She said you two had a date tonight."

"We're at the New Elgan General Hospital. Your mom's in ER." He tried to keep his voice calm and even. "I found her unconscious."

"What happened?"

"I don't know." This time he was not able to hold back the sobs. "They're examining her now."

"Hold on," she said. Her voice was shaky as she spoke to David. "It's Bryan. Something's happened to Mom. She's in the hospital."

Bryan could hear David shout, "We're on our way!"

* * *

Emma and David found Bryan leaning forward with his arms wrapped over his knees. She touched him on the shoulder. "Bryan, do you have any news about Mom?

"Still waiting." He glanced at his wristwatch. "It's been about an hour. Hopefully, we'll hear something soon."

"I'll get us some coffees," offered David.

"Thanks," said Bryan.

Emma sat down and placed her arms around Bryan. "What happened?"

"When I got to your place, your mom wasn't in the house. I searched everywhere, finally finding her outside in the garden." He sighed. "She was unconscious. Her pulse was weak, and her breathing was very shallow. I called 9-1-1."

Although they sipped coffees and tried to distract each other with light talk, the atmosphere among the three was heavy with worry.

They looked up when the emergency doctor entered the waiting room, hopeful she had positive news for them. She looked over her rose colored metal frame eyeglasses and said, "She's had a severe asthma attack."

Emma frowned. "That's unusual. Her asthma condition is mild. She keeps it under control with her inhalers."

"Yes, we pulled her medical records, and we are aware of her asthmatic condition." The doctor paused, "Your mother's bloodwork shows Ketamine in her system."

"What is that?" Emma asked.

"It's a drug known to interfere with asthma medications and obstructs the airways." The doctor eyed them with concern. "It's what led to the severity of the attack."

"What's Ketamine prescribed for?" asked Bryan, suspicion gnawing at the back of his mind.

The doctor hesitated, then said, "That's what's strange. Ketamine is an anesthetic. It's also used to treat depression or to help manage pain. Sometimes used as a recreational drug."

"Mom is one of the most cheerful people I know. She'd never take anything like this. And if she did, I'd know about it."

"It would have been injected." The doctor looked worried. "If Staff Inspector Grant had not found her in time, she would most certainly have died."

Emma's hands flew to her mouth. "Enrico?"

Bryan's eyes flared with fury. "Without a doubt."

Forty

What Now?

DAVID TURNED TO Bryan and asked, "What now?"

"I'm arranging for a police officer to be stationed outside her door while she recovers." His voice was harsh. "I will stop at nothing until I find Enrico Bianchi."

"I won't stop either," said David.

"This is a matter for law enforcement."

"Not when it involves the ones I love. That man has persecuted me my entire life. In my dreams and in real life. This has got to stop!"

"Now will you reconsider the Federal Witness Protection program?"

"Absolutely not." David weighed his words with care. "I am not without means. I earn an excellent income, and with the inheritance from my uncle, if I have to, I will spend every dime of it to find that bastard."

"Look, guys, how about cooling it?" Emma looked at both men with mounting concern. "The nurse said Mom's awake. She said we could go in and see her. Coming?"

David was the first to speak. "Sorry, Bryan. This is all too much."

"I get it. I'm upset, too. Laura is the love of my life." He stopped and caught his breath. "The three of you mean the world to me. You're the family I never had."

David placed his arm around Bryan's shoulder and said, "Let's go."

With that, the three walked into Laura's room to find her sitting up. She was pale and drawn, but still managed one of her brilliant smiles. "My three favorite people."

"Mom, I've been so worried," said Emma rushing into her mom's outstretched arms.

"It's okay, honey. I'm here." Laura said comforting her daughter. "But why am I here exactly? Twice in hospital in less than two months is strange, especially since both times I don't remember a thing."

"Someone drugged you with Ketamine."

"What's that?"

"An anesthetic and also a drug to treat depression," said Bryan. "It can be used recreationally, too."

"The problem is this drug blocks the airways and for asthma sufferers, it can trigger a fatal asthma attack," said David. "I googled more about the drug. It's also used as a horse tranquilizer."

"Bryan found you in time. He saved your life, Mom."

"This is important," said Bryan. "Was there anything unusual about your day?"

"I don't think so." Laura shook her head in disbelief. "I did some grocery shopping in the morning."

"Do you remember anything else?" he prodded.

"Well, there were some real estate people who stopped by in the afternoon to see if I was interested in selling. Which we're not. This is Emma's childhood home we're talking about."

"Anything off about them?"

"I didn't think so at the time." Laura's eyebrows knitted together in concentration. "The woman said she was a gardener. Commented on my beautiful gardens. Said she was in love with the dinnerplate dahlias. Wanted to take a closer look for inspiration." She frowned. "While I was showing the gardens to them, I was stung by a bee."

"Was your back to them at any time?" asked Bryan.

"Yes. The path is a bit narrow, so the woman followed me first, then the man. That's when I was stung. On my left shoulder blade."

"I don't think that was a bee," said Emma, stating the obvious. "The nurse did say it would have been injected."

"Shit," said Bryan. "Did they leave a card?"

"Sure. It should be on the kitchen counter."

"Anyone want to bet the info on the card's bogus?" said David, his voice dripping with cynicism.

* * *

"You failed to kill Laura Jackson?" Enrico's voice was displeased. "A little woman like that survived that high dosage of Ketamine?"

"The police officer she's involved with found her. Rushed her to the hospital." She cleared her throat. "Do you want us to try again?"

"Not yet."

"Just as well. They have a police officer guarding her hospital room."

"Leave any attempts for a few weeks at least. They are on high alert now, but when nothing happens, they'll become complacent."

"Try for Laura again?"

"No, forget Laura for now. Emma's next." His laugh was grating and cruel. "Break David's heart."

Forty-One

David Harris, P.I.

DAVID LOOKED AT his watch and noted the time. It was Wednesday afternoon, and he had a few more hours before it was time to pack it in for the day. He sat up straighter and used his right hand to massage the small of his back. He hadn't been working out as much lately, and his muscles were getting soft. He was obsessed with researching how Enrico Bianchi and his son Alessandro could have disappeared. There had to be a paper trail.

He completed the work for his client and returned to his real job now. Tracking down the Bianchis. He knew that Bryan was doing his best, but David believed his life with Emma could not begin until they saw Enrico and Alessandro behind bars, or better yet, dead.

Unbeknownst to both Emma and Bryan, David had been taking an online private investigator course. The course was fifty hours in length, and once completed would prepare him to take the Ministry of the Solicitor General's provincial exam. Upon successful completion of the exam, he would have his private investigator license and be able to investigate the character or actions of individuals, their businesses or occupations and their location or that of their property. Along with his law degree, he was confident he'd have the tools necessary to find Enrico and his son and remain within the confines of criminal and civil legislation and procedures.

In other words, he planned to do his investigations legally.

His next plan was to take a course in firearms and had noted there was a school near Toronto that would provide live training. The website promised a Tactical Fitness Class which involved circular training and shooting drills to simulate real life situations.

If anything, it will whip me back into shape, David thought.

He knew it was a long game he was playing but was convinced he should be prepared, should he discover the whereabouts of the Bianchis.

He'd confided in Laura, whom he already considered to be his mother-in-law, about his course of action. He had come to admire and respect the tenacious woman who had survived a near drowning and Ketamine overdose, all under the direction of Enrico.

It was now October, almost a month since Laura's last scrape with death, and he was uneasy about when the next attempt to take their lives would be made.

Although engaged, he and Emma had not yet moved in together. They were still talking about whether they'd find a place in the countryside or remain in his large condo in the city. He'd prefer to stay in New Elgan but knew that Emma would not be happy living in the city fulltime. With the sale of his condo in the city, he'd be able to procure a very nice home in a rural area within comfortable driving distance of New Elgan. He could keep his current law office location and set aside an office for Emma so she could conduct her website business from there on the days she needed to see city clients. Driving to work together could be very nice indeed.

For now, they were happy spending Wednesday nights and weekends together. It was getting harder and harder to say goodbye to each other at the end of each date. This past Sunday, as she was getting ready to go back to her mom, she'd said, "I just don't feel like I can make any plans until Enrico is dealt with."

She had become very protective of her mom after the last attempt on her life, and on the nights she spent with David, Bryan stayed with her mom, something Bryan said he didn't mind doing at all. It was curious how the four of them got along so well together. He now believed in soul groups. What else could explain the easy companionship and comfortable feeling he had with Emma, Laura and Bryan? A stab of regret tugged at him as he reflected that two members of this tightly knit family, for how else could they be described, were missing: Sarah and Uncle Liam.

With the workload he'd imposed on himself, it was just as well he had as many nights to himself as he did. It was challenging to catch up on work for his clients while taking the private investigator course, and he had yet to find someone to help with the caseload left by the passing of his uncle.

He'd been spending longer hours at the office even on their date nights, often arriving home late. He was grateful when Emma started preparing their dinners on those evenings, but did feel guilty, knowing he'd been neglecting her.

He promised himself he would make it up to her this coming Thanksgiving weekend. The colors of the leaves were almost at their peak, soon to be bursting into rich hues of gold, orange, and red. He'd planned the weekend away in a cozy cottage on Serenity Lake, close to Algonquin Park, and was delighted that the owners were providing a canoe for their use. No motorboats were allowed on the lake, so he expected a nice peaceful time. *Emma is going to love this*, he thought to himself.

It was approaching six in the evening, and he decided to stop working and surprise Emma by arriving on time. He was looking forward to seeing her cheerful face and enjoying the prospect of telling her about the mini holiday he'd planned for them.

* * *

"You're home early." Emma flushed with pleasure, a faint pink highlighting her high cheekbones. "Dinner's not quite ready. I thought you'd be later."

David pulled her to him and gave her a kiss. "I missed you. Last Sunday seems eons away."

"Silly, it's only been a few days." Her lips curved up in a mischievous smile. "Come on, since you're early, why don't you set the table?"

"I'd be delighted." He rolled up his sleeves and followed her to the kitchen. "It smells good in here."

"Grilled lamb basted with maple syrup for you. Grilled eggplant topped with vegan cheese and tomatoes and garlic for me. I made extra in case you want to try some. Potatoes roasted in rosemary and garlic, and sautéed asparagus and red pepper."

"This is amazing. What's the occasion?"

"It's our Wednesday date night. What more excuse do we need?"

"I'll open the wine. There's a red from California I'd like us to try. The woman at the wine store said it was one of her favorites."

"Sounds great. What's it called?"

"Beyer Ranch Zinfandel produced by Wente Vineyards. From the San Francisco Bay area." David poured a small amount in the wine glass and twirled the stem with his forefingers. "Nice legs on it." He took a sip. "Wow, you're going to love this one."

She looked at the timer on her iPhone. "Dinner will be ready in about fifteen minutes. Pour me a glass and let's sit on the couch for a bit."

"Sounds great."

Every week, they tried a new bottle of wine, giving each other their impressions of that particular vintage.

"Let me know what you think." David handed her the glass of ruby colored wine and said, "It's got great viscosity." The scarlet liquid slid down the sides of the wineglass.

Emma swirled the contents in her glass and said, "You're right about the legs." Then she breathed in the heady aroma and sipped. "Oh my, this is wonderful." Emma took another sip, a little furrow creasing between her eyebrows. "Mmmm… intense blackberry with a hint of spice. Makes my nose tickle a little." Her laugh was infectious. "Your turn."

David smiled at her and took a sip. "Almost like plum jam. Aged in oak."

He put down the wineglass. His face became serious, and he took her hands in his. "Ever since my uncle died… it's been difficult for me.

The caseload at work is heavy." He looked at her with concerned eyes. "I hope you haven't been feeling neglected."

"No, not at all. I get it. Have you found someone to help yet?"

"No, still working on it." He sighed. "Emma, I'd like us to go away this weekend. Up north. I've booked a romantic little cottage on Serenity Lake. There's a canoe."

"Well, I wouldn't consider going if there wasn't a canoe!" She gave him a playful look, then became serious. "Do you think it'll be safe?"

"No reason to think otherwise," he said. "The only ones who will know our plans will be Bryan, your mom and the folks renting us the cottage."

"Okay, that's reassuring. When do we leave?"

"Tomorrow morning; check-in time is four in the afternoon. Checkout is Monday afternoon."

* * *

The assassin, from across the street, put down her surveillance gear, called Enrico and said, "They're headed to a secluded spot up north for the long weekend. The perfect opportunity. No witnesses."

"Excellent. Make sure Emma dies in David's arms." His laugh was sinister and cruel. "Make him suffer."

Forty-Two

Serenity Lake

"THIS IS BREATHTAKING," Emma said as she wiped the sleep from her eyes and viewed the placid lake. Tendrils of early morning fog were reaching out like supplicants seeking benediction. As they rose higher, the brilliant sun dissipated them until they were gone like illusive memories. The reflection of the brilliant chaos of colors was so perfectly produced, it was hard to tell which way was upright or down.

"It really is serene," said David. He came up beside her, carrying two mugs of coffee and handed her one. The curved handle had been shaped to look like a squirrel tail. When she turned the mug around, a little face of a squirrel was carved in relief on the side. "How cute. What's yours like?"

"The handle on mine looks like a raccoon tail." He turned it around. "Raccoon."

"I love these. How novel. I wonder where the owners got them?"

David raised his mug a little higher and looked at the stamp on the bottom. "Says Procyon Wildlife."

"I've heard of them. They're a wildlife rescue and rehabilitation center in Beeton. They do good work. Wouldn't mind volunteering there one day."

She took a sip of coffee. "Do you think we're safe here?" she asked, frowning. "It seems whenever we get too carefree—"

"We can't stop living our lives."

"I guess you're right, but still, I do worry." Her eyes roamed the shoreline and stopped at the dock. "There's the canoe." She smiled with appreciation. "It's a lake canoe. Nice and sturdy."

"Want to go for a paddle after breakfast?"

"I thought you'd never ask." Emma looked at David with faint smile lines creasing at the corners of her eyes. "Let's get breakfast going."

David gently pushed her back toward the railing. "Enjoy your morning coffee. I'm making breakfast."

"You are?" she said with surprise.

"It's my turn to spoil you." He gathered her in his arms and kissed her on the forehead. "You've been picking up the slack because of my late work nights. It's not unappreciated."

She pressed her face into his chest, taking in his musky smell, David's scent. "I love you," she murmured.

"And I love you."

* * *

Emma sat in front on the bow seat of the canoe, while David sat at the stern. They had stopped paddling and were enjoying the gentle rocking of the canoe. "This is so beautiful." Her voice was hushed and reverent. "I feel so close to the Creator when I am immersed in nature."

"Me, too."

"I love it." She sighed with happiness. "Shall we continue?"

"Sure thing."

They reached the end of the lake where it narrowed to a tributary. The stream serpentined through the tall reeds and bullrushes which bordered each side.

"Do you really want to navigate through this?" David looked uncertain. His paddle trailed light rivulets in the water.

"Sure, why not? We might see something of interest."

"What if we can't turn around?"

"You worry too much." Her laugh was soft, melodious, and carefree. A breeze tugged at the curls cascading down her back, whipping her hair into her eyes. She removed the hair bungee from her wrist and secured her unruly hair into a ponytail. "That's better."

David's breath caught in his throat at her graceful movements and thought about how much he loved her.

Emma noticed him staring at her. "What're you looking at?"

"Oh, nothing. Just loving the freedom and the quiet. And the view."

"The view?" Her cheeks flushed pink, as she picked up her paddle.

* * *

The assassin stood at the base of the massive spruce tree. The 1997 Honda Accord she'd stolen had a flat tire and she had arrived later than planned at the hiking trail that led to the lake. By the time she had trekked in and climbed to her roost, the couple in the canoe had disappeared into the tributary.

Her perch was comfortable, and the stock of the barrel rested on the sturdy branch before her. She settled in for the wait, expecting the couple would be paddling back the way they came.

* * *

Emma spoke in soft tones, laced with excitement. "Look, over there! A Great Blue Heron!"

David's city eyes were unaccustomed to the sensory overload of nature surrounding him and was having trouble discerning the bird from the dense reeds. "Where?"

"Camouflaged well." She whispered. "Right over there." She pointed to a spot a short distance away.

He spotted the bird. "Oh, wow. Beautiful."

"They'll be migrating soon."

"Magnificent." He leaned slightly to the side, careful to keep the canoe trim, and pulled the waterproof pouch containing his cell phone from his vest pocket.

The heron noticed the movement David had made, gave the canoeists a wary look and flew off, its large wings gracefully carrying it away from the intruders. David shook his head in disappointment and put the pouch back in his vest.

"Some migrate as far south as Central America or the Caribbean," Emma told him.

"Amazing."

She turned slightly, taking care not to shift the balance in the canoe and gave him one of her breathtaking smiles. "Let's head a little further into the tributary."

"You're the boss."

She picked up her paddle and dipped it into the water.

After another twenty minutes of steady paddling, the tributary widened into a smaller lake. Huge pine trees encircled the lake, their limbs stretching as if to the heavens. The October sun hung low in the cerulean blue sky and cast dark shadows across the western side of the lake. The contrast of light and shadow was startling. The light almost blinding and the shadows dark, jealously guarding their secrets.

Emma and David stopped paddling. "It's like being in mother nature's cathedral." She whispered softly. The canoe floated in the light current.

Suddenly, the canoe began to tremble to the rhythm of David's sobs, the anguish of the last few months being released in a flood of emotions— anger, sorrow, fear and loss.

"I miss them so much."

"I do, too." Emma's green eyes mirrored his sorrow.

"Uncle Liam would have loved this place. Sarah, too."

"I know." She sighed. "Would you like to head back to the cottage?"

"No, let's stay a little longer. Something about this place…" He paused and looked at the trees standing sentinel, witnesses to his catharsis of grief. "This is the first time I can grieve."

"What ever happens, we're in this together." Emma reassured him. "You've got me, and my mom, and Bryan. We'll get through this."

"That means a lot."

The canoe drifted peacefully, little ripples of wind, playfully pushing it about, until Emma gestured toward the sky and said, "The sun sets early this time of year. We should head back."

"It is getting late," he agreed.

David and Emma picked up their paddles.

* * *

The sniper was used to long hours waiting for her quarry to appear and several hours later her patience was rewarded. The couple had come back into view but were still too far away for a clear shot. Based on the speed of their canoeing, she estimated they would come within a comfortable shooting range in approximately five minutes.

She kept the crosshairs of her rifle leveled on the young woman's face and waited.

* * *

The late autumn sun offered little warmth as it made its afternoon descent toward the horizon. A chill spread through Emma.

"It's getting cold fast." She reached forward for the knapsack in the bow of the canoe to retrieve her sweater.

The report of a rifle shot echoed across the lake.

"Emma stay down!" David shouted. He lurched over the stretcher to reach Emma and covered her body with his, the canoe teetering from side to side.

Another shot smashed through the bow of the canoe, missing her face by mere inches. "Oh, my God," she screamed.

The third shot pierced the canoe below the waterline, grazed the calf of David's left leg and exited through the other side of the canoe. Soon the small vessel was flooding with water. He tugged at the side of the canoe facing the direction from where the shots had come, until it flipped upside down, tossing both Emma and him into the water.

He grabbed Emma and drew her under the overturned canoe. "You, okay?"

"Yeah." She coughed out the mouthful of water she'd nearly swallowed.

"You're a good swimmer," he said, keeping his voice calm.

"You know it."

"That's the spirit." He grabbed her face between his hands and said, "Listen carefully. I want you to dive down as deep as you can and swim toward the shore." He pressed his lips against hers. "I love you."

She nodded. Although she was frightened, the resolve in his eyes gave her strength. "I love you, too."

"Good, now go. I'll be right behind you."

Knowing she wouldn't be able to submerge below the surface wearing the buoyant life jacket, Emma pulled it off, and left it floating under the canoe.

She took a deep breath and slipped under the water and began to swim with strong powerful breaststrokes. After almost sixty seconds, her lungs were bursting. She'd have to resurface soon. Holding her breath for another desperate fifteen seconds, she swam toward the surface, careful not to disturb the water. She lay on her back with just her face exposed and gulped in deep breaths of air. Feeling restored, she took one more breath, submerged again, and continued her swim toward the shore.

Fifteen minutes later, Emma dragged her tired body on to the pebbled beach and lay gasping. She was exhausted. But she was alive. She looked about her, her heart beating a frantic rhythm as she searched the shoreline for David. It was getting dark, and she was shivering.

Her cell was in the knapsack she'd lost when the canoe overturned. Overriding the impulse to search for David, she knew it would be wiser to get to the cottage and dial 9-1-1 on the landline. Her eyes scanned the granite rocks and beach one more time, but she still couldn't see David.

Please let him be okay.

* * *

The assassin was losing her cool. After scaling down the massive tree, she had combed the area around its base for the empty shell cases but could only find two of the three. *Damn these pine needles.* She raked her fingers through the pile of organic detritus hoping to find it. With nighttime fast approaching, there was no more time to continue her search since the use of a flashlight might alert neighboring cottagers to her presence.

She was not looking forward to talking with Enrico Bianchi about her latest failure. She packed up her gear and began the hike back to the car. The assassin couldn't believe her bad luck. First the botched attempt on Laura's life, and now this. This whole job had been cursed from the start.

Forty-Three

He's Gone

THE PARAMEDIC WRAPPED the thermal blanket around Emma's shoulders. She couldn't stop shivering. It wasn't just the cold. It was the shock and terror. As each ponderous moment went by, dread clutched her heart with its icy fingers, tightening and squeezing it. She was terrified David was gone.

The rescue crew and canine unit had combed the circumference of the lake thoroughly. She refused to leave her spot on the dock and looked out over the lake with a forlorn expression on her face, her fingers idly twisting the engagement ring on her left hand. *David missing. Perhaps dead, before we could even begin our lives together.* She was devastated.

The fresh-faced police officer from the Serenity Lake Police Service interrupted her thoughts. "Inspector Grant and your mom are on their way."

Emma nodded her thanks. She was too numb to speak.

"Are you sure you don't want to try and get some rest?" The police officer's face creased with concern for the distraught young woman.

"No, I can't go in." Her voice was tired and lacked its usual vibrancy. "What if they find him? I need to be here."

"Look, rest would be helpful to you right now." The officer gave her a kind smile. "I promise we'll call you as soon as we have news."

Emma shook her head. "Thanks, but I'm staying here. I need to know what's happened. If he is alive or—?" She couldn't say the word out loud. She choked back tears and swallowed at the phlegm clogging her throat. "And even if he's found… If he's… I need to be here for him."

Her tear ducts had dried up, and her eyes were red and swollen. The whites in her eyes showed a chaotic road map of crisscrossing fine red lines converging to a highway leading to a world of grief.

****

When David came to, his cheek was resting on a mass of seaweed, their tendrils like slimy fingers leeching heat from his body. He was cold and uncomfortable. His leg ached where the bullet had grazed it. He was about to shout out Emma's name, but something stopped him.

It's because of me that Emma and her mom are in so much danger. And it's because of me that Uncle Liam and Sarah are dead, he thought. *What if Enrico thought I was dead? — No, I can't do that to Emma.*

And yet, the idea began to gain strength, when he realized the advantages if Enrico thought he was dead. There would be no need for that monster to take further revenge on Laura and Emma. There'd be no point. *He's been trying to punish me but if he thinks I'm dead, well—*

He could not even begin to imagine the grief that he would be putting Emma through. A burning pain spread in his gut, as sorrow like an ulcer clawed at the insides of his stomach lining. But there was no choice in the matter. It was better if the world thought he had died. At least for now.

He checked his vest pocket and was glad to discover his cell and several granola bars were still in the waterproof pouch. The phone had not been damaged when he and Emma had been thrown into the water. She had teased him when he'd bought the pouch and called him a boy scout. *Emma. She'll be frantic.*

Grateful there was cell service, he pulled up the browser for a map of the area and located a ranger's cabin, in Algonquin Park, just north of Whitney. *Might be a good place to hide out.* He tapped the online reservations link for the park and was relieved the cabin was available for rent. He stood up, wincing with pain. With the gunshot wound, he figured it might take him a couple of hours to hike to the cabin.

His stomach contracted in pain again as he contemplated the next thing he was about to do. Fingers shaking, he keyed in the message. His index finger hovered above the send icon, a sign of his indecision. A split second later he hit send, his act of betrayal to all whom he loved complete.

* * *

Bryan's work cell vibrated in his pocket. He'd been pushing the speed limit so that he and Laura could get to Serenity Lake as soon as possible. He hated to stop now since they were almost at their destination. Nonetheless, he dutifully pulled over, and retrieved his phone. Laura had been dozing during most of the three-hour trip, so it was fortunate that she did not see the grim expression on his face when he read the text.

She awakened as he opened the driver's door. "Everything okay?"

"Gotta take this call," he said, as he stepped out of the SUV. "It's work."

Laura began to protest. "What if it's news about David and Emma?"

"Don't worry," he reassured her. "I won't be long." He shut the door and walked to the rear of the vehicle and hit speed dial and waited.

"Bryan, thanks for calling back." David's voice sounded raw.

"My God, son, what's going on?" Bryan's tone was heavy with worry.

"Is Emma okay?"

"Yeah, physically she's fine. She's a strong swimmer. She made it to shore."

"Thank God. I've been so worried." Bryan could hear the younger man's exhale of relief.

"But Emma's frantic. She thinks you're dead. Why haven't you called her?"

"About that. I need your help." David cleared his throat. "I gotta disappear."

"What?"

"Can you hook me up with the RCMP's Federal Witness Protection program?"

"Just you?" Bryan was incredulous.

"Yep. If Enrico thinks I'm dead, he'll leave Emma and Laura alone."

What David was willing to sacrifice hit Bryan like a sledgehammer slamming through ice. "You'll break that poor girl's heart."

"Better that than she and her mom dying." David's voice was shattered. "They almost got her today."

Bryan couldn't answer at first. He was still absorbing the impact of what David was proposing.

"Bryan? You still there?"

"Yeah. Just thinking." He hesitated. "Where are you now?"

"I've been following a hiking trail. Hang on."

After a moment, Bryan's phone chimed an alert, and he pressed on the message sent via What'sApp. GPS coordinates and a map showed David's location.

"Thanks," said Bryan. "Looks like if you continue on this trail, it'll take you to highway 60, just east of Whitney."

"Exactly. I estimate a two-hour hike should get me to a ranger's cabin on the outskirts of town." He cleared his throat. "Can you meet up with me there?"

"Of course."

"Um, one more thing."

"Yes?"

"I got shot in the leg. Just a graze, but it hurts like hell."

"My God son, I should be taking you to the hospital!"

"No, I can deal with it. Just bring a first aid kit."

"Okay," Bryan said, unconvinced.

"Thanks, man."

Bryan replaced the phone in his pocket and climbed back in the vehicle.

"Any news?" Laura's eyes glistened like hardened emeralds.

"No, sorry. This was about another case." He hated lying to Laura, but he knew that he had to protect David. Too much was at stake. He admired David's resolve to keep Emma and Laura safe at all costs.

Her eyes probed his. "There's something you're not telling me."

"I can't. Not yet. Please be patient."

* * *

Laura jumped out of the vehicle before Bryan had a chance to come to a full stop and place it in park. "Emma!"

"Mom!" Emma collapsed into her mother's arms. "David—they can't find him."

Laura held her daughter, comforting her with the soft idioms of her childhood, the sympathetic endearments imparting more comfort and meaning than the words themselves.

"I'm here. Just cry. Let it all out."

After a while, Emma's tears lessened. "They're going to drag the lake for his body first thing in the morning."

Laura's heart constricted in grief, as she looked at her daughter, face pale and eyes stripped of joy. "Don't think the worst yet sweetheart."

"After all that's happened—"

Laura cupped her hands around her daughter's face. "Shhhh…"

"Let's head to the cottage. I'll make you a cup of tea."

"I'm so glad you're here." She roughly wiped the tears from her eyes with her knuckles.

Emma looked up when Bryan cleared his throat. "Hi, Bryan. I didn't see you there."

"I didn't want to interrupt." He walked over to Emma and Laura and wrapped a protective arm around each of their waists, and guided mother and daughter up the rocky path to the cottage.

* * *

Once Bryan was sure Emma and Laura were settled inside, he went back out to speak with the officers from the local police department.

He showed his New Elgan Police Service badge and introduced himself to the officers.

Officer Gerard scrutinized the inspector and said, "You're a long way from your area."

"I'm not here officially, but as a friend of the family. Brought the mom up from down south." He gave the officer a conciliatory smile. "Any luck yet?"

"Not so far." Gerard raked through the mass of blond curly hair on his head with long fingers that resembled those of a musician. His blue eyes were hooded by eyelids which squinted with fatigue. "We lose people due to water related incidents every year. Drownings mainly. Usually May to early October. It's the third leading cause of accidental death in Canada." He sighed. "If only people would wear their life jackets."

"I agree. We have the same problem where we're located near South Simcoe Bay. Lotta needless deaths."

"Fortunately, Emma Jackson was wearing her life jacket when their canoe was overturned. She says her boyfriend was wearing one, too."

"That wouldn't surprise me. Those two are used to the water. David sails and Emma is quite a sports woman. Canoes every chance she can. She's also an excellent swimmer."

"That I can believe. She ditched the life jacket though so she could swim underwater to hide from the sniper," he shook his head in admiration, then continued. "She swam quite a distance to shore, and then called us.

"When the nine-one-one call came in she said that she and her boyfriend were staying at the Serenity Dream Cottage for the weekend, and that they'd been paddling in the lake and were shot at."

Bryan's eyes narrowed with concern. "Shit. Not again."

"Say what?"

"We have reason to believe that a gangster by the name of Enrico Bianchi has hired a contract killer to kill David Harris and Emma Jackson and her mother, Laura Jackson."

"Enrico Bianchi?" Recognition gleamed in his eyes. "Now I know why your name sounded familiar. I read about the botched attempt to arrest him and his son in the papers. This past summer."

"Yeah, that's them." He sighed in frustration. "Enrico and his son Alessandro disappeared right after that. Since then, there's been no trace of them."

"Tough break." Gerard's tone was sympathetic. "Coulda happened to any of us in law enforcement."

"Don't I know it. Since their escape, we suspect Enrico ordered the murders of David's uncle - Liam Foster and Sarah Larson. And before that, we think this father and son team murdered Anna Tungsten." He paused. "And we believe Enrico murdered George Larson and Chris Beacon thirty years ago."

"Any chance this contract killer comes back tonight?"

"It's possible."

"I'll arrange for one of my officers to provide a protective detail. Just in case."

"Thanks."

Gerard looked at his watch. "Well, it's getting late. There's not much more we can accomplish tonight." He stifled a yawn. "I'm going for some shut eye. I suggest you do the same. At daylight, we're bringing in equipment to drag the lake." He reached out to shake Bryan's hand. "See you then."

"Until tomorrow." He pulled his cell phone out of his pocket as a way to avoid Gerard's gaze. He pushed away the guilt. He was going to let them drag the lake, even though he knew full well that David was still alive.

Bryan watched Gerard and his team of tired officers walk to their vehicles and drive away, the red taillights of the police cruisers disappearing into the night.

As promised, one of the local cars remained. Bryan grunted with approval when he saw the hefty officer walk up the stairs and position himself in front of the cottage door.

Sure he was now alone, he called David and said, "Hang tight. I'm on my way to you now."

Forty-Four

The First Dawn Without You

THE DAWN OF Saturday, October seventh, rose in a myriad of colors kissing the smooth lake. It was just as beautiful as it had been the morning before. But Emma didn't notice. Her grief was palpable. She was inconsolable. Overnight, her auburn hair had lost its luster and her green eyes resembled opaque stones, impenetrable to light, as if her soul had drowned along with David.

She stood at the balcony and watched without emotion as the men set up the drag hooks in the boat to drag the lake for his body. Next, the three prong hooks were lowered into the water until they rested at the bottom. Slowly, the boat advanced back and forth across the lake dragging the hooks along the lakebed. Whenever resistance was encountered, they would stop, and haul up whatever they had snagged. Apart from submerged logs, and other debris, nothing of interest had been found.

Laura walked onto the deck of the cottage with a steaming cup of tea and said, "Since you won't come in, drink this at least."

Emma took the tea without comment and continued to stare. Laura touched her daughter's shoulder to comfort her, but her daughter shrugged off the gentle gesture. It was as if the endless anguish of the prior night had left her not only drained of tears, but of emotion.

The excited voices of the men in the boat drew the attention of Emma and Laura. Something green shimmered below the surface. The canoe. Emma's steps were rapid as she descended the deck's stairs, two steps at a time, and hurled herself down the hill to the water's edge.

Bryan heard the commotion and ran out of the cottage. "What's going on?"

"They've found something," said Laura.

Bryan followed and caught up to Emma before she reached the men pulling the canoe onto the shore.

"Please, Emma." He grabbed her by the waist to keep her from running forward. "Please. Wait. This is potential evidence. We can't contaminate the scene."

"But what if it's David?" Her breath was wheezy and irregular.

A flood of guilt flooded through Bryan. He had promised David he wouldn't say anything. He hated seeing this sweet young woman tortured this way.

"Please, Emma, just wait," he repeated. "We'll know what they've found soon enough."

"I guess you're right." Her voice was like lead, the hope leeching away with every passing moment.

* * *

Officer Gerard motioned to Bryan to join him. He pointed at the bow, the centreline, and the stern. "Three bullet holes. The one at the centreline was below the waterline."

"Unlike on land, it'll be impossible to know where the bullet came from."

Both men knew the currents would have twisted the canoe around before it settled onto the bottom.

Gerard cleared his throat and asked, "Bryan, do you think Emma is up to talking now? If we knew roughly where the canoe was and approximately where the shots came from, we might be able to determine where the sniper set up."

"Let me try." He looked at Laura who held Emma in a tight embrace.

He walked over to the mother and daughter and took Emma's hand. "Do you remember where you were in the lake, and where the shots came from?"

"It all happened so fast." Her eyebrows creased together. "But I think from over there." She pointed to the high stand of spruce trees. "We were headed back to the cottage. We were midway through the lake." She shook her head in disbelief. "He saved my life. I don't know how he did it. He flipped that heavy canoe over to give us cover. Then told me to swim to shore. He said he would be right behind me." She sobbed. "But he wasn't."

Bryan folded her into his arms, wishing he could tell her the truth about David. Instead, he said, "We'll keep looking." He turned to go.

Emma grabbed his arm; her fiery personality was returning. "Promise?"

"I promise."

* * *

Other than a few false alarms, the crew operating the drag hooks found no further evidence. Even the diving team, who had concentrated their efforts around where the canoe had been discovered, found nothing except for Emma's backpack and her discarded life jacket.

"I'm so sorry." Officer Gerard's demeanor was dejected. "We are calling off the search."

"You mean you won't be back tomorrow?" Emma's voice was high-pitched and uneven.

He shook his head. "I'm sorry. We've done all we can."

Emma placed her hand on her mouth and ran up the hill to the cottage sobbing. "I can't stay here a minute longer. I want to go home." She grabbed her overnight bag, and that of David's and packed. Her right hand trembled as she held the keys to David's MGB.

"Emma, you're too upset to drive," said Laura, her face, lined with worry. "Let me drive." She gently pried the keys from her daughter's clenched hands.

"Okay."

Laura addressed Bryan. "Are you coming back home with us?"

"I'll be right behind you." He reassured her. "Just want to discuss a few things with Officer Gerard before I head out."

"See you soon, then."

"You won't forget your promise." Emma reminded him.

"No, I won't." He walked over to Emma and kissed her on the forehead, then turned to Laura and gave her a gentle kiss on the lips.

He helped carry the bags to the car and loaded them in the trunk.

"Drive safe. Text me when you get back."

"Okay."

I'll see you both soon."

When the bright yellow British car rounded the corner, he turned away. He spotted Officer Gerard among the group of officers packing up their gear.

Gerard noticed the overnight bag slung over Bryan's shoulders. "Heading out?"

"Yeah." Bryan shook Gerard's hand. "Thanks for everything."

"No problem. Hope Emma will be all right."

"With time, I think so."

"Just so you know, we'll be combing the woods where Emma thinks the shots came from." He pressed his lips together in a thin line. "Forensics will also examine the canoe at the lab."

"Good. The hull of the lake canoe was thick; maybe there will be an indication of the type of bullets used."

"Hopefully, we'll come up with something. I'll call you if we learn anything further."

"Thanks." Bryan gripped Gerard's hand. "Appreciate all you've done."

* * *

Bryan exhaled the breath he didn't realize he'd been holding. He looked at his watch. Just enough time to pick up supplies. He put the SUV in gear and headed to the ranger's cabin near Whitney where David was waiting.

Forty-Five

The Ranger's Cabin

DAVID WARMED HIS hands above one of the burners on the wood stove in the chilly, remote ranger's cabin, while two cans of chili heated on the other burner.

"Thanks for bringing supplies." He nodded his head toward the bag of groceries. "Beats the granola bars I had for dinner."

"You're welcome. Not much choice last night. Stores were closed." Bryan motioned to the overnight bag. "We're about the same size. There's a couple of flannel shirts and jeans, thermal underwear, a flashlight, extra lighter fluid, and a thermal blanket." He took off his warm jacket. "You'll need this, too."

"Thanks. It took me hours to get warm. Luckily there was a stack of wood and matches and an old sleeping bag left behind by the previous renters."

"Oh, and before I forget, here's the hand-crank charger you asked me for." Bryan handed David a small black device with a handle that resembled a flywheel from a fishing rod.

"This is great. I'll be able to keep my phone charged." David's voice choked with emotion. "I can't thank you enough."

"How is the gunshot wound?" asked Bryan, changing the subject.

"Feels better than before."

"Have a seat. Let me take a look," he said, picking up the first aid kit resting on the roughly hewn pine table. "It's healing up well. You're lucky it was just a graze." Bryan re-dressed the wound, and said, "Just change the bandages regularly."

"Thanks," said David, wincing as he stood up. "Chili should be ready."

They were silent as they ate their meal. David had polished his off in record time and eyed the older man's half-finished can. Bryan noticed the hungry look, and said, "Here, eat the rest of mine. I can grab a burger later."

"Thanks, I'm still so hungry. This tastes better than a burger could any day."

After they had finished their meal, they began to talk in earnest.

"I don't understand." David's jaw was set in determination. "You were so set on the Witness Protection Program before." He looked at Bryan with annoyance. "Why the change of heart?"

"Oh, I still believe in it. The proposal is that *both* you and Emma enter the program. Laura, too, had she agreed." The older man sighed. "You and Emma belong together."

"Yeah, I know. This won't be forever. Provided we catch the Bianchis."

"We?"

"Yeah. You heard me. I'm working on the case, too."

"You should leave that to the police."

"I'll have you know I've just written the Ministry of the Solicitor General's provincial exam. I'll be a registered private investigator soon." He grinned with grim satisfaction. "I'll have the right to investigate individuals and can work with the authorities on inquiries." He snickered. "I will be my first client."

* * *

Bryan was alarmed at the lengths David was willing to go. "Maybe there's another way besides witness protection," said Bryan. He saw the steely resolve in the young man. "How far are you willing to go?"

"All the way. I want my life back."

"Disappearing like this. Don't you know what this will do to—"

"Of course, I do." His voice was uneven. "There's no choice."

"You're willing to break her heart!" Bryan knew he was being over-protective but had come to view Emma as a daughter.

"It can't be helped. I can live with never seeing her again if it means saving her life." His left hand brushed at the moisture in his eyes before it had a chance to make an appearance. If Enrico thinks I'm dead, there's no more reason for him to go after Emma and her mom. It's why I need to disappear."

"But without you, what kind of life will she have—"

"My mind's made up," interrupted David. "Will you help me or not?"

"Yes," Bryan sighed. "I have my reservations. But yeah, I'll help you."

"Thanks, man."

"Don't make me regret this."

"You won't. Believe me." David braced himself before he asked the next question. "Firearms training. My plan was to take a course in firearms and combat training, but now that I need to stay hidden—"

"I'll train you myself."

"Thanks."

"It's remote here. How long can you stay at this cabin?"

"I've rented it for three weeks." He hesitated. "Under the name Samuel Harris."

"Samuel? You are using George's middle name?

"Yeah. Believe it or not that's my middle name, too."

"Strange coincidence."

"Really, Bryan? After all the weird things we've gone through these last months, I'm surprised you believe in coincidences anymore. I sure as hell don't."

"I guess you're right." Bryan looked at his watch. "It's getting late. I promised Laura I'd be back soon after they got home."

"Yeah. I get it. You should get going. When're you coming back?"

"Can you sit tight till Tuesday?"

"Sure. Looks like you brought enough food for a few days."

"I've got some holiday time coming. I was planning to spend some vacay time with Laura, but I'll tell her I am being sent out of town on assignment."

"What about Laura and Emma?" asked David. "What if I'm wrong and Enrico doesn't call off his assassins? You're not going to leave them unprotected!"

"Don't worry about that. I've got a buddy, Harold Kruger, who owns a security firm. Used to work with me on the police force. Both Laura and Emma will be protected 24/7 by his men."

"That'll go over well," said David. "They are both such independent women."

"Don't worry, they won't even notice Harold's men are there. Besides, after multiple attempts on their lives, they should be more careful now."

"I hope you're right." David paused. "I'm hoping with Enrico thinking I'm dead, that he will call off his dogs."

"Maybe. But don't count on it," said Bryan.

Both men stood up and gripped each other in an embrace.

"Sit tight. I'll see you soon." Bryan turned on his heels and left the cabin.

Forty-Six

Bootcamp For One

DAVID'S BODY ACHED. There was not a single part that didn't hurt. Even his teeth were tender. The intensive training over the last four-teen days had been substantial. He doubted the firearms and combat course he'd originally planned to take could rival the punishment meted out by Staff Inspector Bryan Grant of the New Elgan Police Service. He didn't know whether to love or hate the guy. But he was grateful.

He swallowed a couple of Tylenol and touched his shoulder where the recoil of the rifle had punched into the muscle countless times. He lay down on the sleeping mat which rested on the upper bunk in the ranger's cabin and stared at the play of light and shadows cast by the fire in the wood stove.

As an only child, he'd enjoyed playing this game of seeing objects, which had provided him hours of entertainment. He could find a particular object or a face in almost anything. He didn't even have to try. He just saw them. It was just the way his mind worked. As he grew older, he learned it was called pareidolia and was a sign of keen intelligence.

Nonetheless, David was grateful this would be his final night sleep-ing in these rugged conditions. Bryan was already snoring, fast asleep on the lower bunk.

David reflected on their last night together. Bryan had gone into town to purchase a couple of steaks, potatoes, and a bottle of red wine. He'd touched his metal drinking cup against David's and said, "Here's to the bootcamp for one. You did great. I'm proud of you." Then he paid him the best compliment of all. "Any police department would be glad to have you. With what you've learned, your athletic ability and sharp mind, you'd be a great asset."

Bryan had noticed the uncertainty in his eyes and placed his hand on David's arm. "Plenty of time for you to decide. Let's get that bastard Bianchi and his son, first."

Now, as he listened to Bryan's rhythmic rumbling, sleep would not come, and he reflected on what had been accomplished in a short period of time. Immediately after his disappearance, he'd taken a huge risk and funneled off a sum of his money into a new account under the name Samuel Harris. Although a substantial amount of money, it was small compared to the combined estate of his uncle's and his own.

He reassured himself, should things go wrong and he could not return to Emma, or worse yet, he did die for real, she'd be well cared for. He had changed his will and named Emma as his beneficiary. This last thought comforted him enough to settle down and finally fall asleep.

* * *

David was distraught; he had had the dream again. But it was different this time. Still the eyes, but instead of them being haunting and full of malice, they were now fearful. It was a variation of the surrealistic scene from Pier One at the Simcoe Bay Docks.

David had the feeling that somehow, he now held the advantage over Bianchi. But as he emerged from that heavy dreamworld, he was confused; the dream made no sense at all. He tried to hold onto the dream's message a little longer, sure that something important had been revealed, a clue that would give him the upper hand, but the memory was elusive. *What was it?*

The aroma of Bryan frying eggs on the cast iron skillet on the wood stove, coupled with the morning light shining dimly through the sole window in the cabin, were insistent reminders for him to open his eyes. He strained to see his watch through blurry eyes. Six. No time for reflection now. He pushed away the dream and got up, anxious to start the new day.

* * *

On the drive to Toronto Pearson International Airport, conversation between the two men was sparse. The bond that David and Bryan had developed was strong and the two needed few words to speak.

Bryan pulled up to the departures lane and, parked and handed him a new iPhone. "The KryptAll® firmware has been installed as you requested. Text me when you land."

"Will do."

"You got everything? Passport, money?"

"Yeah, I do, thanks."

Bryan popped the back hatch of the SUV as both men got out from the front. David pulled out the hefty knapsack from the back, slung it over his shoulder and pushed the button to close the rear door.

They grabbed each other in a huge hug, for a moment unwilling to let go of each other. "You take care of my girl." David's voice was husky with emotion.

"You bet."

"I'll be in touch."

"Good luck, son."

David's expression softened at the kind words. "Thanks."

Bryan watched him enter the turnstiles at the airport and disappear into the throng of people headed for international destinations. "Good luck, son," he repeated, his words whispered like a prayer.

He got back in the SUV and pointed the car toward Laura and Emma's home to spend the last day of his time off with them.

Forty-Seven

Days Of Grief

THE PALE JANUARY sun filtered through the room as Emma breathed in the Nag Champa incense. The East Indian scent was derived from the Magnolia champaca and was one of Emma's favorite incenses. In the months following David's disappearance, she had fallen into a deep depression. She'd put her website business to the side and passed her clients on to trusted colleagues in the profession.

She had spent many days of grief alone in David's condo, allowing the memories of their time together to flood in. She'd been surprised when David's lawyer had contacted her informing her that she was named the heir of David's considerable estate. She was under the impression that since no body had been found, his estate would be in limbo until either his remains had been discovered or seven years had passed, at which point he would then be declared dead officially by the courts.

The lawyer reminded her that it would be possible to have him declared legally dead before seven years since he had disappeared under suspicious circumstances. This way the affairs of David's estate could be wrapped up sooner. The lawyer had explained that prior to 2001, the Ontario Declarations of Death Act only provided for declarations of death after seven years. As a result of the 9/11 horrific tragedy where bodies would never be found, Ontario had reformed the statute in 2002. If a person disappeared 'in circumstances of peril' such as the attack on Emma and David at Serenity Lake, it would be possible to declare David officially dead.

"What's the hurry?" she'd asked the lawyer. "I want to wait."

Although David had appointed her executor and heir, that didn't matter to her. She wanted him. And she held out hope that he was alive, although her friends thought this was unrealistic. Even so, she clung to this dream, since his body had not been found.

As time moved on without relent, she refused to allow her convictions to be eroded. She was prepared to wait and with the lawyer's assistance and that of David's financial adviser, she kept David's estate running smoothly.

In the months following his 'death,' she often stayed at his condo, touching his clothes, sleeping in his sheets, and when the sheets finally needed to be laundered, she washed them with great reluctance, afraid to wash away the unique scent that was David. She made sure she used the same laundry soap he had used to clean his clothing, to help her remember him.

After talking with her mom, they decided it would be best if Emma gave herself time to heal. She turned back to the spiritual and meditation practices she and her mom had learned from their dear friend, Anna Tungsten. It was hard to accept the personal losses they had both suffered over the last six months. Christmas had been particularly difficult, but the bright light had been Bryan Grant's love and support. He had become like a second father to her.

She was happy her mom had found love again and tried not to be bitter that she herself had lost her David. She was reminded of Tennyson's poem, In Memoriam, where he lamented the loss of his closest friend Arthur Henry Hallam. He had written in Canto XXVII of the epic poem, *Tis better to have loved and lost than never to have loved at all.* She took comfort in those famous words.

* * *

After her yoga practice, she raised herself from the final posture pose, and settled herself comfortably on her yoga mat. Her body was strong and fluid and peaceful, and she found it easy to transition to the meditation portion of her practice.

Her breathing became more and more relaxed, and each time her mind wandered, she gently nudged it back to reach that special state of Nirvana where her mind was blank, if only for a few seconds at a time.

Once she was fully in the trance, she saw a form consisting of light taking shape before her. Although the features wavered in and out of focus, she knew the apparition was Anna whose words were clear in Emma's mind, even though not spoken out loud.

My darling Emma. Please don't grieve. David is not dead. He's safe. He will come to you soon. Death is only a transition to another state; Sarah and Liam are content and together. There will come a time when we will all be with each other again. Give your mom my love.

No sooner had she heard these words, then the apparition dissipated. Joy radiated throughout her body and a feeling of peace infused her psyche. Somehow, in some way, David would return. Her days of grief would soon be over.

As she awoke, her thoughts became darker. *What about Enrico? If he were to find out David was still alive...* She shivered; after all this time away from each other, they'd still be in danger.

* * *

The assassin thought Enrico was being unreasonable. There was no question that David had drowned. He was either at the bottom of the lake or had washed up on shore for wild animals and carrion birds to scavenge his body. The search team had been thorough, and his body had not been found. Even so, Enrico remained suspicious. She thought otherwise. She had been there. She doubted David could have survived her sniper attack. Still... perhaps Enrico had a point.

To humor her boss, she continued to monitor all incoming and outgoing calls in case there would be some kind of communication from David to either Bryan and Laura or Emma herself.

It was difficult to listen to Emma's nightly sobs. She was beginning to feel sorry for the young woman and found it increasingly hard to push the rebellious idea of helping her away from her thoughts.

She was irritated that she was expected to personally maintain surveillance on Emma Jackson. It had been over three months since her failed attempt to take the life of the young woman and she wondered when Enrico would give up this obsession.

"Missing and presumed dead is not good enough," he'd told her, when she'd explained that David Harris had not made it back to shore.

"What about the girl?" She'd asked.

"For now, keep her alive. And watch her."

"You think David Harris is still alive?" Her voice had been incredulous.

"The fact there is no body makes me suspicious."

"But it could have been caught in the undercurrents, washed to shore and eaten by wild animals."

"Maybe. But I doubt it. Watch her. If he's alive, he'll contact her eventually."

"For how long?"

"As long as it takes. Years, if necessary."

Forty-Eight

Our Anniversary

IT WAS THE anniversary of the day David had met Emma. July 26th. One year ago. How could time have gone by so quickly? And yet on the other hand, time had also inched along with the same indolence as the slow-moving sloth which filled the view finder on his camera. The three-toed sloth moved with deliberation up the cecropia tree with her baby clinging to her. Sloths often fed on the large, juicy leaves of these soft wood trees, their main source of food.

Emma would love this, he thought to himself, a stab of sorrow piercing him.

Since November of last year, he'd been posing as a photographer during the daytime, and in the late afternoons and evenings, when it was too hot to be outside, he would study the financial records that Bryan had sent to him by encrypted email. He was looking for a money trail that might indicate where the Bianchis had fled. Several years ago, a large sum of money had been transferred into cryptocurrency making it impossible to trace where the funds had gone. This was a sign that Enrico and Alessandro might have had an established escape plan long before the trouble had started with him discovering the killer of George Larson, his previous reincarnation.

Out of sentimentality, knowing this was a country that Emma loved, he'd chosen Costa Rica to hide out while he worked on his plan with Bryan to destroy Enrico and Alessandro.

Back in New Elgan, Bryan was investigating Bianchi's oldest son, who was considered belligerent and ruthless but without the cunning and intelligence his father and younger brother possessed. Although it was obvious Lorenzo had no idea where Enrico and Alessandro were hiding, Bryan was convinced that Lorenzo might know more than even he realized.

During their last conversation, Bryan told David, "I'm keeping the surveillance in place on Lorenzo. Word has it he's been trying to gain control of the real estate empire during his father's and brother's absence," he paused. "How are you doing?"

"Okay, lonely in paradise." He gave a cynical laugh. "Wish Emma was here. I miss her."

"I get it. Keep the faith."

"Will do."

"I'll be in touch."

"Thanks, man."

* * *

Emma was humming. Ever since Anna had visited her back in January, and had reassured her that David was alive, it was hard not to keep the lightness out of her step. She was compelled to keep her vision secret. Even from her mom and Bryan. Just in case Enrico's people were still watching, she wanted to act the part of the grieving girlfriend. When she was alone in David's apartment, she was free from prying eyes.

One year ago, today, was when they had first met, and she couldn't stop thinking about how they had become connected so quickly. She knew David was her soulmate and had been for many reincarnations. She just wished there would be more to their story in this lifetime. She didn't want to wait till her next life; she wanted to be with David now.

Her reverie was interrupted by the vibrating cell phone in the back pocket of her jeans. She frowned, wondering who it might be. She hadn't socialized much since David's disappearance. One by one, her friends had lost interest in trying to spend time with her when she rebuffed their repeated attempts to go out.

"Maybe, it's Mom," she wondered out loud.

The banner on the screen showed the alert:

Unknown Caller.

No doubt yet another call to sell me duct cleaning services or tell me the Canada Revenue Agency is about to arrest me, she thought with annoyance.

She shrugged and was about to disconnect, but it was as if a hand had physically arrested her from pushing the key. Instead, her index finger pushed the accept call icon.

"Hello?"

There was a silence on the line, loaded with expectation. The person on the other end, cleared their throat. "Em, it's me."

"David?"

"I couldn't not call. On the anniversary of the day we first met."

"Oh, David." She released a long breath. She had not been this happy since that last October morning together, when they'd shared coffee, enjoying the view of Serenity Lake, and planning their outing in the canoe. "Where are you?"

"It's not a good idea to tell you that." There was silence again, and she heard a deep sigh. "I love you."

"I love you, too."

"You don't seem surprised to hear from me."

"I saw Anna in a vision. She told me you were safe. Alive. That I'd see you again."

"Wow."

"Don't think I haven't suffered though." She stifled a sob.

"Emma, my love, please don't be upset."

"I'm not. Not really. I'm only crying because it's such a relief to finally hear your voice."

"I've gotta go."

"Oh, please don't—"

David interrupted her. "I'll call again. Soon, I promise."

Emma stared with fascination at the screen which had gone blank. She checked the recent calls option on her iPhone but found no history of the number. Disappointed there was no redial number, she acknowledged that it was safer this way.

* * *

The assassin hit speed dial and called Enrico. "You were right."

"About?" Enrico sounded short of breath and annoyed.

No doubt torturing some other hapless prostitute, she thought.

"David Harris is not dead."

"Grab your clothes and get outta here." She could hear a sharp slap and a frighted woman yelp. "It's your lucky day," he snarled.

"Pardon?" asked the assassin.

"Not you. Talking to someone else."

"Do you want me to call back?"

"Nah, she's left now."

The assassin suspected her call had just saved some unwitting woman from a miserable and painful death. She was surprised her boss was taking the interruption so well.

"So, tell me what you've learned."

"He contacted Emma today. Their first-year anniversary of having met. The stupid guy got lonely."

"Go on."

"I couldn't tap into the call. Looks like he's using the same kind of encryption software we do. I could only hear Emma's responses using the wireless listening device."

"Humph. What did you find out?"

"Not much yet. Said he'd call her back. Soon."

"I'd like you to interrogate Emma."

"I don't think she knows anything."

"Perhaps, but let's make sure."

"Okay." She hid the reluctance from her voice.

"Find out what you can. By any means." His laughter was disgusting. "Make it painful. Make the bitch suffer. Don't kill her though. She might be useful as bait."

"I'm on it."

"Oh, and one more thing. Get rid of that meddlesome detective, Bryan Grant. He's been poking around my stupid son."

"There's more risk involved in killing a police officer."

"Do you think I give a shit? After all your fuckups? Fail me one more time, and I'll kill you myself." He disconnected the call.

The assassin sat back in shocked silence. An icy hand clamped around her heart. She had never experienced this type of fear before. She liked it; it made her feel alive.

Forty-Nine

Scared, Please Hurry

"HOLD THE ELEVATOR!" called out an urgent female voice. The doors to the elevator were about to close just as the light-haired woman in the jogging suit came into view. Her hair was damp from perspiration, perhaps from a mid-afternoon run.

"Sure thing." Emma pushed the button, and the elevator doors slid back open. She looked thoughtfully at the attractive woman. "You seem familiar."

"So do you." The woman gave an earnest smile as she pushed the button for the seventh floor.

"I wonder where," said Emma.

"Probably in this building. Although I've been out of country this past year. Europe." The woman's laugh was easy and friendly.

"I would have been visiting my boyfriend." A shadow crossed her face.

"What's wrong?"

"Nothing." Emma looked at the fresh-faced, blue-eyed woman and liked her straight away. "It's just... my boyfriend drowned in a canoe accident last year."

"Oh, I'm so sorry. Do you live here now?"

"Yeah, so to speak. A few days per week. It's taking time to settle his estate. I like staying here. Makes me feel closer to him."

The woman looked away, her discomfort obvious and said, "Sorry, I shouldn't have pried."

"Don't worry about it; you couldn't have known."

The elevator stopped at the seventh floor and the doors slid open.

"See you around," said the woman.

* * *

The assassin walked along the hallway with purpose. She waited till the elevator doors had closed and then headed toward the stairway and descended the seven flights of stairs and exited through the backdoor. Once outside, she headed to the surveillance apartment across the street to plan her next move.

* * *

Emma opened the door to the condo and was surprised to see the woman from the elevator. She had changed into an elegant black pantsuit which showed off her sleek runner's figure. Her long sandy-colored hair was tied in a ponytail. The serviceable black bag which hung over her right shoulder marred an otherwise perfect ensemble. Nonetheless, she was stunning and exuded power and confidence.

"Hello," said Emma, hiding her confusion.

"I'm Rebecca Blake," she said as she flashed her RCMP badge and pocketed it before Emma could see it fully.

"How can I help you, Officer?" said Emma.

"You're David Harris's girlfriend, aren't you?"

"Umm, yes," she said, her voice laced with concern.

"We are investigating his disappearance. We don't believe he drowned that day at the lake. We think he's still alive."

"No, that can't be," Emma's voice was filled with anguish. "After all this time—"

"I'm sorry, I didn't mean to upset you." The woman gave a disingenuous smile. "But you're going to want to hear what I have to say."

"Okay," said Emma, trying her best to conceal her mounting panic. *Had David's secret been discovered?*

"I also have information about Enrico Bianchi."

"I don't understand." Emma choked back a sob.

"Invite me in and I'll explain."

"Fine. Come in and have a seat." Emma relented and gestured toward the living room. "Would you like some tea?"

"Sure. Can I help?" Rebecca asked.

"No, just make yourself comfortable. I'll be right out. I was already making a pot."

Emma returned moments later carrying a tray laden with sugar-free cinnamon oatmeal cookies and a teapot containing one of her special blends of tea. "I hope you'll like the tea. It's from my garden. Chamomile, bergamot, also known as bee balm, spearmint, and stevia which serves as a natural sweetener."

* * *

The aroma of the tea permeated the room as Emma poured the amber liquid into the delicate Royal Doulton teacups.

Rebecca took a sip of the fragrant tea. *Not bad,* she thought.

"Do you like it?" asked Emma.

Rebecca nodded, and said, "Yeah, but would you have a little bit of honey I could add?"

"Hang on. I'll bring some honey. It's from my mom's neighbor's beehive."

Of course, it is. What a goody-two shoes. She was a little disgusted but mostly bemused. And envious. Imagine growing up in a sheltered and privileged world like that. She pulled the vial containing the fast-acting sedative out of her pocket and poured it into Emma's teacup.

* * *

By a lucky twist of fate, Emma turned around to ask Rebecca what type of honey she'd like in her tea, as she had two types to offer. She stood stone still as she watched Rebecca, or whoever the hell she was, pour the unknown contents into her teacup.

She withdrew further into the kitchen and leaned against the wall, deciding what to do. She picked up her cell which was on the counter, put it on silent, and tapped out an urgent message to Bryan: *A woman's here. Says she's Rebecca Blake from the RCMP. Claims to have information about David's disappearance. Tried to slip something in my tea. Scared, please hurry, E.*

Sit tight. On my way, B.

For now, she'd play along and wait for Bryan to arrive.

"Sorry I was so long. I've got two kinds of honey. One made from clover and one from wildflowers. Both are wonderful," said Emma.

"Oh, how lovely," exclaimed Rebecca. "May I try the wildflower?"

Emma handed her the honeypot and smiled timorously. She raised her teacup to her lips and mimicked taking a sip. Setting down her cup, she lifted the cookie tray and said, "Cookies? I baked them myself."

"Lovely. Thanks." Emma caught the poorly disguised derision in the woman's voice and facial expressions.

"So, you mentioned you've been overseas?" asked Emma politely.

"Yeah, on assignment. Getting back into the routine."

"So, do you actually live in this building?"

"Yeah, for the last five years."

"Nice." Emma's look and tone was without guile. "You said you have information about David."

"We believe that David is in hiding. That he didn't die."

"So, you've already said." She gave a sigh of frustration. "What makes you think this?"

"We're aware that the two of you have been in contact with each other." Emma flinched at Rebecca's hard stare.

"Impossible." Emma swallowed at the lump in her throat.

"It's okay, I understand your reluctance to speak up," said Rebecca. "The danger is over. We've apprehended Enrico Bianchi." Emma flinched inwardly at the bold lie. Rebecca placed a comforting hand on Emma's. "David can come home now."

A jolt of energy pulsed through Emma, as Rebecca's thoughts flooded her mind. *"Damn you Enrico. I'm no good at this. I'm better when I'm looking through my rifle scope. And when is the twit going to take a real sip of that tea?"*

"You mean David can come home?" stammered Emma, knowing she should play along, but finding it hard to mask her fear.

"Yes—"

Their conversation was interrupted by the intercom.

"Expecting anyone?"

"No." Emma put her teacup down. "Would you excuse me, for a moment?"

"I'll be here." Rebecca reassured her. Her smile faded when she heard Emma speak.

"Uncle Bill," Emma gushed. "What a nice surprise. Come on up."

Still tuned into Rebecca's thoughts, she heard, *"Emma doesn't have an uncle. This could be a trap. Better play it cool for now."*

"My uncle is in town for business," she explained to Rebecca. "I don't often see him. I hope you don't mind."

"Not at all. Perhaps I should get going. I can come back another time."

"I wouldn't hear of it." Emma placed her hand on Rebecca's shoulder and smiled. "My uncle has been a great support to me. He'll want to hear what you have discovered about David."

The doorbell chimed.

"That'll be him." Emma got up to answer.

"It's so good to see you, Uncle Bill." Emma fought to keep her voice light and cheerful. "I've got company. I'd like you to meet RCMP Officer Rebecca Blake. She lives on the seventh floor." She spoke in a bright cheerful tone. Under her breath, she muttered, "I'm glad you're here." Her face was pale and frightened.

Bryan mouthed to her, "Go now."

Emma nodded and ran out into the hallway and was greeted by officers who rushed her away.

Fifty

Rebecca

REBECCA WAS UNABLE to hide her shock when instead of Emma and her 'uncle,' Staff Inspector Bryan Grant and six officers walked in.

Bryan's eyes scanned the tea service with suspicion, his right hand resting on the gun in his holster.

Self-preservation became foremost in Rebecca's mind, and with one fluid motion, she hurled the teapot at the inspector. He ducked to avoid the projectile hurtling toward him. Moments later, the teapot hit the wall and shattered into dozens of shards before showering onto the plush carpet, staining it with splotches of the amber-colored tea.

She reached for her purse and launched herself behind the couch, pulled it on its side to serve as a barrier, and struggled to open her handbag to access her handgun.

"There's no way out. You're on the fourteenth floor," Bryan told her, his gun aimed at her head. "Toss me your purse, put your hands where I can see them and come out from behind the couch."

Rebecca knew she had no choice. With reluctance, she did what Bryan asked.

* * *

At the police station, Bryan scratched his head. The woman who called herself Rebecca refused to talk. He was perplexed. Her fingerprints were not in any of the databases, and there was no identification in her wallet. He had even run her image through a facial recognition program and that too had yielded no results. She was a ghost.

In addition, no one matching her description lived on the seventh floor of the condo building David Harris had called home.

Examination of the contents of her purse had yielded a Glock style polymer Smith & Wesson Miliary and Police (M & P) gun. The very kind used by his department and many military and police forces. The interchangeable grip used was clearly for someone with a smaller hand.

Analysis of the tea Emma had almost consumed contained Rohypnol, a powerful sedative, also known as the date-rape drug. *What had Rebecca been up to? Kidnapping? Interrogation?* Bryan asked himself for the hundredth time.

The ringing of the desk phone interrupted his thoughts. "Staff Inspector Bryan Grant speaking."

"Hey, Bryan."

"Hi, Emma."

"You free for lunch?"

"Sure. Any place you have in mind?"

"Yeah, somewhere public. Café Mokka?" Emma knew it was a risk to be out in public but had become stir crazy staying in the apartment.

"I could use a break." Bryan looked at the analog wall clock. "I have a few things to finish up. How about one o'clock?"

"That'll be fine. See you soon."

* * *

EMMA WAVED AT Bryan when he walked through the door, signaling him to join her at a table tucked near the little bistro's kitchen. Nearby, sat one of the bodyguards from Harold Kruger's firm that Bryan had rehired to accompany her whenever she was in public. Once he was seated, Megan, the barista, walked over to their table.

"What can we get you?"

"Coffee black with a couple of sweeteners. Stevia if you have it," said Bryan.

"Sorry, we just have Sugar Twin. That okay?"

He nodded. "That'll be fine."

"Anything to eat?"

"The chicken, onion and avocado wrap."

They turned to Emma. "What about you, Em?"

"I'll have an iced tea and the veggie wrap."

Megan used the stylus to enter the details of the orders into the digital device and hit send.

"That new?" Emma tilted her head toward the tablet Megan was holding.

"Yeah, the boss said to start using it. We love it. As soon as we hit send, the order pops up on the big screen in the kitchen. The staff can prepare the orders faster." They grinned. "No one has to guess about our messy handwriting anymore."

"Cool."

"I've missed seeing you. Feel like grabbing a drink after work sometime?" asked Megan.

"Maybe," replied Emma. She was reluctant to explain to her friend why she still felt uncomfortable in public.

"Okay," said Megan, their voice disappointed. "We'll be back with your orders soon."

When the server left their table, Bryan asked, "Good friend of yours? She seems nice."

"They are."

"They?"

"Yeah, Megan identifies as non-binary."

"Sounds like they miss you."

"I know, I feel guilty about it—but after David, well you know." Her voice trailed off. "I stopped seeing friends. I was so depressed."

"Lately you have seemed happier."

"I have been. Ever since—"

"There's something you should know."

"I already do." She rested her hand on his forearm. "David called me a few days ago."

Bryan leaned back in his chair. "Ah." He looked down to hide his surprise. "I'm sorry. I couldn't tell you. He insisted it was safer that way."

"I get it." She straightened her shoulders. "I already knew anyway."

"You did. But how?"

"Anna. Back in January. She came to me while I was meditating. Told me David was alive."

At first, Bryan was speechless and took a few moments to compose himself. "When she was alive, she helped us with cold cases. I was skeptical at first, but soon realized that her talents were genuine." He raked his fingertips through his salt and pepper hair. "I never imagined she would reach out from beyond the grave."

"It was so hard for me to accept he was gone. There was a part of me that just would not believe it."

"I know you took this hard. I didn't breathe a word about David still being alive to anyone." His eyes shone with tears. "I hated seeing you suffer."

"Yeah, I understand. But when Anna reached out to me, well, it all somehow made sense." She gave a wry laugh. "The lawyer just doesn't understand why I don't want to proceed with probate."

"I wondered why you were waiting but was glad you did." Bryan placed his large, calloused hand over hers and said, "There is something more you should know."

"Oh?"

"David and I have been working together to try to track down the whereabouts of the Bianchis."

Emma's eyes lit up with excitement. "Really? Have you made any progress?"

"Somewhat. David's been able to ascertain that they funneled a large sum of money from their real estate holdings into cryptocurrency accounts. From there it's been very difficult to trace where the money ended up."

"So, in other words, you've hit a dead end," said Emma with disappointment in her voice.

"Yes, for now."

"I wanted to see you for another reason, though," said Emma. "The woman you apprehended. I've seen her before. About a year ago."

"Interesting," said Bryan.

"I guess she doesn't really live in David's condo building and that her name probably isn't Rebecca."

"You guessed right," said Bryan.

Emma paused when she saw Megan approach their table with their orders. "Thanks, Megan. This looks delicious."

"Enjoy." Megan's smile was reserved as they headed back to the kitchen.

"I've disappointed them," said Emma, nodding toward Megan. "It's just been too much; living with the fear and uncertainty."

"If Megan's a good friend, they'll understand."

"Yeah, I guess." Emma sighed, "I just wish life would get back to normal."

"You and me both."

"Don't you think it's a little strange that the moment David contacted me, that woman showed up at my doorstep?" She looked at Bryan thoughtfully. "Is there any chance she may have used a listening device?"

"It's possible." Bryan considered her question. "Emma, do you mind cutting lunch short? There's something I'd like to check at David's condo."

"Sure. What do you have in mind?" she asked, unable to hide her curiosity.

Bryan pushed away his plate and pulled out his wallet. "My treat."

Megan noticed that Bryan and Emma were ready to go and hurried over. They noticed the half-eaten meals. "Didn't you like your lunches?" The space between their eyebrows was scrunched together with concern.

"We liked them just fine," Emma said.

Bryan said, "We did. Wouldn't mind taking the rest with me for a snack later."

"Me, too," said Emma.

Megan's smile brightened. "Sure, no problem. Let me get you a couple of carry-out boxes."

Emma looked over at the bodyguard, "Ready to head back to the condo?" He nodded, "Sure thing."

* * *

Bryan and Emma's bodyguard searched David's spacious condo for bugs and listening devices but found nothing. Perplexed, Bryan turned to Emma and said, "When David called you, can you tell me where you were sitting?"

"I was right here by the window." She pointed at the rocking chair with padded cushion. "It's nice and sunny. I enjoy looking out the window at the activity in the street below."

Bryan gazed out the large picture window and noticed the apartment building across the street. "I wonder," he said.

"Wonder what?" asked Emma.

"We canvassed and questioned all the residents in this building, but I hadn't considered the building across the street."

"What do you have in mind?"

"Emma, I think it's highly likely David's condo was bugged. I did a cursory search just now, and didn't find anything, but I'm going to send in a team to look more thoroughly." He stopped for a moment, deep in thought. "And I'm going to have the building across the street canvassed from door to door. Rebecca may have used a long-range listening device."

Fifty-One

But Can We Turn Her?

DAVID AWOKE TO a night vision. In it, Enrico held a knife to Emma's throat. As is so often the case with dreams and nightmares, his own movements were sluggish, as if walking in a thick viscous atmosphere, his legs mired in molasses. In the dream, he was not able to get to her in time, and he watched with horror as Enrico slid the knife edge across her neck, the blade so sharp it left only the thinnest necklace of red against her delicate throat.

"David—" She reached her right hand toward him, her left holding Enrico's blade arm, in a bizarre motion of victim holding onto assassin for support.

It was an intimate moment of death. Her gaze was penetrating, and her voice was a whisper caught in the wind tunnel of time and space, where the dreamworld and the waking world converge.

"He knows you are alive," she said. "Be careful, my love."

David tried to wrest himself from the horrific details, but the bright morning tropical sun filtering through the fronds of the palm leaves did nothing to assuage his terror. The memory of Enrico's eyes, cesspools of evil, and his malicious laughter remained vivid in his mind.

He reached for his journal to record the details, but then flung it away in irritation. *Something was wrong.* It had been several days since he and Bryan last communicated. He picked up his secure phone.

Moments later, Bryan answered and said, "David, I was just about to call."

"Emma? Is she okay?"

"Yes, she's safe now."

"Now?" David exploded. "What does that mean?"

"Calm down." Bryan tried to soothe the younger man. "She had a close call. But she's smart. She called me before anything serious could occur."

"Tell me what happened!" David demanded, his anger simmering below the surface.

"Sure, but take a deep breath."

"Okay," said David, trying to settle his temper. "I'm listening."

"A woman showed up at your condo claiming to be a Rebecca Blake from the RCMP and that she was investigating your death which she believed had been staged." Bryan cleared his throat. "Emma invited the woman in for tea to try and learn more. Fortunately, she noticed the woman slip something into her tea."

"Damn it! I went into hiding to protect Emma. We've been so careful."

"True, but it looks like she's been stalking Emma for quite a while."

"Why contact her now?"

"Well, Emma told me you called her on your anniversary."

"You don't think—"

"Yeah, I do."

"But I called on a secure encrypted line."

"Emma was the one who figured it out. Wondered if her phone or the condo had been bugged."

"Really?"

"She thought it was too much of a coincidence that this woman made contact with her the same day you called." He cleared the phlegm from his throat. "Based on the Rohypnol in the tea, we assume the goal was to kidnap Emma. If she hadn't seen the woman pour the contents from a vial into her tea, we would be having a very different conversation."

"Thank God for that," muttered David.

"We didn't find any bugs in your condo." Bryan paused. "It got me thinking about the apartment building across the street. We discovered that apartment number 1413, which is directly across from your condo, had been sublet. The description of the woman seen going in and out of the apartment matches the person we have in custody."

"Did you search the apartment?"

"It took a couple of days to get the search warrant, but yes, we have."

"Find anything?" David was anxious to hear more.

"We did. A packet of cocaine matching the same chemical markers found in your uncle's bloodstream, vials of Ketamine, the horse tranquilizer used in the attempt to kill Laura, and Rohypnol, the date-rate drug that was found in Emma's tea."

"Quite an accomplished killer."

"Yes, very." Bryan cleared his throat again. "The coroner has reversed his original findings that Liam and Sarah's deaths were accidental and agrees with my suspicions that they were indeed murdered."

"So, their case has been reopened?"

"Yes."

"Did you find anything else in the assassin's apartment?"

"We also found surveillance equipment, a cache of handguns and ammunition, but most worrisome; a long-range sniper rifle."

"What kind of LRSR?"

"One of the best. An M107 Semi-Automatic."

"I can't believe this," David moaned.

"The sniper's been watching your condo for months. Even before you disappeared. Our theory is that Enrico never believed you were dead. He had this woman watch Emma just in case you contacted her. Which you finally did."

"His patience paid off." David's voice was grim. "What else did you learn?"

"We had a piece of good luck. The police department up north discovered where the shots had come from when you and Emma were shot at in the canoe. The sniper had hidden up in a tall spruce tree. When they combed the area at the base of the tree, they found a discarded bullet shell which had been hidden under the pine leaves."

"Sniper must be a hell of a shot. That had to have been over 1,500 meters."

"True. The LRSR has a range of 2,000 meters, so the shot was well within range. But a shot like that takes great skill." Bryan's voice was gravelly. "The casing we found matches the ammo in the apartment."

"So, we know the sniper is likely this Rebecca woman?"

"Very likely. And because of that we can keep her in custody for quite some time."

"She's in a world of trouble."

"Yeah, she is. But so far, she's not talking."

"There must be something we can do to turn her."

"The Crown might lighten her sentence somewhat, if we can get her to divulge where the Bianchis are hiding."

"Do we know who she really is?"

"Not yet. She doesn't show up in any of our national databases."

"Could she be ex-military?"

"Quite possibly, and not necessarily from the US or Canada." We have also contacted Interpol to see if they can be of assistance."

"Someone has gotta know her."

"Indeed."

The two men finished speaking, allowing a silence to fall: the anger and frustration they shared remaining unarticulated. The stillness over the phone was deep and impenetrable.

"David, are you still there?" Bryan finally asked.

"I'm getting on a plane and coming back. I can't believe Enrico's people got so close to Emma." He moaned. "I can't lose her. I need to be there to protect her."

"It's best you remain hidden," said Bryan.

"But—"

"Just hear me out. Emma's safe. The woman's in custody." Bryan made a sharp exhale. "We have guards on security detail to protect both Emma and her mom wherever they go."

"I can't take this!" David exploded. "I should be with them!"

"Give it a few days. Just be patient."

"Don't think I can." David disconnected the call.

Fifty-Two

Coming Home

DAVID'S HEART HAMMERED in his throat when he presented his passport to the Security Police, but they only gave his identification and his face a cursory glance. He hadn't expected any issues with the high-quality forgery and held back the sigh of relief when he passed through without incident. He watched his carry-on bag pass through the X-ray machine, then picked it off the conveyor belt and flung it over his shoulder.

He confirmed his gate and headed over to sit in the chaotic waiting area. The excited laughter of people ready to head home after adventures of ziplining, surfing and gastronomic delights was distracting. Contributing to David's massive headache was a shuffleboard game being played by a father and his young son and several other people who were riding stationary bicycles to recharge their electronic devices.

His tension escalated when a canine unit approached the travelers. One by one, the dog gave the sniff test to the carry-on luggage strewn at the passengers' feet or stowed in chairs beside them, with the odd word of encouragement issued to it by its handler.

David stiffened when the handler pointed at his bag, and he held his breath while the dog did its work. It wasn't that he was carrying anything illegal, only his guilty conscience. He was nervous traveling under an assumed name and was jumpy. He knew the best thing was to remain calm, as were his fellow travelers, and allow the canine to do its job. David's anxiety ebbed away when the dog moved off to another waiting area further on.

He looked at the clock on his iPhone for the umpteenth time and hoped there would be no delays to the departure time posted at the flight counter.

As he was about to return the cell phone to the rear pocket of his jeans, he was surprised to feel it vibrate in his hand. Glancing down, he saw the image of Bryan Grant displayed on the home screen. He was torn about answering since he was coming home to Canada despite Bryan's advice. After a moment of indecision, he accepted the call and said, "Look Bryan, my mind's made up. I'm coming home."

"You are?" asked Emma.

"Em, how did you—" He was astonished to hear her voice.

"I borrowed Bryan's phone." She sighed. "I miss you." She paused. "Is this true? You're coming home?"

"Yeah. I am."

"Oh, David, is it safe?"

"Probably not, but since Enrico now knows I'm not dead, there's no point hiding. I don't want to be away from you for another minute. I miss you too much."

"I can't wait to see you, either." She hesitated. "Where are you?"

"In the airport lounge. Should be leaving in about forty-five minutes."

"Where have you been all these months?"

"You've got three guesses, but only the first one counts."

"No? Really? Costa Rica?"

"Yep. It's just as beautiful as you described."

"Umm… since you're there—"

"Chocolate is already in my carry-on luggage."

"Ah, you remembered." He could here the smile in her voice. "David, Bryan wants to talk to you now."

"Put him on."

* * *

Emma handed the phone back to Bryan. "Thanks so much for this," she said softly.

"Don't thank me just yet. This could get very dangerous. For all of us. You and David in particular."

He nudged the phone between his shoulder and ear and said, "David, I understand you're coming back. Can't say I'm surprised." Bryan tried not to sound annoyed. "Text me your flight number. We'll be waiting for you in arrivals." He paused. "There have been some developments we should go over as soon as you get back."

Fifty-Three

We Work Better As A Team

SINCE IT WAS several hours before David's flight would be landing, Bryan had said to Emma, "I'll drop you off at your mom's place. Then when it's time, the three of us can head over to pick David up from the airport."

"Sounds like a plan," said Emma. "It's only a fifty-minute drive to the airport."

"After I've dropped you off, I have to head to the station for a bit." He glanced at his watch. "But I'll be back in a few hours."

As Emma made to get out of the passenger seat, Bryan gripped her arm and said, "I can't stress this enough." His tone was stern. "Don't leave the house under any circumstances."

When Emma began to protest, he had said, "I know how you and your mother can get."

He had called out to the two security men from Harold Kruger Security who were stationed outside Laura's front door and said, "Don't let them out of your sight."

***

Emma sat in the lotus position, preparing to meditate. After having spoken with David on the phone earlier, she had found it difficult to relax. All she could think about was seeing him again.

Emma drew in a deep breath and cleared her thoughts. She recalled the 2010 University of Kentucky study which showed that people who meditated needed less sleep and that an hour of meditation could be the equivalent of two hours of sleep. Using the techniques Anna had taught her, she fell into a meditative state, concentrating on the even rhythm of her breath.

Soon, she went even deeper, the boundaries of the walls in the room, beginning to expand to an endless horizon. It was as if she was aboard a raft floating on a vast ocean. Although she didn't see Anna, she sensed her presence and as before, could hear Anna speaking to her in her mind.

My dear, Emma, I have much to tell you, but I need a circle of spiritual believers to amplify my message.

"You mean hold a séance?" Emma's mind reached out across the abyss between the physical and spiritual world to understand Anna.

Yes. Must have all of you there.

"All of us?"

You four are strongest when together. You, your mom, Bryan, and David.

When Anna had conducted séances when she was alive, she had explained that choosing a tool to contact the dead like a spirit board, pendulum or spirit rapping could have good results. Choosing an experienced psychic medium to be a conduit, however, was by far the best way and it was always Anna who had taken on that role.

"But who will be the medium?" asked Emma.

You.

"Me?" Emma said, startled. "But I am not ready!"

It must be you.

"But—"

Even though Emma's connection to Anna's spirit began to fade, a faint murmur remained, reassuring her that she was the one meant to amplify Anna's messages.

She unfolded her crossed legs and stood up and walked to her mom's sewing studio.

"Mom?"

Laura removed her foot from the pedal of the sewing machine, swiveled the chair toward the door where Emma stood and looked up at her daughter. "Honey, did you have a good rest?"

"Yes. I did, but—"

Laura noticed the shadow of uncertainty flash across Emma's face. "What is it?"

Emma dragged the spare chair from where it rested against the wall and positioned it so she could sit opposite her mom. She took her mom's hands in hers, and said, "I have been having clairaudient experiences."

"You have?"

"Anna has been in touch. Twice."

"Ah, Anna." Laura smiled at the thought of her dear friend contacting Emma. "What did she have to say?"

"Well, the first time was in January when she told me David was still alive."

"I see. That's about the time you started pulling out of your depression."

"True. Knowing he was okay bolstered my spirits. It made me feel that life was worthwhile again. That we could have another chance. Although, it has still been so lonely." Tears sprung into Emma's eyes.

Laura stretched out her hand and stroked her daughter's cheek. "But why didn't you tell me." Emma could hear the hurt in her mother's voice. "You said you heard from her a second time?"

"Just now."

Laura's mouth rounded in surprise. "Just now?"

Emma nodded. "She wants the four of us to hold a séance so she can communicate with us to find the Bianchis and bring them to justice.

Maybe then we can get on with our lives." Her eyes took on a distant look. "There's one problem."

"What is it?"

"She wants to speak through me."

"Oh my. How do you feel about this?"

"I am terrified." She straightened her back with resolve. "But I am going to do it anyway."

Fifty-Four

Don't Think Of It As Eerie

"YOU WANT TO do what?" David was incredulous. "Em, this could be dangerous. Remember what happened when Anna regressed me?"

"That was different." Her lips were pressed together in annoyance.

"What if another spirit takes over?"

"Only Anna will be given permission to speak through me. It will be just us four, and Anna, of course."

"I don't know what to say."

"Just say, yes." She pressed her index finger to his lips. "What harm can it do? And we might get answers."

"I'm still not sure." David was conflicted and said, "Bryan, what do you think?"

"Anna was a huge asset to the department when she was alive and helped us solve multiple cold cases." Bryan gazed at David with thoughtful eyes. "If she can do the same thing from beyond the grave, who am I to argue?"

"So, you're in?" asked Emma.

"Yeah, I'm in," Bryan replied.

"And you, Mom?"

"Yes, of course, dear."

"David, please?" Emma's expression was anxious.

"How can I ever say no to you?" His voice was brittle. "Just promise me you'll be careful. We stop if we sense there's any danger."

"Yes." Relief washed over Emma.

"When do we do this?" said David.

Laura interrupted. "It's past midnight. You must be jet-lagged, David."

"There's only a two-hour time difference between here and Costa Rica, but even so, it was nearly a twelve-hour trip from door to door." He yawned. "It would be good to get some rest."

"How about tomorrow night?" suggested Emma. "After dark."

"Here?" asked David.

"May I suggest we hold it at Anna's home in the city?" Laura inhaled a deep breath. "Her estate is still tied up in probate. As her executor, I have a key to her house."

"That's a great idea, Mom. Anna always said it's best to hold a séance in the home of a loved one who has passed."

"Everyone in agreement?" asked Laura.

"Yeah, I'm on board. A little spooky though," said David "But what you say makes sense."

"Don't think of it as eerie," said Emma. "It's more like 'spiritual' wireless technology, giving us a link to loved ones who have passed."

"Let's call it a night, then," said Laura. "See you in the morning. Sleep in. You both need your rest." She turned to Bryan and asked, "Staying tonight?"

"Yes, my love."

Once Bryan and Laura left the living room and headed upstairs, David turned to Emma. "Finally, alone."

"I've missed you so much," she whispered.

He pulled her into his arms and kissed her. Her breath was sweet and had a faint taste of the raspberries and the chocolate they had snacked on earlier.

"Come," she said, pulling away from his embrace and tugging on his hand to follow her to her bedroom.

They fell onto the bed in a tangle of arms and legs, kissing with urgency, anxious to fulfill the longing they had endured over the last nine months apart from each other. Two hearts now reunited. Bodies entwined as one.

Afterward, her words soft and gentle, she said, "I missed you so much."

"As did I," he murmured. His hands caressed the graceful features of her heart shaped face, tracing his fingers from her hairline to her forehead, along her Grecian nose, to her full lips and delicate chin. When he reached her long neck, he shuddered, as he recalled the vicious dream and the thin trail of blood the knife had left along her throat.

"What is it?"

"Nothing, just got a chill."

"In the summer?" She teased. "Let me warm you." She snuggled closer, and he held her even tighter. "I am never letting you out of my sight again."

They both fell into a dreamless and gentle sleep, safe and secure in the knowledge they were together. They did not rise until the late morning sun filtered through the venetian blinds in a joyful horizontal pattern of light and dark.

Fifty-Five

The Séance

THE SOFT LIGHT of dusk had yielded its last rays of illumination to the nighttime. It was approaching nine-thirty in the evening, and Emma was making final preparations. She had meditated earlier and had been relieved when she had heard Anna's disembodied voice tell her that she would do fine and not to worry about tonight's proceedings.

They chose Anna's quiet room that she had used to conduct séances when she was alive. The scent of cinnamon incense used to attract spirits wafted in the air and she had lit violet candles to enhance psychic powers and blue candles to enhance communication. Four chairs surrounded the table, and the table itself was uncluttered save for Anna's favorite Chrysanthemum Damask linen tablecloth. Emma closed the curtains to prevent any ambient light from entering and turned the dimmer switch down until the room was bathed in a soft light.

"Everything's ready," she said with some trepidation. "David, please sit to my right. And Bryan, to my left. Mom, please sit opposite me." Emma took in a deep breath. "Good. Now, everyone please join hands."

The four of them grasped each other's hands.

"Before we begin, I'd like to cover a few things. First of all, has everyone prepared their questions? Remember, they should be as specific as possible. Our time with Anna may be limited. Anna chose the four of us because we are all believers in the spiritual world. Our chances for communicating with her are much greater because of this. Have faith.

"Also, by being here in the room she loved best, we will feel her presence more easily." She looked at the face of each person. "And no matter what, don't let go of each other's hands.

"We are not using Ouija boards, or pendulums, but if the strength of our connection weakens, we can use the spirit rapping method. This will consist of asking simple questions that require a yes or no answer. The spirit will rap once for yes, and twice for no.

"Finally, I want you to know I love the three of you very much and I am grateful you are willing to try this." Her smile was gentle. "Shall we begin?"

Everyone nodded.

"Great. I want you to clear your minds, by concentrating on your breathing. Become aware of your breaths, by saying with me, 'I am breathing in, and I am breathing out.'"

Laura, David, and Bryan spoke in unison with Emma.

"Good. Now, please say, 'My body is breathing in and breathing out.' Observe your body doing this. This allows us to become objective."

"Perfect. Now repeat these mantras in your mind only."

Soon, only the sound of deep and relaxed breathing could be heard. After a few more minutes, Emma was compelled to speak.

"Anna, we are welcoming you into our circle. I give you, and you alone, permission to speak through me."

The air became cooler, and the atmosphere took on a viscous feel. Time and sound and other sensations began to recede until only the sound of soft inhalations and exhalations could be perceived.

Emma's body shook slightly, not with the dramatic thrashing seen in movies, but almost imperceptibly. Her youthful features changed in the soft light and became older and more serious.

David swallowed the gasp that rose to his throat. He was looking at Anna.

Laura also noted the change in her daughter's face but was not alarmed, as she had witnessed this type of manifestation before.

Bryan took it all in with stoicism.

"Anna, thank you for joining us," said Laura.

Emma began to speak, but not in her usual voice. It was Anna's older, more mature, and deeper intonation that was heard. "It's been a while, friends." Her wry laughter and no-nonsense voice were unmistakable. "You may call me Spirit Anna."

"Thank you for being here, Spirit Anna," said Bryan. "Like old times, when you helped out on cases."

"Yes, it sure is." The room filled with delighted laughter.

"May we ask you questions?" said Bryan.

"Yes."

"Can you tell us the true name of the one who calls herself Rebecca?"

"Yes."

Bryan looked at Laura with a puzzled expression.

She mouthed the words, "Be more specific."

He nodded in understanding. "Please tell us the true identity of Rebecca."

"Jasmijn Bakker."

"Where is she from?"

"The Netherlands," said Spirit Anna.

Laura's eyebrows raised in surprise when Spirit Anna, without prompting said, "Check missing children's records."

"Thank you," said Bryan.

David, having learned from Bryan's experience, formulated his question more specifically. "Spirit Anna, where are Enrico Bianchi and his son, Alessandro?"

"The Maldives."

Laura spoke next. "Will the Bianchis be apprehended?"

Her question was met with silence. She sensed the connection was weakening. "Spirit Anna, please rap once for yes, two for no."

Relief flooded through her when there was a single steady knock on the table.

"Will Emma and David remain safe from harm?" asked Laura.

This time there was no rap in the affirmative or negative. The temperature in the room warmed, Anna's features faded, and Emma's youthful features returned.

"She's gone," said Emma now alert. "What did we learn?"

"Spirit Anna says our unknown woman is named Jasmijn Bakker," said Bryan.

"And the Bianchis are in the Maldives," added Laura.

"Interesting," said David. "If I remember from my geography classes in school, the Maldives are a series of coral islands in the Indian Ocean."

He released Emma and Laura's hands and got up from the table to retrieve his tablet to do a google search on the Maldives. "Found it. Almost twelve hundred coral islands grouped in a double chain of twenty-seven atolls."

"Well, that narrows it down," said Bryan, his voice laced with sarcasm.

Fifty-Six

You Can Call Me Jazzie

THE MORNING FOLLOWING the séance, Bryan contacted the International Commission of Missing Persons, stationed in The Hague, the Netherlands. The International Commission on Missing Persons was the only international organization tasked exclusively to work on the issue of missing persons.

After being connected from one sympathetic person after another, he finally spoke with an official who confirmed that in 2006 a preteen by the name of Jasmijn Bakker had gone missing while walking home from an Amsterdam school.

"She was only eleven years old." The woman sounded sad.

"I know it's a long time ago. Can you tell me who the officer in charge of the case was?"

Bryan could hear tapping on the keyboard as he waited.

"Most of the officers on the case have died or retired."

"Most, but not all?"

"Johannes Nota was a young officer. He's now the Chief of Police for the Regional Police Unit in Amsterdam."

"Do you have the number for the Amsterdam police unit?"

After another series of clacking of keys, his patience was rewarded. "I have it here, sir. Would you like me to email you the information?"

"That would be great." Bryan recited his contact details and said, "Thanks for your help with this."

"My pleasure, sir. If you get any news about the whereabouts of Jasmijn Bakker, please share it with us. My records here show her parents are still alive." Bryan could hear another sad sigh. "It's the waiting and never knowing that hurts the most."

Moments later, his cell pinged, notifying him he had email. He hit the number that appeared on the screen and waited to be connected to Johannes Nota.

"Chief Nota, speaking." The intonation was firm but polite.

"Chief, this is Staff Inspector Bryan Grant of the New Elgan Police Service in Ontario, Canada."

"How can I help you, Staff Inspector?"

"I am working on a case that may be related to a missing child case dating back to 2006. I was hoping you can help me."

"I'll try. Tell me more."

"We recently apprehended a woman for attempted kidnapping and for murder. We believe she may be Jasmijn Bakker."

There was a long pause on the line before Nota spoke. "I remember that case. The child's parents were distraught. She disappeared while walking home from a school for gifted children. Appeals were made to the public and a reward offered, but she was never located." As was the case for most Dutch people, his English was impeccable. "How did you learn about the Bakker case?"

"Her name came up while conducting a murder investigation."

There was a long silence before the Dutch chief finally said, "Interesting. What aren't you telling me?"

"I'm afraid I can't reveal my source."

"Then there is not much more I can do to help. Goodbye—"

"Wait—"

"Yes?"

"Look, I'm desperate. The name was given to me under very unconventional circumstances." Bryan decided to take a chance at the risk of being ridiculed. "It came from a psychic. I know that sounds crazy."

"Ah, not so much. You have heard of Warner Tholen?"

"I can't say that I have."

"He was a psychic here in Holland. Died in the early eighties. He helped solve many cases. I was just a young officer when he died, but he was a legend." Bryan heard the man take in a deep breath. "So, tell me more about this case."

"Prior to her death, Anna Tungsten was a psychic who helped our department solve cases. Unfortunately, last year she was murdered. The suspect's name is Enrico Bianchi." Bryan nudged the phone between his ear and shoulder more securely and reached out to take a drink of coffee and nearly spat out the cold concoction. "She had made contact through one of her former protégées, Emma Jackson, and had requested she hold a séance. We learned that Bianchi may be in the Maldives, and the woman we apprehended is likely Jasmijn Bakker. She had no identification on her person, or in the apartment she was renting, and insists we call her Rebecca."

"Rebekka? That's odd." Jan's tone was charged with excitement. "That was Jasmijn's mother's name. She called the little girl Jazzie."

"Coincidence?"

"Not likely. Each year we review our cold cases. In the case of missing children, it is customary for us to use face-aging and rejuvenation software. Looks like the most recent face aging was done for Jasmijn Bakker in March of this year."

"Would you mind sending those results to me?"

"Certainly. And in return, can you send me a picture of the woman you have in custody? I'd like to run the images through our facial recognition software to see if there are any markers that match."

"Will do," Bryan said. "Before we sign off, can you send me the full names of the parents?" He paused for a moment as an idea came to him. "And if you've got them, family photos of Jasmijn and her parents."

The two police officers, two continents away, exchanged their personal contact details with each other. Both shared an optimism they had not experienced for some time. Hope in solving a missing child's case that had plagued the Dutch Chief of Police for years and hope also prevailed in Bryan's heart that he and David were one step closer to apprehending the Bianchis.

* * *

Through the one-way observation glass, Emma and David watched Staff Inspector Bryan Grant enter the interrogation room. Bryan had invited them to observe, hoping Emma might receive some intuition and insight into the woman, who insisted she be addressed as Rebecca. She sat in a plastic chair, and her hands were restrained in cuffs that were bolted to the table.

"Good morning, Jazzie," said Bryan.

"Say again?" The woman's face blanched, her expression befuddled.

"You heard me, Jazzie."

"I told you before. My name is Rebecca."

"Jasmijn Bakker. Born in the Netherlands."

"Stop calling me that." She turned her face away from him and stared at the wall to her right.

Bryan continued. "Jasmijn Bakker. Disappeared at the age of eleven."

"Seriously? That all you got, old man?" She laughed with derision.

He slid a folder across the table and said, "Open it."

Several photographs fell out of the file as she picked it up. A look of confusion briefly crossed her face before she smirked and leaned back in her chair as far as the restraints would allow, her face an impassive mask.

He pointed at a family portrait of the young Bakker family. Young Jazzie was sitting on her mother's lap, her father stood behind them, his arms protectively encircling both mother and young child. "Parents Rebekka and Joop Bakker."

Bryan waited for her reaction and was not disappointed.

The woman's ice-blue eyes flashed with fury and narrowed to slits. "That's not how you pronounce my dad's name."

"Oh?"

The words rushed out. "You don't pronounce the 'j' like that. It's a 'yuh' sound and the 'oo' is a long 'o' sound. Not a 'u—" she stopped speaking, realizing her mistake.

Jasmijn folded over the table, not noticing the shackles binding into her upper body. The years of pent-up anger and fear were draining away. She began to sob, quietly at first, until it reached a crescendo of soul-shattering grief. Her lost childhood and lost identity. Even her lost womanhood. She was consumed with sorrow, shaking violently as her mind accepted for the first time the loss and sacrifices she had been forced to endure.

Bryan watched, his eyes patient, for the sobbing to stop.

When she spoke next, her words were so quiet he had to strain to hear.

"I don't really know who I am." She shuddered. "But you may as well call me Jazzie."

* * *

Bryan left the interrogation room, locking it behind him and joined Emma and David.

"That was quite a breakthrough," said David.

"Yeah, we made progress."

Emma watched Jazzie through the glass. "She's exhausted. She's breaking down." She tilted her head to the side, as if listening to a private conversation. "Spirit Anna's here. She wants me to work with Jazzie."

"How so?" Bryan looked at her with concern.

"She thinks I can get her to open up about her past."

"As a civilian, it would be unorthodox having you interview her."

"Oh, that's too bad." Emma looked crestfallen.

"Though it would be helpful to find out how she went from a kidnapped child in Holland to an assassin for hire," said Bryan.

"And what happened to her during those years she was missing," said Emma.

"I still don't think this is a good idea." Bryan looked at her pensively. "She tried to kill you and your mom—"

"You don't think I can be impartial." Emma's tone was hurt.

"I suppose I could bring you on as a consultant. I would need to be always present."

"It will be less threatening and put her at ease if I go in alone."

"Okay," said Bryan with reluctance. "I will be right outside observing the interview closely."

"You better be," said David. "I don't like this idea at all."

"David, it'll be fine. Bryan will be close by."

"So will I," replied David.

Bryan glanced at his watch. "It's late. See you both back here at nine tomorrow morning?"

"Sure. You staying at Mom's tonight?"

"Yeah, I am. You two enjoy the evening."

Emma and David exchanged worried glances. "We will. See you soon."

They turned to walk away, their security detail waiting outside to escort them to the condo.

Fifty-Seven

Jasmijn Bakker's Story

BRYAN CHECKED HIS watch and calculated it was just before midnight in Holland. When they had ended their telephone conversation earlier in the day, Johannes Nota had reassured Bryan he could call at any hour of the day if he'd learned anything useful.

"The older I get, the less sleep I need," he'd said. "I live and breathe my cases, much to the chagrin of my ex-wives."

The cell rang only once before Johannes answered. "Inspector Grant. You must have news." His voice was just as alert as if it was midday and not midnight.

"Yes, I do. And please call me Bryan."

"As long as you call me Jan."

Bryan was pleased they were on first-name terms. He liked this man. "We have confirmed the identity of the woman calling herself Rebecca. She is indeed Jasmijn Bakker. She had a breakdown while we were interrogating her, and we're letting her rest now. We will be working with her again tomorrow morning to find out where she has been for the last seventeen years."

"She was a highly intelligent child." Bryan could hear Jan's hesitation. "When she was abducted, we feared the worst. That she had been sold into slavery for the sex trade. But now I wonder. She had a high aptitude for mathematics, linguistics as well as athleticism."

"All excellent characteristics required to become a sharpshooter."

"Indeed. Did you know that UNICEF, the United Nations Children's Fund has estimated that between 2005 and 2020 more than 93,000 children were verified as recruited and used by parties in conflicts around the world? And UNICEF believes that number is conservative." Jan sighed with frustration. "Where has she been all this time?"

"Hard to say. Hopefully, we'll know more tomorrow."

"Oh, by the way, thanks for sending the current image of Ms. Bakker. We are waiting for the results of the facial recognition program looking specifically for facial markers. I'll send you the results when they come in."

"Thanks."

"Bryan, I really appreciate your call. If you learn anything more on your end—"

"You'll be the first to know."

"Great. Never knowing what happened to their daughter has been hard on Jasmijn's parents. This will provide closure of some sort."

* * *

Emma walked into the interrogation room carrying two takeaway cups of tea and a paper bag containing an oatmeal muffin and napkins. Her body posture was relaxed and non-threatening while Jazzie's was defensive. She had been hunched forward, her chin nestled against her collarbone, and raised her head when Emma sat down across from her.

For a few minutes the two stared at each other.

"Here to gloat?" Jazzie eyed Emma with suspicion.

"No, just here to help."

"There's no helping me." Her tone was acidic. "Unless you plan to take me away from this fine establishment." She gestured around the room, like a real estate agent expounding the merits of a plush home.

"They found the sedative in the tea. What were you planning?"

"Wouldn't you like to know?" Jazzie snickered.

"Yeah, I would. All of it. I can't imagine what you've been through all these years." Emma looked at her with such sincerity that Jazzie's derisive laughter faded abruptly.

"You've no idea."

"My instincts are that you are a good person who was thrown into an impossible situation. You did what you did to survive." She straightened her shoulders and said, "How about we start again?" She smiled and reached her hand out to Jazzie and said, "I'm Emma."

After a moment of indecision, Jazzie returned the handshake, the shackles limiting her range of motion. "I'm Jazzie."

"Tea?"

"You and your tea." Jazzie's laughter this time was without sarcasm. "Got any honey?"

"Nah, just cream and sugar. And an oatmeal muffin. I hope you like blueberry." She slid the bag containing the muffin, the napkins and packets of sugar and containers of cream across the table. "I'll bring honey next time."

"That'll be great." Jazzie opened the bag and took in a deep breath of the fresh baked aroma. "Thanks for this." The handcuffs strained at her wrists, as she lifted the muffin to her mouth to take the first bite. "Mmmm..." Her eyes partially closed with appreciation.

"Time to talk," said Emma, her body language quiet and non-threatening.

Jazzie wiped her fingers on the paper napkin and nodded, "Sure, what do you want to know?"

"What do you remember about your kidnapping?"

"It was so long ago." Her sigh was heavy. "Certain parts are so clear, and other parts I barely remember." Her hands cradled around the Styrofoam cup as if gathering strength from the warmth imparted by the tea.

"I understand you were taken while walking home from school."

"Yeah, that's right. From the Amsterdamse School voor Hoogbegaafde Kinderen. A school for gifted kids." A soft smile played on her lips. "I loved going to that school. My favorite subjects were math and languages. And gymnastics."

"I really liked school, too. Math and art and swimming were mine."

"I was learning a difficult floor routine and I stayed later than usual. I'd just left the school property when a dark sedan pulled up beside me. Two men jumped out, threw a hood over my head, and that was it." Her voice became bitter. "My life as I knew it was over."

"What happened next?"

"Brainwashing first. Lots of beatings whenever I cried for my parents. And the threat they'd be killed if I was disobedient. My name was no longer Jazzie. Just the reference number J-216.

"Then dawn to dusk school. But not what I was used to. Hand to hand combat, mixed martial arts training, munitions training, life or death challenges. Math and languages still. Learning was no longer fun, but a necessity to survive."

"Where did they take you?"

"In the early days, I never knew. We were moved around a lot. Throughout the middle east."

"Were there many of you?"

"There were never more than ten in our unit. If one didn't make it, he or she was replaced." She took a sip of tea. "There was this kid—"

Emma grew pale and her eyes shifted slightly out of focus as the vision of the child struggling played out to cinematic perfection. His feet were bound by heavy coils of rope, then the thick cord was looped over a large pulley attached to the ceiling. A group of children in their early teens pulled on the rope until the poor kid was suspended upside down. She gasped when a small, robed figure moved forward and slashed a knife against the child's throat.

"B-293," Emma said softly. "The kid's name was Bobby."

"What?" Jazzie's eyes grew large with surprise. "You psychic or something? How could you know that?"

"They killed him because he refused to give up his name."

"True, only—I was the one who killed him." Fear flickered across her features.

Emma shook her head. "They made you."

"No excuse. We— no— *I should have helped him!*"

"You had no choice." Emma placed a comforting hand on Jazzie's. "You would have been dead, too."

The space between Jazzie's eyebrows was creased. "What just happened?"

"Sometimes, I have visions."

"And you saw Bobby."

"Yes, I did." Emma's expression was sorrowful.

"That's not a 'gift' I'd like to have."

Emma shrugged her shoulders. "With training, you get used to it."

"I guess." Jazzie eyed Emma with wariness.

Emma changed the subject. "How long did you remain in the unit?"

"I never got out. There's just three of us left from our original unit."

"You still work for these people?" asked Emma, surprised.

"Sure. The threats made against our families when we were children remain valid today. We've no choice."

"Who are they?"

"They call themselves the *Dark Hands of Anubis.*"

"Seriously?"

"No word of a lie."

"And what's Enrico Bianchi's role in this?"

"Just a customer who has such deep pockets I've been on loan from Dark Hands for over a year."

"Surely the authorities can help."

She gave a wry laugh. "We're criminals. Assassins hired out by the group that kidnapped and trained us."

"There has to be some way—"

"You don't understand. Their power is not insignificant. Just by having been apprehended my life is forfeit. They always assume the worst. It's why I decided to talk to you. Nothing left to lose." Her sigh was heavy. "My life was over eighteen years ago."

Emma took both Jazzie's hands in her own. "I can't imagine what your life's been like, but please don't give up hope."

For the second time in as many days, Jazzie wept. Emma got up and walked to where she was seated and placed a comforting hand on her shoulder. "You're not alone anymore."

"Thank you." Jazzie's voice was almost childlike. "Can I rest now?"

"I'll let them know we're done for the morning. I'll come back this afternoon." She paused. "Just one more thing, are you willing to help us track down the Bianchis?"

Jazzie wiped the tears from her cheeks and met Emma's gaze. "Nothing would give me more pleasure."

Fifty-Eight

What Do I Need to Do?

JAZZIE STARED AT the four walls of the detainment cell in the New Elgan Police Service. Despite Staff Inspector Grant and Emma's assurances, she knew she would never be safe.

The Dark Hands of Anubis had infiltrated various levels of law enforcement in many countries. She didn't believe New Elgan would be the exception and doubted she would be alive by the end of the week. Unless she found a way to outwit Emma and the inspector.

Other than the muffin and tea Emma had provided her in the interrogation room that morning, she had refused to eat. She eyed every meal and beverage offered with suspicion, and for this reason, today's lunch tray remained untouched. Over the past several days, a significant amount of weight had dropped from her already slender frame.

There were no clocks nearby, as it was not customary for prisoners to be given the time. Her internal clock helped her ascertain that it might be a little past one in the afternoon. Possibly another forty-five minutes before she was due to meet with Emma again.

* * *

Bryan leveled his gray eyes at Jazzie.

Beside him sat Emma, who smiled at Jazzie and said, "Before we begin, I've brought pizza and bottled water for you. I am sure prison food must be just as awful as hospital food."

"God, that does smell good," said Jazzie eying the slice of pizza Emma had placed on the paper plate. "I'm so hungry."

"Aren't they feeding you?" Bryan asked, a note of irritation creeping into his voice.

"Umm, yes, but—"

"You're afraid to eat the food." Emma completed her sentence.

"How does she do that?" said Jazzie, between mouthfuls.

"It's a gift," said Bryan. "Let's get started."

Jazzie reluctantly put down the partially eaten pizza.

"Emma tells me that you are willing to help us track down the Bianchis."

"Yeah." She sat up straighter.

"I've spoken to the Crown Attorney and although you are facing serious charges and significant jail time, they are willing to broker a deal with you if you help us locate the Bianchis. After sentencing, part of that deal would entail you being transferred to Holland where you would complete your time."

Jazzie frowned, "Why there?"

"You'd be close to your parents." He cleared his throat. "The Dutch government is willing to provide counseling and care as you were the victim of a kidnapping. You didn't choose the life you were thrown into."

"I see." Her voice was flat and without expression.

"There's one more thing," Bryan said.

"Oh?"

"As we speak, they are making arrangements to come see you."

"Who? *My parents?*" The young woman's panic and surprise was palpable. "I'm not sure I want to see them or for them to see me—"

Bryan interrupted her mid-sentence. "Right now, you are facing charges for the first-degree murders of Liam Foster and Sarah Larson-Moody and one charge for the attempted murder of Laura Jackson,

Emma's mother, two counts for the attempted murders of Emma Jackson and David Harris." He took a deep breath, "And finally, for the attempted kidnapping of Emma Jackson."

Jazzie gazed at the table while Bryan spoke. When she glanced up at him her lower lip was trembling. "What do I need to do?"

"Cooperate fully with us so we can apprehend the Bianchis. Then we need you to work with Interpol and the Dutch police to shut down the Dark Hands of Anubis."

"Fine," she stared at him with a mix of tears and defiance. "Just keep my parents out of this. I don't want them to come. Dark Hands will kill them, should they learn I'm assisting you."

"I'll contact Jan Nota, the Amsterdam Chief of Police and have him explain the situation to your parents."

"Thank you." Jazzie directed her gaze at Bryan and said, "I'll need my phone back. I assume you have my computer. And I'll need internet access."

"Okay," agreed Bryan reluctantly. "But only under our supervision."

Her smile was grim. "I suspected this day might come. I've been keeping tabs on Dark Hands. And Bianchi. Before you arrested me, I was close to pinpointing Bianchi's location."

"Good."

"Bianchi is accustomed to communicating with me via our encrypted cells. Once we have determined his location, may I suggest laying a trap?"

Emma shifted uncomfortably in her seat as she cocked her head to one side and listened to Spirit Anna.

* * *

Through the observation glass David watched the interrogation intently. He noticed Emma incline her head and wondered what Spirit Anna was advising. He knew Emma was a kind-hearted person, which is why he loved her as much as he did, but he worried that she was too forgiving and naive.

He was willing to admit Jazzie had gone through a lot, having been kidnapped at an early age and then trained to be an effective assassin. Clearly, she was a chameleon who had molded herself to unfavorable situations to survive. This made her very dangerous.

Emma could be forgiving, but he could not. At lunch that day they'd had words.

"Jazzie is an instrument of murder, no different than a gun or a knife," Emma insisted. "She was just following orders."

David shook his head. "So were the Nazis when following Hitler's command to eradicate the Jews and others not fitting the pure Aryan image."

"That's hardly the same thing," she'd retorted.

"At what point should the damaged child, now an adult, take responsibility for his or her own crimes?" he'd asked in anger.

Emma had glared at him, but when she saw the pain in his eyes her gaze softened and she'd begun to say, "I'm sorry—"

"Emma. Do not forget. She killed Uncle Liam and Sarah. Nearly killed your mother. Almost killed us both. Tried to kidnap you."

"You're right. I really am sorry." She'd gotten up and wrapped her arms around him. "I've lost sight of the full picture. Please forgive me."

"She's destroyed so much." He'd held her tight. "I can't afford to lose you, too."

Thinking back on the conversation, he was resolved to be cautious about Jazzie. Under the orders of Enrico Bianchi, she had taken so much from him. It was unforgivable. He was not interested in being part of the hit-woman's redemption and rehabilitation. For now, he'd play along with Emma and Bryan, but given the chance, he wouldn't hesitate to exact revenge.

His thoughts were interrupted when the door to the interrogation room opened, and Emma slipped out.

"What did Spirit Anna have to say?" he asked.

Emma's cheeks reddened. "Jazzie will help us to a point, but she warned us to be careful."

"Uh huh," David grunted. "Why am I not surprised?"

"Please don't say I told you so."

Bryan, who had also left the interrogation room, heard the tail end of the discussion, and asked, "Told who what?"

"Spirit Anna said we shouldn't trust Jazzie," David had another headache coming on and massaged both temples with his fingers to try and alleviate it.

"I concur." Bryan considered his next words. "David, you've spent significant time on this case, but now that you are a private investigator, I'd like you to officially work on my team as a consultant."

David straightened his shoulders, "Thought you'd never ask."

"I know this may be difficult, considering Jazzie is responsible for the deaths of your family, but I'd like you to work with her and a team of technicians on tracking down Enrico."

"I'll do whatever is necessary." His tone was resolute.

Fifty-Nine

An Offer Not To Be Refused

JAZZIE SHIFTED UNEASILY in her chair. Emma's psychic abilities made her nervous. Although she appeared sweet, Jazzie now knew there was an inner core of steel within Emma not to be underestimated. In addition, David's hate for her emanated from him in waves that made her feel suffocated and nauseous. *I don't have to be psychic to know that man hates me,* she thought. *If Enrico could see me now, he'd be furious. He'd kill me as surely as one of his disposable whores.*

Used to working alone, she disliked having David and Bryan's IT team examine her every move and tuned out their annoying questions. Put out by the distraction they were causing; she was vaguely aware of David speaking.

"Say again?"

"I said, what kind of spy software have you used to track down Enrico's location?"

"It's called VirtualSpy; it turns a cell phone into a bugging and tracking device. Without it, we won't be able to track Enrico's location." Her smile was smug. "Not dissimilar to the software the New Elgan Police Service uses."

The IT team leader shifted nervously in his seat but ignored her comment. "Didn't you say both you and Enrico installed KryptAll® on your phones? Won't its algorithms prevent you from tracing the call?"

"Normally, yes, but I found a way to override the autodestruct safeguards of the KryptAll® firmware already installed on Enrico's VoIP enabled iPhone."

"Impressive," David said.

"Well, watching your condo for months on end left me a bit bored. Had lots of time on my hands to puzzle this out."

David bunched his hands into fists and looked away, attempting to control his flaring temper.

To diffuse the hostilities, one of the technicians said, "Heard you were a math whiz." He tried to keep respect for the assassin genius out of his voice.

"Numbers never lie," Jazzie gave him a haughty smile. "Math is the only thing I could ever rely on."

David moved to the phone on the wall and dialed the internal number for Bryan. "We're ready to make that call."

"Excellent. Emma and I will join you momentarily. We're ready, too. The script is complete."

* * *

"I don't talk like this," said Jazzie, throwing the script onto the table with disgust. "Enrico will know this conversation is fake."

Bryan leveled a stern gaze at her. "Okay, so what do you suggest?"

Jazzie's pulse raced at this possible chance for escape. Her freedom was paramount. If an opportunity presented itself to warn off Enrico, and sacrifice David, Emma, and Bryan, she wouldn't hesitate. It might also ensure her financial freedom and her parents' safety.

"First of all, he'll know something is off if I'm too polite. This script is ridiculous."

"So, say what instead?" asked Emma, lightheaded with concern.

"All our business transactions are done via encrypted texts or calls." Jazzie gloated inwardly when David winced at her casual reference to murder for hire as a mere business transaction. "I go on the offensive. Skip the clandestine stuff. Ask for an in-person meet."

"Won't that warn him off?" David asked.

"The exact opposite. I'll make him think he has no choice."

After Jazzie outlined her plan, Bryan said, "That could work." He rubbed the pepper-and-white stubble on his chin and stared at her. He was exhausted.

It had been days since he'd had a proper sleep, let alone a decent shower and shave. Although he'd taken the previous night off, he had not been able to relax, and instead, had stared for hours at the ceiling, feeling the warmth of Laura's body beside him. Just before dawn, he had drifted to sleep, only to be awakened an hour later by the birds beginning their early morning summer songs.

He shook off the weariness and said, "David, Emma, you're with me." The legs of three chairs scraped against the floor in mutual discordance as they got up and left the room.

* * *

Once outside, Bryan turned to Emma and David. "Come on you two, let's get coffees. I need to clear my head."

Once they were seated in the police department cafeteria, Bryan asked Emma, "What do your instincts tell you?"

"I don't trust her. While we were in there, Spirit Anna told me to go along with her but be careful."

"What do you think, David?" asked Bryan.

"I agree with Emma. Something is off."

"I know." He sighed with frustration. "But we're at a stalemate if we don't move forward."

"If we do locate the Bianchis, what do we do next?" asked David.

"When Enrico and Alessandro escaped last year, we asked Interpol to issue a Red Notice, but nothing turned up."

"What's a Red Notice? asked Emma.

"A Red Notice is issued by Interpol and is a request to law enforcement around the world to find and conditionally arrest a person, pending extradition." Bryan took a sip of the hot coffee and continued. "It all depends on if the country they are hiding in has an extradition treaty with Canada. The Maldives probably do not, since normally the country admitting them has an obligation to advise the Canadian authorities of an attempted entry."

"Unless they used false passports," said Emma.

"Exactly, and evidence thus far indicates that's likely what they did," added David, referring to the hours he had spent tracking down the financial records of the Bianchis, until he'd reached a dead end.

"So, if they are hiding in the Maldives, like Spirit Anna said, and there is no extradition treaty, what do we do?" asked Emma.

"Actually, I checked already, the Maldives has no extradition treaty."

"Oh," Emma frowned. "That's disappointing."

"We can ask Interpol for help, and for the Canadian authorities to mediate and work with the host country via diplomatic channels, but odds are we won't have much success," said Bryan.

"Plus, we'll lose the element of surprise," replied David.

Bryan rubbed his tired eyes with the heels of his hands and said, "True. We'll work on a new script with Jazzie to lure Enrico into a trap. Once we know the Bianchis' location, if it is indeed the Maldives, we'll decide what to do."

* * *

Several hours later, after heated discussions between Bryan and Jazzie, the final script had been prepared. The iPhone had been blue toothed to speakers and a separate recording system had been set up for analysts to review later. Bryan's team of technicians had confirmed the trojan tracking software installed on Jazzie's iPhone was working and would not alert the KryptAll® firmware to its presence. Their head technician had cloned the two phones so any data on Jazzie's phone would be mirrored to the one that Bryan now held.

"Ready?" Bryan asked.

Jazzie nodded and said, "Ready."

Bryan, David and Emma focused their attention on Jazzie as she punched in the sequence of numbers to route the encrypted call through the global network of servers.

Everyone held their breaths as the phone rang.

Enrico's gravelly voice came over the speakers. "Heard you were in jail."

"Just got out," Jazzie told him. "They got nothing to hold me on."

"Where are you now?"

"Ready to leave town. Now that my cover is blown, I'm outta here."

"Your bosses won't like that," he warned.

"At this stage, do you really think I give a shit about the Dark Hands of Anubis?"

"Then why are you calling?"

"Just a courtesy and a reminder to pay me what you owe me for the Foster and Larson-Moody job."

"Really? I don't owe you a bloody thing. You incompetent little bitch—"

"Shut up, you stupid bastard." Jazzie's voice was cold and flat. "You think I don't have transcripts of all the dirty jobs you've had me do over the last year? Besides, you'll want to hear my offer."

"Offer? You're in no position to bargain with me, little girl."

"That's where you're mistaken. Once you hear me out, you'll pay me triple what you already owe. Consider this an offer you can't refuse."

Jazzie saw Enrico's geolocation flash across her screen and quickly glanced up to meet Bryan's eyes. He nodded slightly, acknowledging he'd also seen the information.

"Okay. Start talking," said Enrico, his voice sounded irritated.

"Nah, this meeting has to take place in person."

"Absolutely not."

"I know where you are," she taunted him.

"What the fuck?"

"Don't try to leave." She snickered. "I'll know if you do. One call and I will let the authorities know exactly where you are."

"You little—"

"Your secret's safe," she reassured him. "Just want to be paid what I'm due."

"You'll pay for this if you try to double-cross me."

"See you in forty-eight hours." She disconnected the call and grinned. "The Maldives is lovely this time of year."

Sixty

There Are No Guarantees, Honey

"SPIRIT ANNA WAS RIGHT," said Bryan. "Enrico and his son are in the Maldives."

Emma and David mirrored his enthusiasm.

"When do we go?" David had trouble controlling his excitement at the prospect of finally bringing Enrico and his son, Alessandro, to justice. One way or another.

"Look, I can't ask the two of you to take this risk. You two are like the kids I never had." Bryan's voice was choked with emotion. "My career is coming to an end, but your lives are just beginning."

"Our lives won't ever get started if we don't get rid of the Bianchis." David's jaw was set in determination. "Besides, you're going to need our help."

Emma reached out her hand to caress David's face. She turned to look at Bryan and said, "He's right. We're in this together."

Tears welled up in Bryan's eyes at the tender gesture. He shook his head in disbelief. "We're going to have to do this on our own. The Bianchis are too much of a flight risk. There is a strong chance that corrupted individuals in the Maldives government may warn him off. We need to be very careful."

"A year ago, I would never have considered such a thing," Emma told him. "But a lot has changed. I've never done anything against the law. I've never even had a parking ticket."

"Growing up in a home with lawyers, it's been the same for me. But there's a higher moral authority we're following. Call it justification, or better yet justice. We need closure on this. And it's never going to happen until Enrico and his son are dead and buried," said David.

Bryan searched for a way to be tactful, and then decided to just say his piece. "I am worried you're motivated by revenge. I need to know that you're going to keep a cool head."

"Yeah, I can do that." David glanced toward Emma and said, "We both can."

Bryan cleared his throat a second time. "I'd hoped Emma would not be coming."

"After what we've been through, I am never letting David out of my sight again. It's either live or die for both of us."

"It's settled then. We're headed for the Maldives," Bryan announced. He thumbed through his cell, "The first flight out is with Air Canada. Leaves at ten fifty tonight. I'll book it now and text you both your e-tickets and flight details."

David placed his hand on Bryan's arm. "Let me pay for the tickets. I've got funds put aside for this."

Bryan nodded in appreciation. "Thanks, David. This would not have been easy on my cop's salary." He looked at his watch, "Okay kids, pack your bags. Let's meet at Emma's mom's place for a quick farewell dinner, then we'll head to the airport together."

"Kids?" Emma smiled at Bryan.

"You know how I feel about the two of you." He gave them both hugs, his face turned away so they couldn't see his flushed face. "Now get going," his tone was brusque, as he attempted to hide his emotions.

"See you tonight," said Emma, as she pecked Bryan on the cheek.

"With any luck this will be over soon," said David.

"How nice it will be to not have bodyguards shadowing our every move." Her body shook with relief. "To not be fearful every minute."

* * *

Laura picked up the ginger cat, gently placed it on the floor and motioned for Bryan to join her on the love-seat in her bedroom.

"Sarah's cat is adjusting well to his new home," commented Bryan as he scratched behind the purring feline's ears.

"Snuggles is a lovely cat," she smiled as the cat brushed against her legs.

"Sarah would be glad you gave him a home."

Laura nodded. "I still can't believe she and Liam are gone." She nestled into the crook of Bryan's arm, her face pressed up against his chest. Her voice was muffled. "I'm going to miss you." Tears sprung into her eyes. "Promise you'll keep Emma and David safe?"

"There are no guarantees, honey. You know that."

"Yeah, I know, but lie to me a little bit, okay?"

"Sure." Bryan held her tighter. "I'll do everything I can to keep them both out of harm's way." His voice cracked with emotion.

"Thanks, I needed that," she whispered. "Come on, let's head downstairs. The lasagna should be ready now." Laura pulled away from his embrace and stood up. "This may be the last time we're all together for a while, sharing a meal." She choked back a sob. "Maybe forever—"

Bryan caught her hand and pulled her back onto the seat. "Wait a moment, Laura—"

"Yes?"

"Will you marry me?"

"Will you stop making me cry?" This time she brushed away tears of joy.

* * *

The flight to Dubai International Airport was uneventful but long. Bryan had never been able to sleep on planes. He'd picked up a book at Toronto Pearson International called *Outfoxed – An Inspector William Fox Adventure.* The book, by up-and-coming author Peter Thomas Pontsa, was an international, globe-trotting adventure and helped pass the time during the tedious fight. Bryan wished he had a man like William Fox on his side for what they were about to embark upon.

From time to time, he would look up from his book and watch the two lovers sleeping. Emma's head nestled into the space between David's shoulder and chin. Their faces were soft and slack, making them appear much younger and more fragile than when they were awake.

The plane was jarred by turbulence as it began its descent toward Dubai, and startled Emma and David awake.

"Are we already getting ready to land?" Emma asked, yawning, as she massaged the crick in her neck. "A plane is not the most comfortable place to sleep. I'm surprised I did."

"You both fell asleep from the moment the wheels were up."

David nodded. "It feels great to have had some shuteye. But it'll be good to stretch my legs."

"How about you Bryan, did you sleep?" asked Emma.

"Not a chance," he said. "But I had a good book to keep me company."

The wheels hit the tarmac with grace, to the thundering applause of the passengers. The soothing voice of the flight attendant over the intercom system was barely heard as the applause continued. "Welcome to Dubai. The current temperature is thirty-seven degrees Celsius with sunny skies. You may now use your mobile devices, but please remain seated until the plane comes to a full stop."

"I didn't think people applauded the captain anymore," said Emma.

"I didn't think so either, but it's nice to see the tradition continuing," said Bryan, as he turned on his mobile device. His face darkened instantly.

Emma noticed the change in his expression and asked, "What's happened?"

"Jasmijn Bakker has escaped."

<h1 style="text-align:center">Sixty-One</h1>

<h1 style="text-align:center">A Generous Snifter Of Camus XO</h1>

JAZZIE SMIRKED AS she climbed the stairs to the private jet. She settled into the plush seats of the luxurious plane and gloated at how easy her escape from the New Elgan Police Service holding cell had been.

Bryan, David and perhaps Emma, were likely already on their way to the Maldives. It had been urgent she escape police custody and arrive in the Maldives before they did.

She had known it was a matter of time before she would be transferred to a higher security detention center to await trial. She calculated her best chance to escape would have been to overcome a guard before or during prison transfer. Once in a higher security jail, her chances of escape, although not impossible without procuring outside help, would have been far more difficult. When the opportunity, almost laughable in its simplicity, presented itself, she'd stifled a giggle.

The New Elgan Police Service, like police services in so many small-town Ontario communities, was struggling to survive on a limited budget. Consequently, the building housing the police force had not been upgraded and its holding cells were antiquated and not furnished with surveillance cameras.

While laying on her back on the uncomfortable cot, she noticed one of the ceiling tiles was slightly askew. She stood on the cot to take a closer look and discovered distinctive scratches and scores at its edges. She looked around the room for an object to poke at the hole but found nothing suitable.

The cot was secured to the floor, however, due to poor upkeep, or lack of inspection, someone had pried two of the bolts loose. Jazzie made a rueful smile. No doubt it had been a fruitless endeavor for them, but she hoped to benefit from their previous effort.

After the lights were turned off at ten, moonlight filtered through the tiny cell's window. She had tugged at the bed frame and was surprised that the legs released without much resistance. With another hefty tug, she was able to lean the cot against the wall.

She used the tilted bed frame as a ladder and was able to reach the ceiling. She shoved at the compromised tile and was pleased it was not fixed down but had been positioned over the metal supporting frame to hide a person-sized hole. She tested her weight against the supporting rods and once confident they would support her, she raised herself up to better examine the opening to the ventilation duct.

Confirming she would be able to crawl through the duct, she pulled herself in, waited a moment to adjust to her surroundings, then began to creep. Every so often she stopped to listen for any sign her presence might have been detected.

After thirty minutes of inching her way along the metal duct, she came across another duct opening, and moved closer to inspect. The grate had been attached with screws from the outside, leaving the sharp pointed edges exposed on the inside. With her thumb and forefinger, she twisted the screw points, ignoring the stabs of pain. Each time a screw fell to the floor below, she held her breath and waited, concerned the small ting of metal against ceramic might have been noticed. Before the final screw was completely loosened, she grasped the grate firmly to prevent it from falling to the floor, bent it slightly and then pulled the grate into the ventilation duct.

She lowered her athletic frame, honed by years of gymnastics and training to become a top sniper, through the opening and landed, cat-feet light on the ceramic floor.

Although her maneuver had been noiseless, she had nonetheless startled a female police officer who had just turned into the corridor.

"Stop there!" the officer had shouted.

Within seconds, Jazzie had immobilized the officer with a series of efficient Muay Thai kickboxing moves. She pulled the unconscious woman into a nearby unoccupied office and closed the door.

Jazzie was pleased to see that they both were blond, and close in size and appearance. She pulled the officer's ID and badge and examined it. Officer Stacey Janneck. *I can work with that*, she thought.

She stripped herself and the woman down and exchanged each other's clothing. Next, she pulled on Janneck's duty belt which held a Glock firearm, pepper spray, a Taser, radio, surgical gloves, a baton, and handcuffs. She considered using the handcuffs to secure the officer, but decided there was no need, as she expected Officer Janneck would be unconscious for quite some time. With any luck, her escape would not be noticed until morning.

From there, it had been child's play. She had sauntered by the police department's front desk, the receptionist's friendly voice saying, "Have a good evening."

Moments later, she had passed through the station's front door and strolled out into the warm August night, just another officer out on patrol. She had walked to the safe house she maintained for emergencies; one of which not even Enrico Bianchi nor the Dark Hands of Anubis were aware.

Searching on the safe house's Virtual Private Network, she had hacked into the airport's servers and discovered that Bryan, David, and Emma were on tonight's flight for Dubai via Air Canada, with a connecting flight the following day to the Maldives.

Only once she had chartered a private jet for Dubai, with departure first thing in the morning, had she allowed herself to relax. She would arrive in the Maldives ahead of the three budget-constrained travelers.

After a home-made dinner of Pad Thai, she indulged in a wonderful bath and rewarded herself with a generous snifter of Camus XO. The cognac's intense floral aromas, along with flavors of dried and candied fruit, gave off a pleasant heat as it traveled to her belly. She had sighed in satisfaction; her body warm on the outside from the bath and on the inside from the cognac.

Now seated in the comfortable jet, her musings were interrupted by the polite flight attendant, who held a bottle of Moët et Chandon. "Would you like a refill?"

Jazzie nodded her approval, leaned back in her chair, feeling content and relaxed.

The attendant smiled and poured the golden colored liquid into the champagne flute. "Would you like to see the menu?"

"Yes, please." After a quick perusal of the menu, she said, "I'll have the salmon, asparagus and roasted garlic potatoes. Followed by crème brûlée."

"Very good. I'll inform the chef."

Yes, booking the flight was an extravagant expense, however she had the funds to cover it. And besides, it was essential she overtake Bryan, David, and Emma before they arrived at their destination in the Maldives.

* * *

The color drained from Emma's face. "But how could this have happened?"

"She escaped through the tiled ceiling in her cell. Made her way through the network of ducts." Bryan shook his head in disbelief. "Then she overpowered a police officer. Officer Stacey Janneck. Good kid." He wiped tears from his eyes. "She's in a coma."

"Do you think Jazzie's on the run?" asked David.

Emma's head tilted to one side, a sure sign she'd just heard from Spirit Anna. "No, she's coming after us."

"At least we have a head start," reasoned David.

"I'm not so sure about that," said Emma frowning.

Sixty-Two

The Maldives

"WE'VE GOT ALMOST a seven-hour layover," said Bryan. "Our flight to the Maldives leaves at seven forty-five this evening." His hands trembled as he rubbed his tired eyes.

"Bryan, you're exhausted," Emma told him. "Why don't you head to the Plaza Premium Lounge and try and rest?"

After Emma realized their first leg of the flight would be nearly thirteen hours in length, she had prebooked the luxurious lounge for the three of them. Even though she and David had slept well on the plane, the level of exhaustion on Bryan's face made her glad she had made the booking.

"Good plan," said Bryan, trying to rally himself.

"Come on, we'll go with you," said David. "I wouldn't mind getting a bite to eat."

After David and Emma coaxed Bryan to eat and got him settled into the plush and comfortable chaise lounge, Emma said, "Let's go for a walk."

David took her hand and said, "Sure thing."

After ten minutes of walking through the bustling airport, David asked, "Why did you say you thought Jazzie was going to catch up with us?"

"Spirit Anna sent me a mental image of Jazzie boarding a luxury aircraft." She shuddered.

"What is it?" David asked, concerned. The nightmare where Enrico held the knife to Emma's throat flashed in his mind, reminding him that they would never be safe until the killer was apprehended.

"I don't know." She shivered again. "I can't explain it. I just feel ill at ease."

"Let's assume your impression is right and figure out how Jazzie could get here so fast," he suggested. He pulled her closer to him as a large group of boisterous tourists passed by.

"Okay."

"Here is what we know." He tapped his right index finger on the palm of his left hand as he made each point. "One; it is believed Jazzie escaped from police custody somewhere between ten and wake-up call at six thirty in the morning. Two; she'd need to hide out somewhere. But where would she go?"

Emma raised her eyebrows. "Something like a safe house, maybe?"

"Yeah, I think so. Okay. Three; we can assume she has deep pockets."

"That makes sense. She's a chameleon. No doubt keeps a stash of cash and false identities."

David chuckled.

"What?"

"You watch too many spy movies," David joked.

Emma smiled and teased back. "Can we stay focused, Private Eye David Harris?"

"Right, and I agree with you by the way." He grinned at her. "She's got to have serious funds at her disposal."

"And four?" prompted Emma.

"Four; she's hired a private jet."

"I was thinking that, too." She pulled out her iPhone to search for flights. "There's a company called AerojetMe." She whistled. "Forty-one thousand Euros to fly to Dubai, then another thirty-seven thousand to fly from Dubai to Maldives."

"Interesting," he said, then tapped his palm one more time. "Five. Even if she left a few hours after us, she wouldn't have to contend with the seven-hour layover we do."

Emma's face flickered with fear. "Which means she would arrive before we do."

"Come on." David set his jaw in grim determination. "Let's head back to the lounge. We need to talk with Bryan."

* * *

Their flight from Dubai International Airport left on time and arrived a little over four hours later, just after midnight at Malé International Airport. They had booked rooms at the Samann Grand, a boutique hotel in Malé City, as it was less than two kilometers from the airport.

Check-in was a blur, as the three weary travelers navigated the charming lobby of the hotel, barely noticing their posh surroundings. For practical and safety reasons, they had reserved the two-bedroom family suite with private balcony.

Once in the hotel suite, Emma pulled off the shawl covering her head, and flopped herself down on the couch. "Finally, here; that was an exhausting trip."

Bryan glanced at his analog watch. "I've adjusted the time on this thing so often, I have no idea what time it is back home."

"It's past midnight here," said Emma, looking at her iPhone, which had adjusted itself automatically for the local time zone. "It's only just after three in the afternoon back home."

"So, today here is yesterday there," groaned Bryan. "I'm so jet-lagged, I can't think straight."

"I'm wired up, too," agreed David.

Bryan walked to the hotel bar fridge, opened the door, and perused its contents. "Darn. I forgot they don't serve alcohol here." He gave a heavy sigh. "I sure could use a drink."

"When we arrived, I noticed there's a mosque right beside the hotel," said Emma.

"Well, overtired as we are, we better try and get some shuteye," said Bryan. He got up from the couch, kissed Emma tenderly on the cheek and gave David a hug. "See you guys in the morning."

"Goodnight, Bryan," Emma murmured. "Get some rest."

"Will do. Don't stay up too late."

* * *

EMMA AWOKE JUST before six in the morning, to the hauntingly beautiful incantation of the Islamic call to morning prayer. She threw on a midcalf length dress and matching jacket and placed the shawl over her head and shoulders. She drew open the sliding glass door and crept onto the private balcony. She leaned against the wall so she could remain out of sight and listened.

Even though she was not of Muslim faith, she was mesmerized by the soothing and melodic qualities of the morning prayer. The final notes of the prayer faded away from the minaret, just as the red ball of sun rose above the horizon.

The balcony door slid open, and David emerged. "That gave me chills. A little noisy first thing in the morning, but exquisite."

"Good morning, David." She nestled up against him as he wrapped her arms around her. "Had a good night?"

"Very good night."

"Do I smell coffee?"

"You sure do. Come inside. I'll pour you a cup."

"Thanks. Bryan up yet?"

"Not yet. It's early, let him sleep a bit longer."

She settled on the couch, tucking her legs underneath her, and took a sip of the aromatic coffee. "Nice. Remind me again. What time does the charter company open?"

"Eight this morning."

"Good. We've got time." She put the empty cup on the table, stretched her arms above her head and got up and headed toward the private bath in their bedroom. "I need a shower. Coming?"

* * *

Emma was annoyed with David and Bryan. "What? You want me to remain at the hotel while you track down Enrico on his private island." Her eyes flashed with fury. "No way are you leaving me behind."

"Em, I promised your mom I'd keep you safe," said Bryan, trying to reason with the headstrong young woman.

"Look. There's no point trying to dissuade me." She punctuated her next words carefully. "I. Am. Coming."

David and Bryan exchanged uneasy glances, knowing it was useless to argue further, as it would only cause more delays.

"At least stay here in the room until we've chartered the boat," pleaded Bryan. "The less conspicuous we are the better."

"Okay," Emma said with great reluctance. "I'll agree to that."

"Don't worry, it'll be fine," reassured David.

She nodded, fear making the words stick in her throat.

He gathered her in his arms, "You'll be safe here."

"Yes, but will you and Bryan be?"

* * *

Jazzie set down the surveillance equipment and smiled with satisfaction that David and Bryan had left Emma behind in the hotel room. They'd be gone at least an hour, time enough to put her plan in motion.

Back in New Elgan, under the pretense of helping the police locate Enrico, she'd had access to David's phone and had cloned it. She picked up the phone and sent the text.

* * *

The polite desk clerk at the charter company looked at David and said, "Sir, it will be easier and less expensive for your party to book a seaplane to go to Hulhumalé Island than a private yacht."

"Yes, but I am a sailor, and I have always wanted to sail in the Maldives."

Except the island they were headed to was not Hulhumalé, but Enrico Bianchi's private island. Taking a seaplane would only alert Enrico and his guards to their approach. Coming by boat would be far more prudent, allowing them to keep the element of surprise.

"As you wish, sir." He hesitated. "With or without a skipper?"

"Without," replied David.

Half an hour later, after mountains of paperwork, including proof of David's navigational skills as a skipper, he was handed nautical maps and charts and the keys to the catamaran.

"What time would you like us to take you to the boat?" asked the clerk.

David glanced at the clock on the wall behind the clerk's desk. "One hour, okay?"

"Most certainly, sir."

* * *

Emma was getting restless. *What is taking so long? Should I go look for them?* She wondered. She paced back and forth through the spacious hotel room, winding herself up with anxiety, blocking her ability to receive empathic impressions from Spirit Anna.

She jumped when she heard her cell ping and glanced at the message: *We're ready to go. Meet us in the lobby, David.*

Perplexed, Emma sent her reply: You're not coming up?

No need. Grab your stuff and meet us down here.

Okay. See you in 5.

Emma was curious why David had asked her to come to the lobby rather than coming to get her. She tried to still her thoughts and confer with Spirit Anna but couldn't get a definitive reading on what she should do, other than a general feeling of unease. *The jetlag could be interfering with my psychic abilities,* she decided. Telling herself there was no danger, she carefully placed the headscarf on her head, put the hotel key card in her purse, slung it over her shoulder and exited the hotel room.

She rushed down the hall, pushed the elevator button and was pleased when the door slid open immediately. She hurried inside and joined one other occupant, who was also wearing a hijab. Emma's expression darkened with fear when she recognized Jazzie's startling blue eyes staring at her through the headscarf. She turned to exit the elevator but was too slow to react and watched with panic as the doors slid closed.

"We have to stop meeting like this," said Jazzie.

"What—?" said Emma.

"You know, in elevators," she interrupted. Jazzie's smile was sarcastic, as she laughed at her own lame joke.

"What are you doing here?" stammered Emma, completing her previous question.

"You should know; you're the psychic. Don't ask stupid questions." Jazzie advanced, causing Emma to retreat until her back was against the rear wall of the elevator. She jabbed the needle containing the sedative into her neck smoothly. "You're my bargaining chip." The sharp prick was as inconsequential as a mosquito bite. Within moments, Emma was woozy and lightheaded.

* * *

When the elevators slid open at the main floor, Jazzie guided the semiconscious Emma through the crowd in the busy lobby.

"Excuse me, please," she announced with urgency in her voice, "My sister is sick! I need to get her to the hospital!"

"May we call an ambulance?" enquired the concierge.

"No time. I have a taxi outside waiting."

"Allow me to assist you."

"Thank you so much." Jazzie gave him her best impression of fright and worry.

The concierge gently took Emma's left arm, while Jazzie supported the half comatose woman on the right. Once at the taxi, the concierge helped Jazzie get Emma settled into the backseat.

"Is there anything else I can do to help?" he asked.

Jazzie shook her head. "No, thank you." She wiped phantom tears from her eyes, pulled the door to the taxi closed. Energized by her charade, she told the driver, "Take me to the Velana International Airport. My sister and I have a plane to catch."

"Does she not need medical attention, miss?" asked the cabbie, his forehead creased with concern. "I thought I was to take you and your sister to the hospital."

"Nah, she's just hungover." She held back the chuckle that was building in the back of her throat. "She'll be just fine." *For now.*

Sixty-Three

Where Is She?

"I DON'T UNDERSTAND," David's voice was panicked. "Where is she?"

Bryan surveyed the room. "There's no sign of a struggle."

"Where did she go?" David rubbed at his temples, and massaged the back of his neck, trying to assuage the onslaught of an instant headache.

"Maybe she went for a massage or a swim?"

"I doubt it. She hates massages. If she'd gone for a swim, she'd have texted me." David picked up his cell and called her. He frowned. "No answer." He tapped out a rapid-fire text and hit send. "She promised she'd wait."

"I'm calling the front desk," said Bryan. After a few moments, he said, "My daughter, Emma Jackson, who is staying with me is not in our suite. Did she leave the hotel?"

"Daughter?" mouthed David.

Bryan placed his hand over the mouthpiece and said, "Less explaining to do." He listened to the person on the other end of the line, then said sternly, "She doesn't have a sister."

"A sister?" David's heart raced.

After another long pause, Bryan said, "Call the police. This is a kidnapping. The woman who took her is wanted by Interpol and is a killer."

David's world crumbled at Bryan's angry tone. His head spun.

"I want to talk with the concierge right now," Bryan demanded.

"Oh no, not Emma," David swore under his breath. "This was my worst fear." His body shook with rage and out-of-control adrenaline.

"Pull yourself together." Bryan's tone was firm. "Focus that anger and energy into getting her back."

David shook off the anxiety, straightened his shoulders, and said, "Let's go see that concierge."

* * *

When David and Bryan entered the lobby of the Samann Grand, the concierge rushed up to them, looking defeated. "I am so sorry, sir." His Adam's apple bobbed up and down nervously. "She said she was the young woman's sister. She was so convincing—"

Bryan interrupted, his manner brusque and impatient. "Have the police been called?"

"Yes, they are on their way."

"Tell me exactly what happened," Bryan commanded.

The concierge shook. "The woman was wearing a hijab. She called out for help, said her sister was sick. I offered to call an ambulance, but she refused." He raked his hands through his hair and moaned. "I'll lose my job."

"That is minor compared to my daughter being kidnapped," said Bryan.

David grabbed the concierge's collar and pulled him so close their faces were inches apart. "That young woman means everything to me. We're getting married. Tell us what happened!"

"I helped the sister get the ill woman into the cab."

"She's not Emma's sister," David reminded him.

"Right, sorry," the concierge stuttered.

"Where were they headed?" demanded David.

"The taxi headed east. Toward the airports. The opposite direction of Indira Ghandi Memorial Hospital—"

"Airports?" Bryan asked. "There are more than one?"

"Malé International Airport and Velana International Airport. They're adjacent to each other. The seaplanes fly out of Velana."

"Get us a cab right now," said David.

"But sir, the police are on their way," stammered the bewildered concierge. "They'll want to speak with you."

David's reply was abrupt. "Then you tell them what happened. We're going to find my fiancée."

Their taxi pulled out of the hotel's porte-cochère and headed toward the airport just as the two officers from the Maldives Police Services arrived.

David averted his head away from the police vehicle, and said softly, "Don't look now, but the police have arrived."

The two men ducked slightly to remain out of sight. Both sighed with relief when the cab entered the main thoroughfare.

Bryan tried to ignore the stab of guilt from evading the officers. "They could've helped."

"We'd only be wasting precious time," said David.

"Possibly. But the more help we get the better prepared we'll be."

"They'll only slow us down," he insisted. "There is only one possibility; Jazzie's taking her to Enrico."

"That is likely the most logical scenario."

"Emma was taken in by her and thought she could be reformed," said David.

"I had my doubts. From my years on the force, it's been my experience that reform is rare for people who are used to just one sort of life."

David rubbed his temples. "Damn this headache." He reached into his back pocket and pulled out a couple of Tylenols and dry-swallowed them.

Just as the cabbie pulled in front of the entrance to the Velana International Airport, David's cell phone pinged. Emma's profile image flashed across the screen. His face darkened in anger as he read the message. "Take a look at this." He handed the phone to Bryan. "It's from Jazzie."

Bryan's eyebrows creased together with concern as he read the message: *We have Emma and want a trade. You and Bryan for Emma. Come to the island, J.*

"Shit!" said David, taking his phone back. "Bryan, how do I respond?"

"Tell her you want proof of life."

David's fingers flew over the phone as he typed his reply: Send proof of life.

A few seconds later his phone opened to a live video message showing a zoomed-in image of Emma's tear-streaked face.

"David?" Although her grief was obvious, the expression in her green eyes was strong and determined.

"We're coming for you, honey."

"David, please don't. They'll kill you and Bryan." She swallowed at the lump in her throat. "Then they'll kill me any—"

A man's impatient voice cut in. "Enough!"

"Enrico," David barked. "Let her go."

The video feed turned sideways, became blurry and choppy, just before the connection was severed.

Moments later his cell pinged again with another message from Jazzie: *We have your geolocation. We know you're at Velana airport. A private seaplane is on standby to take you to the island, J.*

David stabbed out his answer: Don't you dare hurt her!

Get going, J.

David turned to the cabbie and asked, "What do I owe you?"

"Nothing, sir," he replied, eyes filled with fear. "Just go with your friends."

"What friends?" he frowned.

Two large muscular men approached the vehicle, each man taking a position beside each rear passenger door. Blocking the sunlight, the man on David's side tapped the window with one hand and moved his jacket away with the other hand to reveal a gun.

"I guess we're going to lose the deposit on the catamaran," David quipped, feigning a bravery he did not feel, his guts churning inside.

Bryan raised an eyebrow. "Stay cool, kid. These guys are lowlifes. We'll get our chance at the big boss."

Sixty-Four

Snacks, Anyone?

DAVID AND BRYAN did not notice the sunlight playing on the shimmering aquamarine sea as they walked along the pier toward where the De Havilland Twin Otter seaplane was docked. A woman and two men stood at the entrance of the cabin. The pilot and co-pilot were both barefoot and smiled. The woman, possibly the flight attendant, motioned them to enter.

"Here, you'll need these, gentlemen," she said as she handed them each a small bag containing a pair of earplugs. "The flight will be noisy."

"Are they even aware we are being taken against our will?" David whispered, wondering about the courteous behavior.

"I doubt they care," Bryan replied.

David hesitated before entering the cabin and was reminded by the barrel of the gun pushing against his spine that this was anything but a pleasant flight in paradise.

The cabin could accommodate sixteen passengers, but besides Bryan and David, the only souls on board were the flight attendant, the pilot, and his co-pilot, and of course, their two captors.

* * *

As they were forced into their seats, Bryan placed a comforting hand on David's arm and muttered under his breath, "I know how to deal with their kind. Be ready to follow my lead."

David gave an almost imperceptible nod while Bryan made sidelong glances at their captors, assessing their strengths and weaknesses. Once seated, the younger of the two pulled out his cell phone. After a stern look of disapproval from his partner, he placed the phone back in his pocket with an adolescent sigh of annoyance.

Good. Easily distracted, thought Bryan.

At start up, the interior of the cabin shook with its twin engines' heavy vibration. The take off was rougher and noisier than what is usually experienced on land, as the sea dragged at the plane's pontoons with ponderous insistence. Droplets of sea spray dotted the windows and were whipped away by the wind once the plane was airborne. The plane banked and flew over the heavily populated island of Malé, over the yachts nestled in the manmade bay and out over the sparkling Indian Ocean.

Whispery white clouds passed by the cabin window, as the plane flew on, over the coral tips of the oceanic volcanic mountain range rising above the waters to create what is known as the Maldives, an area comprising approximately 1,192 islands. The breathtaking, bird's-eye view of the archipelago was an experience lost on the two captives and was met with indifference by the cabin crew and the two gangsters.

"I checked out our options when we were deciding on coming in by catamaran or seaplane. This flight should take thirty minutes at most," said David, struggling to be heard over the engines. "I estimate we'll arrive in another ten minutes or so."

"Shut up," said the older thug. He glanced over at his younger counterpart who was busy tapping away on his cell phone and swiped the phone out of his hand. "I told you to put that away!"

"Hey!" The younger one focused his attention on his colleague instead of on Bryan and David.

"Now," Bryan shouted.

He lunged forward out of the seat and grabbed the older man's arm and twisted it behind his back, while David leaped from his seat and gave a square punch to the chin of the cell phone addict. The kid must have had a glass jaw, because his eyes rolled back until only the whites were visible. He slumped down, banging his temple against the cabin floor.

Meanwhile, Bryan was struggling to take down the burly man. "A little help here!"

The irregular motions of the fighting caused the seaplane to see-saw back and forth. The pilot shouted commands at the co-pilot to stabilize the aircraft.

David jumped up on the seat and launched himself in the air. Using his legs, he grabbed the man around the neck using a wrestling technique he hadn't used since his high school days, taking the giant down and putting him to sleep. The plane gave a shudder at the sudden motion and made a vertical descent until the pilot corrected course.

"Impressive," said Bryan.

"Thanks." David extricated himself from under the dead weight of the unconscious man, searched his pockets and confiscated the man's gun, a knife, and a phone.

Bryan stood up, rubbed the small of his back and said, "I'm getting too old for this." He hooked the second thug's gun into the back of his belt and trousers and pocketed the cell phone. "We need some rope to secure these two characters."

David rummaged through the cargo area and found a coil of strong nylon rope. He used his newly acquired knife to cut off a length and handed it to Bryan.

The flight attendant had been cowering near the cockpit. She regained her composure as she watched Bryan and David tie up the men, and said, "Snacks, anyone?"

Sixty-Five

═══════════

The Labyrinth

THE REMAINING FIVE minutes of the flight were uneventful as the pilot skillfully landed the seaplane in rough water, then taxied toward the waiting berth on Enrico Bianchi's private atoll. White sand and palm trees dotted the shoreline.

The engines ceased, the propellers stopped their whining and the plane glided to a full stop.

"We've got a fighting chance now," David said, his eyes steely and resolute, his confidence restored knowing he and Bryan were now armed.

"No turning back now," said Bryan.

"How do you want to play this?" asked David, as he viewed the small greeting party gathered at the dock.

"We rush out. You take the two on the right, and I'll take the one on the left."

"Two?"

"You're the younger one. Keener eyesight and a better shot."

David nodded. "Okay, let's go!" He swung open the cabin door holding the gun securely in both hands. The three men holding their semi-automatics looked up with surprise to see David instead of one of their men. Before they had time to react, he had shot one between the eyes and the other in the torso. Bryan was on the stairs, flanking

307

David on the right and had fired at the same time. All three men lay on the sun-bleached deck, their blood trailing like viscous red ribbons into the sea.

The flight attendant screamed hysterically. The pilots just stared in disbelief. The co-pilot reacted first, pulled the cabin door shut, turned on the engines and taxied back out to sea and in minutes they were airborne.

"Guess we lost our ride," said Bryan.

"Maybe not." David nodded toward a catamaran docked a few meters away. "If things go right, that's our way out."

"Let's get Emma," replied Bryan.

* * *

Bryan and David followed the Corallina-tiled path to a gate entwined with red and pink bougainvillea vines. Through the ornate design of the entrance could be seen a massive villa surrounded by an intricate pattern of walls constructed from volcanic rock.

Bryan stopped and said, "We should split up."

"Approach from two sides?"

"Yeah."

"We'll need to scale the walls."

"I'm getting too old for this," groaned Bryan. "If I get out of this alive, I'm retiring."

"Hang in there, old buddy."

"You, too."

The two men grasped each other by the forearms in a rough embrace.

"See yah on the flip side," said David.

Bryan rolled his eyes at the cliché.

"What?" grinned David. "I always wanted to say that. Besides, a little comedic relief can't hurt."

* * *

David approached the villa from the west. Upon closer inspection, he realized the walls would not be too difficult to climb. He hoped Bryan was encountering an equally easy ingress.

He scaled the wall with ease and realized that the intricate pattern of walls was a labyrinth. Thinking back to his undergraduate days, where he had taken a Greek mythology course, he recalled the hero Theseus who followed the Minoan maze to its heart where he slayed the Minotaur. *Was Enrico Bianchi his Minotaur?*

As he continued to follow the maze, he heard noise ahead of him. He pulled out the gun and aimed, before coming face to face with Bryan.

"Ah, it's you," he said.

Bryan blew out a relieved breath. "We're in a friggin' maze."

"Indeed." David held his finger up to indicate quiet. "I hear something," he whispered.

He cocked his head to one side. "Voices. Male and female."

They walked in silence toward the voices. David stopped, flattened himself against the wall and pulled Bryan back with him.

"There's Emma."

Emma sat on a chair with her hands bound in front of her. Her hair was unkempt, but she appeared unhurt, and looked calm and peaceful.

"That's my Em," David said. "She's meditating."

"She's got company. Jazzie, Enrico, and Alessandro are here."

"What do you say we drop in?" said David.

"What're we waiting for?"

The two men inched forward toward the final opening to the center of the labyrinth and froze when Enrico called out, "Come on in, gentlemen. We've been expecting you."

When Bryan and David stepped into view, confusion flickered in Enrico's eyes before the impassive veil was reasserted. "Where are my men?"

"Dead," said David, keeping his voice aloof.

Enrico took two powerful strides forward. In one fluid motion, he pulled Emma out of the chair and held the knife against her neck, just as in David's dream.

"Let go of her," David shouted. "We're here to make the exchange."

David quickly glanced over to his left and saw that Bryan and Alessandro had aimed their guns at each other. Stalemated, the two men just stared, each waiting for an opening to get the upper hand.

"I've had a change of heart." Enrico snickered. "My men not being present tells me you've dispensed with them. All five." His voice was puzzled. "How did a washed-up cop and a weaselly little lawyer accomplish that, I wonder?"

"They got everything they deserved," said David, through clenched teeth.

"Maybe so. Incompetence should be rewarded with death. It's hard to find good men." He shook his head, annoyed. "I'll kill you both and keep this one as compensation," he said, tightening his grip on Emma. Enrico's voice was sinister. "Until I tire of her."

Emma made an involuntary gasp and tried to wriggle away but stopped when Enrico pressed the flat edge of the blade even tighter against her throat.

"You're not going to get away with this," David said as he realized Jazzie was threading her way along the far wall. *What was she up to?*

"Oh yes, I will. We chose the Maldives as our new home for a reason. No extradition treaty, and lots of playthings available."

"You're nothing but a sadistic creep," Emma's words squeezed out of her constricted throat.

"Mind your manners, my dear."

"I'm not your dear." Emma kicked her heel against his shin, then yelped, as the sudden movement caused the knife edge to nick her skin.

"You are quite the feisty thing," said Enrico. "I like that. You and I will have some fun later."

Jazzie now stood directly behind Enrico. Without hesitation, she hurled her body against Enrico's and wrapped her arms around his neck, using her weight to pull down on his windpipe. Enrico dropped the knife and let go of Emma. He clawed at Jazzie's hands, trying to break the chokehold.

"Run, Emma!" Jazzie shouted. "Run!"

Emma ran toward the passageway of the maze, disappearing around the corner. David registered that Emma had escaped and kept his gun trained on the struggling Enrico, unwilling to take a shot that might also hit Jazzie, who had just saved Emma's life.

* * *

Meanwhile, taking advantage of the distraction Jazzie had caused, both Bryan and Alessandro opened fire on each other. Bryan felt a searing pain in his gun hand and dropped the gun to the ground. *This is it*, he thought, trying to stop the flow of blood streaming from his hand. Bryan ran toward Alessandro, expecting to be raked down by gunfire, but hoping to buy some time for David to complete his shot. Instead, he heard the unmistakable sound of an empty clip and saw Alessandro hurl his useless gun away.

Enrico, still struggling to get away from Jazzie, called out to his son, who, roaring with fury, raced to help him. Bryan ran after him, hoping to tackle him to the ground, but the younger man was too fast for the aging policeman, whose right hand was slick with blood. In one fluid motion, Alessandro picked up the fallen knife and stabbed Jazzie in the back. Her arms went slack, and she slipped to the ground like a marionette whose strings were cut. Seconds later, Bryan tackled Alessandro and they tumbled to the ground.

* * *

David seized the opportunity and fired at Enrico who was so enraged he didn't register that the bullet had ripped through his arm, pulverizing tendons and muscle. He kicked at the lifeless woman and turned his fury toward David, his breath choppy and uneven. "You need to stay dead, *George*."

"Thought you didn't believe in past lives—"

"Anna was quite convincing before I snuffed out her—"

"You bastard!" David stared into Enrico's evil eyes—the eyes he'd recalled for far too long, spiraling him into the abyss, as had happened so many times in his dreams.

This is not a dream, he reminded himself. He pulled back from the depths of hell and said, "You took a young man's life thirty years ago. Mine. It's payback time."

"You think I care about that? Whatcha gonna do when I kill you again? Don't think for a minute I can't get to you." His laughter was maniacal. "Gonna try again when I'm ninety?" He tried to raise both fists menacingly, but the right arm dangled, useless at his side.

* * *

Alessandro stopped struggling with Bryan when he noticed his father's blood loss and said, "*Basta.* Enough." He looked at David whose gun remained pointed at him, then turned toward his father, and said, "It's over, Babbo."

The sound of police helicopters approaching almost snatched away his final words.

Sixty-Six

What's Next?

"SO WHY DID Jazzie help you?" asked Laura.

Bryan sat on the couch with his arms around her, while David and Emma sat on the opposite love-seat.

"I don't think Jazzie wanted me dead. We might have been friends if circumstances had been different."

"Who needs friends like that?" said David.

"I think she may have had a split personality. Rebecca *and* Jazzie. Rebecca was the dominant personality, the tough one who took care of them 'both' during her years having been kept captive and trained as an assassin. Jazzie was the diplomat, but still a willing participant."

"Well, it's all conjecture now, isn't it?" said Bryan.

"So, I'm curious, which one kidnapped you?" asked Laura.

"Jazzie was under Rebecca's control, so it was still Jazzie, but it was Rebecca who gave the orders." Emma took a sip of her herbal tea, appreciating the mix of chamomile, bergamot, and mint.

"And how did she trick you into leaving the hotel suite?"

"I got a text from David saying to meet him and Bryan in the lobby." She tilted her head and gave a rueful smile. "Just got chastised by Spirit Anna. I had misgivings but ignored them. I was so sure the message was from David."

"It wasn't your fault," said David. "We know now she cloned my phone when we were working at the station tracking Enrico's location."

She wiped her eyes. "I know, but I shouldn't have ignored my intuition. It's too bad Jazzie didn't make it. It was a brave thing she did. She saved my life."

"True. She sacrificed her life and stopped two evil men from killing again." Bryan looked thoughtful. "The good part is the Republic of Maldives government agreed to cooperate with the Canadian government. Enrico and Alessandro Bianchi will be returned to Canada to stand trial."

"And why did the Maldives government look the other way?" Laura asked, puzzled. "After all, you killed three men."

"They were more worried about maintaining their image as a safe vacation spot," explained David.

"The three dead men were wanted criminals, and the two men we restrained on the plane were arrested and will stand trial," added Bryan.

"It's a relief this nightmare is over," said Laura, her eyes misting over. "I am so happy everyone is back home, safe."

Bryan cleared his throat. "I have an announcement to make."

Three pairs of eyes settled on him expectantly.

"I am retiring from the force at the end of September." He paused. "It's been a great career, but I am ready for a new chapter in my life."

"And I'm selling the law practice," said David. "Now that I have my Private Investigative license, Bryan and I will be working together. Emma, too."

"Oh?" Laura raised her eyebrows in surprise.

"Our plan is to start an investigative business using paranormal means and good, old-fashioned detective work to solve cold cases. We've offered our services to the New Elgan Police Service, and they are interested in taking us on as consultants," Bryan told her.

"Wow, that's fantastic." Laura directed her gaze at Bryan.

Bryan nodded. "We'll be working with Spirit Anna, as before, even though she's in the spirit world now, with Emma as our medium."

"Mom, we wondered if you'd join us," said Emma.

"I like the idea." She paused, "I was thinking of a new challenge. My eyes are getting too old for the seamstress work, but I have good business sense." She sparkled with delight. "Need a bookkeeper?"

"I have one more announcement to make," said Bryan.

"A night full of surprises," said Laura.

"Yes, it is, my love." He held Laura's hand in his. "Before Maldives, I asked Laura to marry me, and she said yes." His voice choked with emotion. "We decided to wait to tell you until we were sure we'd come out of this alive."

"Thank God you did," Laura whispered.

Emma jumped off the couch and embraced her mom. "This is wonderful news." She turned to David, "What if we all got married at the same time?"

"I know a great place in Costa Rica," grinned David. "Double wedding on the beach?"

END

About the Author

Angela van Breemen

Angela van Breemen is delighted to have completed her first novel, Past Life's Revenge, a crime thriller with a twist of spiritualism.

She is an avid writer of poetry, belongs to the Wordsmiths Writers' Group based out of New Tecumseth, Ontario, Canada and is a member of the Crime Writers of Canada and the South Simcoe Arts Council.

Angela is a Soprano Soloist. A firm believer in giving back to the community, she often sings for different charitable organizations.

Music and poetry have been an integral part of her life, and in early 2024 she launched her debut album, In The Breeze. Celtic in nature, it includes three original pieces of music, based on her poetry.

Angela volunteers for Procyon Wildlife Rehabilitation and Education Centre, a group dedicated to the rescue, rehabilitation and safe release of orphaned and injured Ontario wildlife.

She lives in Loretto, Ontario with her husband Peter Thomas Pontsa, author of *Outfoxed - An Inspector William Fox Adventure.*

You can connect with Angela on:

https://angelavanbreemen.ca
https://www.facebook.com/angela.vanbreemen.5
https://www.instagram.com/stories/angelapearl55/
https://x.com/breemenangela
https://wildsongbird.ca

Subscribe to her newsletter:
https://angelavanbreemen.ca/contact-us

Preview of Revenge is Not Enough

A David Harris and Emma Jackson Mystery - BOOK 2

One

SQUEALS OF LAUGHTER permeated through the dense forest. The girl turned her head around to look at her pursuer and tucked the tendril of light-colored hair behind her right ear. "Catch me if you can," she taunted.

The boy stopped in his tracks transfixed by her beauty in the soft light of dusk filtering through the trees. Thin, new subtle curves hinted at the fuller shape she would soon possess.

"Come on," she said. "We're almost there." She turned on her heels and started running, strong and supple as she wove through the tangled vines interlacing the pathway in the woods which led to the old gristmill.

The boy picked up his pace and raced after her, unwilling to be left behind in the growing dim. "Wait up," he shouted, breathless from the exertion.

"Last one there is a dirty rotten egg," she teased.

That final goad did it, and the boy's long legs closed the distance. When he was within an arm's length of her, he reached out and grabbed a long strand of her golden hair, stopping her from running.

"Hey," she screamed. "That hurt!"

He roughly whipped her around and grabbed her around her slight waist with one hand and still clenching a fist full of her hair, mashed his lips against hers and forced his tongue down her throat, causing her to gag.

"Yuk!" The girl jerked her face away from his and coughed. She tried to wriggle free, but he wound her hair even tighter around his fist, making it impossible for her to move her head. "You're hurting me." Her voice was thick with fear and terror.

"Stay still." He could feel the panicked hammering of her heart against his chest which made him feel strong and superior. The more pain he caused, the more intense was this new-found pleasure which coursed through his body.

He kicked her feet from under her and pushed her to the ground. The flailing of legs and arms against his body only aroused him more. He released her hair and, in a fluid, motion grabbed both her wrists and pinned them to the ground. He rammed his mouth against hers again and this time bit her lower lip hard. He savored the iron taste, as the warm velvety blood gushed into his mouth. He moaned with excitement and whispered,

"Maggie."

* * *

Emma groaned in her dream and kicked David hard in the shin. He switched on the nightlight and watched her squirming in her sleep, her breathing erratic. Worried, he placed his hand on her shoulder, to calm her, but she continued to thrash, her eyes open, but clearly seeing something other than their cozy bedroom.

He shook her shoulders gently. "Emma, honey. Wake up." He was relieved when her breathing returned to normal and the haze of fear in her eyes dissipated. He helped her sit up and adjusted the pillows behind her.

"Bad dream or a vision?" he asked.

"Vision." Her voice cracked with emotion. "David, it was awful." She buried her face in his chest, her hot tears staining his dark blue silk pajama top. When her sobs had subsided, she pulled away, and said, "I'm sorry."

"It's okay honey." He filled a glass from the crystal pitcher of water resting on the nightstand. "Here, drink this."

Her hands shook as she took a few sips. "Maggie," she whispered and handed the glass back to David. He gently placed the glass on the nightstand and waited for her to continue. "Her name was Maggie."

He handed her a notepad and pen and said, "Here, write everything down."

She nodded, leaned forward, and with trembling fingers took the pen and began to write in the notepad. When she had finished, she leaned back against the pillows and said, "That's all I can remember." She closed her eyes, dark circles punctuating the depth of her exhaustion.

"Let's try and get some rest." David took the pen and notepad and slid them into the drawer of the nightstand. He shut off the light and adjusted his body, until he formed a protective spoon around her. He looped his top arm around her protectively, kissed the nape of her neck and waited till he heard the soft rhythm of her breath.

As usual, sleep was never an easy companion for him, and his thoughts were preoccupied with Emma's burgeoning psychic ability. He worried he wouldn't be able to protect her. Was it only last year that they had first met, fallen in love? It seemed a lifetime ago. Together, they had pursued Enrico Bianchi, the man who had murdered him in his past life. Sometimes he wondered if his quest for revenge had been worth it. They had lost loved ones in their pursuit to bring Enrico to justice and not one day went by that he and Emma didn't miss Anna, his Uncle Liam and Sarah.

He questioned their decision to work cold cases together. Perhaps this idea to work on decades old cases of missing people and murders using the help of spirit guides, such as Spirit Anna was flirting with a danger best left alone. He checked the time on his phone, only three a.m. Even if sleep might elude him, at least he could keep watch over Emma and comfort her if her night vision recurred. In the morning he'd call Laura and Bryan Grant, his in-laws and his and Emma's business partners of their newly formed company, Jackson, Grant & Harris Investigations. Was it time to reconsider this venture? Wasn't Emma's safety, her sanity worth more than trying to solve cold cases the police had abandoned years ago?

* * *

REVENGE IS NOT ENOUGH

BOOK TWO

AVAILABLE IN 2025.